CU00559020

DAUGHTERS
OF THE SEA
SEA
HR MASON

TANGLED TREE PUBLISHING

For information, contact the publisher, Tangled Tree Publishing.

www.tangledtreepublishing.com

Editing: Hot Tree Editing

Cover Designer: BookSmith Design

E-book ISBN: 978-1-922359-46-9

Paperback ISBN: 978-1-922359-47-6

Hardback ISBN: 978-1-922359-74-2

This book is dedicated to all the women in my family, both past and present. Thank you for passing along your strength and wisdom. As always, this is for my daughters and husband. You're my inspiration.

"When shall we three meet again? In thunder, lightning, or in rain?"
–William Shakespeare, Macbeth

A NOTE FROM THE AUTHOR

Did you know that most of my story ideas begin with a question? Often, I don't even realize I've asked the question until I start looking for the answer. Once I begin digging, it's only a matter of time before the real story surfaces and the characters begin to speak to me.

When I began writing *Daughters of the Sea*, I started out on an entirely different path from where I eventually ended up. I've always been a bit obsessed with Salem, Massachusetts, and witches. The idea that so many people could be wrongfully accused and put to death without any real concrete evidence has always blown my mind. I wanted to write something that had to do with history, because I adore historical research, but I wanted to throw in a bit of the supernatural as well. Salem and witches seemed to be the perfect fit.

I began digging into witch trials, and I was shocked at all

the details that came up in my search. Witch hunting was so much broader and much more widespread than I had ever realized. It went far beyond Salem and happened much earlier in other parts of the world. About that same time, I was also digging into my own family history, and I had just come across a connection to my Norwegian heritage. It was the perfect storm for two of my passions—history and genealogy —to collide.

As I was searching, I learned about a witch trial in Norway, and the details wouldn't leave me alone. Given my newly discovered family connections to the country, I was intrigued. I began reading, and what I found was shocking. In the remote region of Troms og Finnmark, in northern Norway, lies a coastal village called Vardø, with the catchy moniker "Witch Capital of Norway." Needless to say, I was hooked.

Between 1593-1692, there were more than 140 witch trials in this small community. Ninety-one people were found guilty of witchcraft and executed. While that number might not sound like much, given the fact that the area is sparsely populated, it is an astronomically high number. They even have a monument, The Steilneset Memorial, which was constructed 348 years after the trials as a way to commemorate the horrible events.

As I began to read about the trials, my first thoughts were ones of anger and sadness. It seems unthinkable that so many innocent people were condemned and executed. I tried to imagine what it would have been like to live in that village, waking up in fear every day that you might be the next one who was accused. It must have been such a feeling of help-lessness, especially for the women of Vardø, who made up the vast majority of those accused and condemned.

Then another thought popped into my brain—what if you were a woman who actually was different? What if you were a woman who had some kind of power that you couldn't explain? What if all the women in your family had the same power? That would certainly be a death sentence. What would you do to survive?

Daughters of the Sea was born from my research and endless questioning. It blends the historical with the supernat-ural in a way that I hope you'll love. Perhaps it will leave you with some lingering questions of your own. Maybe someday I will still write that book about Salem witches, but for now, I give you the Norwegian ones.

HR MASON

PROLOGUE

Helga ran, her lungs exploding with pain. The frigid air nipped at her cheeks and sliced razor blades into her feet, cutting straight through the soles of her leather boots. Not daring to stop for even a second, she ventured a furtive glance behind her. Relief flooded her upon realizing she had momentarily escaped the band of angry men in her wake.

Ducking behind an abandoned barn, Helga plastered her small body against the splintered wood. Struggling to catch her breath, she gazed across the field of snow-covered ice. The bitter howling wind of the Barents Sea scattered snowflakes all around, the flurries obscuring her vision. She listened as the waves crashed in the distance, pounding against the rocks along the rugged shore. Her home, Vardø, felt cut off from the rest of the world.

The steady rhythm of the ocean hummed in every cell of her body. She breathed in the salty air and worked to calm her pounding heart. The village had always been her safe haven, and until recently, she couldn't imagine living anywhere else. But the panic set in and everything changed. If Helga didn't get away soon, she wouldn't get away at all.

Glancing around, she stealthily slid along the length of the old shack and quickly ducked inside. She climbed the rickety ladder leading up to the barn's loft, moving carefully, knowing the weight of her slight body might be too much for the rotting wood floor. Crouching in the corner of the loft, Helga peered through the cracks in the wall.

The men were approaching, each carrying a torch, their flames flickering in the polar night sky. The silhouettes of their bodies were awash with the blue-and-green northern lights flickering in the heavens above. Helga could feel the pulsing colors of the nordlys vibrating within her own body. The rainbow of lights had always given her a sense of complete connection with nature, seeming to bridge the gap between her and all of creation. They gave her the strength to do what she must.

A rippling sensation trickled through her body, her pale blonde hair lifting and swirling as a sudden breeze made its way through the barn. She breathed deeply, closing her blue eyes and envisioning the breeze turning into a gale-force wind. Picturing the wind in her mind, Helga imagined it extinguishing the flames of the men's torches.

"Så det. So be it," she whispered.

As the thought entered her mind and the words came out of her mouth, every torch flickered before going out completely. Helga smiled to herself as the familiar flow of electricity coursed through her body. The men's angry voices echoed in the night as they stumbled, trying to figure out what happened. She waited quietly, and after several minutes, the men headed back toward the fortress of Vardøhus.

Exhaling heavily, Helga sank onto one of the bales of hay at her feet. She must follow the plan, even if she didn't want to. If she failed, she would find herself on trial, like so many other women in her village. The panic had spread like wildfire, and she tried her best to remain in the shadows. Unfortunately, her gift had a way of thrusting her into the light.

She had always been proud of her abilities, so much like those of her mother and grandmother yet distinctly her own. Her twin sister, Bekka, also had the gift. Together, the girls had been a powerful force. Their mother, Else, called the twins "The generation of two," believing their magic was unstoppable.

The problem was that the "generation of two" had to sacrifice something in order to be granted such power. In their case, the sacrifice had been too great; Bekka was taken away, the payment for the possession of intense magic. When Bekka drowned as a young girl, Helga nearly died of grief herself. Losing her twin was a wound she would bear forever.

The women in Helga's family were part of a legacy. She

was simply one link in a long chain of women whose special abilities couldn't be explained. Helga believed her powers came from God. Others believed their origin was darker. Else said their gifts were given so they might serve others, just as they had done for generations. But now their gifts were misunderstood, putting them all in danger.

The tragedy began when several fishermen perished at sea in a deadly storm. Because no one could explain the events, the women of the village were blamed. They were accused of sorcery, of making pacts with the Devil. It was said that the women opened their wind knots, blowing up a storm to make the fishermen's boats sink.

Since then, Vardø had become a dangerous place, filled with murmurings and finger-pointing. One terrifying word struck fear in Helga's heart as it was hurled throughout the town—witch.

As more innocents were accused, Helga's worry grew. The people in the village knew of her abilities. She had used her gifts to help the townspeople since she was a small girl, always willing to do what she could to ease her neighbors' pain, to take their discomfort upon herself, to feel the sickness leave their bodies as she gazed into their eyes. Now those eyes bored into her, viewing her not with gratitude but with anger and fear.

She wasn't safe, and she wondered whether she ever would be again. Her gifts could only cause her harm. If she wanted to stay alive, she had to leave Vardø. She would follow

Else's final instructions—sneak to the harbor and sail away with Finn, the Dutch fisherman who believed Helga could control the weather. Else had promised Finn her daughter's hand in marriage. She had sweetened the deal by convincing him that Helga would ensure the safety of himself and his crew.

It was Else's final act of love, a dangerous effort to keep her daughter safe. Helga had no idea what awaited her beyond the shores of Vardø, or if she would ever return to her beloved village. She didn't even know if she had the strength to carry out the plan. But she had to try.

When the angry band of men dragged her mother away, Helga knew Vardø could no longer be her home. Else's hastily whispered final words before her death gave Helga the way out. It was risky, but it was her only chance.

Helga crept from the barn, bracing herself against the chilling wind. As she ran toward the shore, she remembered the last time she spoke to her mother, just moments before Else was burned at the stake.

"I will not leave you, Mother. I must stay," Helga cried as she gripped her mother's hand.

"Take this. It is your legacy. It will keep you safe." Else removed the Ansuz rune necklace from her own neck and placed it around Helga's.

"I can't leave you," Helga sobbed as she rolled the pendant within her fingers.

"I am not long for this world. You must go." Else's beau-

tiful blue eyes were wild with determination. "Do you have it?"

"The book?"

"Yes. That book is all we have left. Guard it with your life."

"Why is the book so important, Mother?"

"It tells our story. You will add yours to its pages. Continue our legacy."

"Yes, Mother." Helga nodded as she sobbed.

"My blessed daughter, I am at peace because you will survive."

"How can you be sure? Have you seen it in a vision?"

"I have seen it clearly," Else answered with a smile.

"Where will I go?"

"That I have not seen. But one thing I know for certain— no matter where you go, you will always be min datter av havet."

"Your daughter of the sea," Helga repeated.

ONE

R una Brandon hated change. In her mind, there was nothing better than the perfect sameness of an ordinary day. She loved predictability and routine, preferring to always do the same thing. She was afraid of rocking the boat and venturing into the unknown.

Maybe it was the fear of the unfamiliar that prevented her from moving forward, instead keeping her stuck in the quagmire of the past. It was the only excuse she had for staying with her abusive, controlling ex-fiancé for as long as she had. Runa had a knack for holding on when she should simply let go.

Glancing nervously around the storefront, stacked from floor to ceiling with boxes, Runa fidgeted with the ring on her right hand. The sterling silver Ansuz rune symbol was given to her by her mother, Asta, for her sixteenth birthday.

A follower of all things mystical, Asta said the ring would inspire insight and wisdom. So far, Runa didn't think it had done much good. She thought Asta's beliefs were a bunch of hocus-pocus, but she cherished the jewelry because it came from her mother.

"Here's another box. Where do you want it?" Asta, slightly out of breath, blew a strand of wayward hair from her eyes.

"I'll grab it. Thanks."

Runa hefted the box from Asta's hands and stacked it on top of the glass counter.

"I don't know about you, but I'm beat." Asta sighed. "I'm too old for all this physical labor."

"Old? I don't think so, Mom." Runa laughed.

Asta grabbed her nearby water bottle and took several large gulps. Runa grinned as her mother wiped beads of perspiration from above her upper lip. At forty-seven, Asta didn't look a day over thirty. She certainly didn't appear old enough to be the mother of a twenty-nine-year-old.

With their long pale blonde hair, blue eyes, and overall Nordic good looks, the two women were often mistaken for sisters, which never bothered Runa. She had always been proud to look like Asta. But although they were nearly mirror images of each other, their resemblance ended at the physical.

Asta, a massage therapist and energy healer, was confident, bold, and fearless. She grabbed life with both hands and held on for the ride. She knew exactly who she was and what she wanted. Runa had always envied Asta's mettle and secretly wished some of it would rub off on her.

In contrast, Runa was fearful, questioning, and uncertain. She was a bit naïve, too kindhearted for her own good, and had a hard time seeing the bad in anyone, qualities which made her the target of abuse in more than one relationship.

When Runa finally ended things with her fiancé, it was long overdue. She'd been broken for so long she couldn't remember how it felt to be whole. When Runa told Asta she was leaving Portland, Oregon, and moving to the tiny coastal town of Departure Cove, her mother thought she'd lost her mind. But opening Runa's, her upscale clothing boutique, felt like the right thing to do. It was the first decision in a long time of which Runa felt certain.

Although she was supportive of her daughter's plan to start a new life, Asta was openly uneasy about the town in which she'd chosen to do so. Departure Cove was a new town for Runa but a far too familiar one for Asta. It was the town in which she'd grown up, the place she'd told Runa she couldn't wait to leave.

For Asta, Departure Cove held too many bad memories, and she'd shared her wishes that her daughter choose anywhere else. She'd suggested several alternate locations, but Runa remained steadfast in her plan, knowing Departure Cove was the right place for her to set up shop.

"I can't believe we're standing here, in your boutique, in my hometown."

Asta shook her head slowly, trying to wrap her brain around it.

"It's perfect, isn't it? I know Departure Cove wasn't your first choice for me, but it's going to be great, Mom." Runa smiled.

"I'm sure you're right, sweetie."

Asta smiled, but Runa noticed the expression didn't quite reach her mother's eyes.

Runa had visited Departure Cove only once in her life before moving there. She'd been a girl of only ten years old when she and Asta had gone for her grandmother, Celine's, funeral. Runa had only seen a picture of her grandmother, but she still felt a connection to the woman who so closely resembled her and her mother.

Although the visit to Departure Cove had been brief and long ago, it made a lasting impression on Runa. She was drawn to the gray skies, frequent drizzle, and sound of waves crashing on the shore. She felt compelled, called by the water. She'd always wanted to live near the ocean but had never been willing to take the plunge. After the breakup, it was time to make a change. As much as she feared the unknown, something pulled her toward the small seaside town.

What Runa hadn't shared with Asta was that she'd been dreaming of Departure Cove since she was a child. She'd always known she would end up there, although she didn't understand why. About a year ago, the dreams began occurring frequently—vivid dreams of Departure Cove and Runa's place in it. She saw herself living there and operating a business. She dreamed of the house she would move into and the building where she would open Runa's.

When she began searching for houses and storefronts, she'd found the exact home and business she'd dreamed of on the classified page of the *Departure Cove Sentinel*. They were there, waiting for her. Everything had happened quickly. Runa signed the rental contracts on both the house and business within a week.

In spite of her reservations, Asta was nothing but supportive of her daughter. She'd taken time off, traveled the two hours from Portland to Departure Cove, rolled up her sleeves, and helped Runa move into her new life. That was the kind of mother she was, and Runa was grateful. She knew she couldn't do it alone.

Runa loved Asta fiercely. Her mother had been the one constant throughout her life, and she was thankful for the woman's strength. Asta was Runa's true north. She needed her, especially now when her life was in a state of complete chaos. They had always been a tight unit, a team. It was the two of them against the world.

Just eighteen when Runa was born, Asta had left Departure Cove and never looked back. She never mentioned Runa's father, and Runa didn't ask. When she was young, it hadn't really mattered. Asta was father and mother all rolled into one, and Runa never questioned a paternal absence.

As she got older, she became curious. She brought up the

subject once, and Asta told her he was dead. The sadness she'd seen in her mother's eyes made Runa never speak of him again.

"I guess it's time to start unpacking these boxes and making this place look like a boutique instead of a storage unit, huh?" Runa twirled her hair around her finger as she looked around the room.

"You'll get it whipped into shape before you know it. You've always had a knack for making things pretty," Asta answered as she popped open the cardboard box at her feet.

"I hope so. If not, I'm in the wrong line of work." Runa laughed, smiling as she looked around her shop.

The women began unpacking boxes and hanging the beautiful clothing on rolling racks. Runa was pleased with her inventory, and she couldn't wait until she was able to open.

"I'm going to grab some more boxes out of the car, Mom. I'll be right back."

Runa pushed open the glass door and stepped onto the sidewalk. The afternoon had grown overcast, and it was raining. Normally she loved rain, but not when she had to transport boxes of expensive clothing from her car to the building.

Looking up at the sky, Runa watched the gray clouds swirling above.

"It would be nice if it could stop raining long enough for me to get the last boxes inside the store," she said aloud.

Suddenly a trickle of energy ran down her spine. She shivered, having never felt anything like it. It was like a jolt of electricity. The current radiated through her body as the rain-drops slowed to a stop. The clouds receded, and the sun peeked out from behind them. As quickly as it had come, the electrical phenomenon made its way out of her body.

"What in the world was that?" Runa asked as she looked around, wiggling her fingers as they tingled. "Weird. It stopped raining."

Remembering she was headed to her car, she continued down the sidewalk. Out of nowhere, a large body plowed into her from behind, causing her to lose her balance and topple to the pavement below.

Caught off guard, she sat on the ground trying to gather her wits.

"I didn't see you there," a deep voice said from above. "Let me help you up."

Reaching to grab the man's hand as he pulled her to her feet, Runa smiled as her eyes met his. "Thank you. No real harm done, I suppose."

Rather than return her smile, the dark-haired man gaped at Runa, a look of shock overtaking his stunning features as his face grew pale. Slowly, he shook his head, as if trying to dispel the image of Runa from his mind. His body began to tremble, and he shoved her hand away with a force that nearly sent her tumbling back to the pavement.

Without another word, the man took off running, not even glancing back. He couldn't seem to get away quickly enough.

"Well, that was rude. What's his problem?" Runa steadied

herself and brushed off her jeans. "He looked like he saw a ghost."

TWO

Two weeks later, Runa took one last glance at her inventory list and dropped the notebook onto her desk. Closing the office door behind her, she walked to the front of the store. Her eyes scanned the room, and she smiled. A wave of pride washed over her as she took it all in. She had actually done it. It was opening day for Runa's, and she had pulled it off. Her dream was finally coming true.

Fixing her eyes on the clock, she breathed deeply before opening the front door and flipping the sign from Closed to Open, signaling the start of business. Waves of excitement washed over Runa, and her stomach knotted in anticipation.

The one downside to the day was that Asta wasn't there to share it. She had stayed in Departure Cove for two weeks, unpacking, moving, and helping her daughter settle in. As much as Asta wanted to be there for Runa's grand opening, she'd needed to return to Portland. She had her own business to run, and she couldn't afford to be away from it any longer.

"It's all right. You can do this," Runa whispered to herself. "All you need is customers."

Runa had no way of knowing whether opening day would be busy or slow. She realized it might take a while for people to come in and check out the store, and she'd tried to mentally prepare herself for that. She'd run an ad in the newspaper, plastered signs all around town, set up social media sites on all the platforms she could find, and tried to get the word out as much as possible. All she could do was wait and see.

Asta warned her that the people of Departure Cove were slow to warm to newcomers. At first that hadn't deterred Runa. However, after having been in town the past few weeks, she had to admit Asta was right.

Runa had experienced the town's frigid reception first-hand. As a general rule, she wasn't an outgoing person. For the most part, she kept to herself, preferring her own company to a crowd. But knowing her business depended upon the residents of Departure Cove, Runa had tried to socialize. She'd done everything she could to take herself outside of her comfort zone since she'd arrived. She drank coffee every morning in the diner next door, even going so far as to strike up awkward conversations with those around her. Most people barely acknowledged her existence, and she'd tried not to take it personally when folks didn't engage.

As a last resort, she'd gone out the night before to the local pub. She'd had dinner, a glass of wine, and dessert. She'd tried to smile and appear open and ready for interaction, but in the end, she'd spent the entire evening sitting alone at a table in the corner. No one even glanced in her direction. In a last-ditch effort to do something out of the ordinary, she'd settled for leaving a stack of business cards next to the sink in the women's restroom.

Runa had trudged home, discouraged and more than a little concerned about her future in Departure Cove. Normally she would have called her mother to complain, but she didn't want Asta to know she'd been right. In spite of everything, Runa loved the little town. So far, it seemed the affection was one-sided.

"Today is a new day. Things are going to be just fine, and customers are going to come into my store," Runa whispered to herself.

No sooner had the words escaped her lips than her body began to tingle. It was similar to that day on the sidewalk, but that had been more of a jolt. This time it was a hum, like her skin was vibrating. As the tremor passed through her body, Runa felt her discouragement leave, and in its place was a sense of calm.

"Why is my body tingling? Maybe I'm getting sick. I've been working myself too hard."

The feeling wasn't altogether unpleasant, but it was more than a little disconcerting. Trying to ignore it, Runa busied herself behind the counter. After a couple of minutes, the sensation faded. She was straightening her display case when the bell on the entrance door jingled. Runa's stomach clenched as she realized she had her first customer.

Glancing up from her work, she was surprised to find the man walking through the door was the same one who had knocked her down a couple weeks ago. Runa frowned, her nose crinkling with distaste. She thought he was a very rude man, and she didn't know why he had come into her store. Nevertheless, he was a customer, so she forced a smile and greeted him.

"Hello. Welcome to Runa's."

The man stopped about halfway to the counter and stared at her. Once again, his face grew pale and his Adam's apple bobbed up and down as he swallowed hard. The look on his face was a mixture of sadness and disbelief. He didn't move from his spot on the floor as he shook his head and took a deep shuddering breath.

Not sure what to do, Runa decided she would try again. "Is there something I can help you with, sir?"

"I… uh… well…," the man stammered as he pulled a silk handkerchief from the breast pocket of his designer suit and wiped beads of perspiration from his forehead.

Runa noticed the man looked like he was going to pass out. "Sir, are you all right? Do you need to sit down?"

He dabbed his forehead once again, gently folded the handkerchief, placed it slowly back into his pocket, and took a deep breath. "Thank you, but I'm quite well."

"You don't look at all well," Runa persisted.

She was worried about what she might have to do if the man fainted on the floor of her store.

"I'm sorry. I'm just fine. I guess I must be overheated or something," he said with a wave of his hand.

Runa thought that seemed unlikely, as it was cool and cloudy outside. Rather than argue with the man, she reminded herself that she was a businesswoman and he was in her store.

"Well then, welcome to Runa's. You're officially my first customer," she said with a tentative smile.

"Is the store named after you?" He took several steps forward until he was standing across the counter from her.

"Yes, I'm Runa Brandon," she answered with a nod.

"Well, Runa Brandon, it's nice to officially meet you. I'm Chase Everwine."

"It's nice to meet you, too. What can I do for you?"

"To be honest, I stopped by because I had to get another look at you," Chase blurted, looking a bit embarrassed as the words left his mouth.

"Get another look at me? I don't understand what you mean, Mr. Everwine." Runa bristled.

"I'm sorry. It seems I just keep making an even bigger mess of things," Chase said with a sigh. "What I'm really trying to do is apologize for my behavior the last time we met."

"You're referring to the day you knocked me to the ground

and ran away?" Runa demanded. "You acted as if you'd seen a ghost."

"A ghost... yes...." A strange look covered his face, and he cleared his throat loudly.

"Well, I don't believe in ghosts," Runa stated matter-of-factly, her hands on her hips.

"I didn't think I did either," he mumbled under his breath.

Runa gazed at Chase. He was tall, standing well over six feet. His hair, the color of mahogany, framed a jawline that was square and chiseled. His brown eyes, pools of melted chocolate, were deep enough for a woman to get lost in if she wasn't careful. He was one of the most handsome men Runa had ever seen.

He exuded an air of sophistication, and a sense of brooding magnetism practically rolled off his perfect skin. She had taken an immediate disliking to him after their first encounter, but now he seemed kind, if not a little disoriented. Perhaps she'd judged him too harshly.

"Are you looking for something specific, Mr. Everwine, or did you come in simply to apologize?"

"My poor behavior has bothered me since that day. I assure you I'm not usually this awkward, and I'm sorry I ran off like that after I knocked you down. I was... well... uh... in a hurry, I suppose. But that's no excuse," he offered, shrugging his broad shoulders.

"Apology accepted. Let's forget about it," Runa said with a dismissive wave of her hand.

"That's very kind of you, Ms. Brandon."

"Please, call me Runa."

"Very well, but that means you must call me Chase. What brings you to Departure Cove, Runa?"

"I needed a change of pace, and this place seemed to fit," she replied, giving the most basic of explanations.

"And how are you enjoying our little town so far?"

"You mean besides random men plowing into me as I walk down the street?" Runa asked with a grin.

"Yes, besides that, of course." He chuckled.

"Well, I think it will take some getting used to. It's quite a change from Portland, and folks seem slow to warm up. I'm hanging in there, though, and I'm hoping I'll be able to drum up some business and make a go of it," she explained, surprised at the ease of their conversation. She hadn't expected that.

"Give it some time. Before long, everyone in Departure Cove will be smitten with you."

Chase gave her a lingering look, then turned abruptly on his heel.

"I wouldn't be so sure about that." Runa chuckled.

"Why not? I already am."

Smiling at the look of surprise on Runa's face, Chase gave her a quick nod and walked out the front door.

THREE

W ith one final straining push, Ella screamed as her baby entered the world. Panting, she wiped sweat from her forehead as her weary body collapsed onto the bed.

"It's a girl," the midwife said with a smile as she worked to quickly clean the screaming infant.

"I know," Ella replied with a sigh. "I've always known."

"She's a fighter. Listen to those lungs. This girl's a healthy one," the midwife declared as she placed the squirming bundle into Ella's arms.

The infant squealed angrily, and Ella raised her shift. The baby rooted around until she found her mother's breast. Content, she latched on greedily.

"All of the women in our family are fighters. We've had to be," Ella replied as she watched her daughter closely.

"Indeed. Women like you don't have it easy."

"What do you mean, women like me?" Ella asked, *a hint of worry in her voice.*

"Women with powerful gifts," the midwife answered evenly.

"Gifts?"

"Magic runs through your veins, ma'am. I could see it in your eyes from a mile away."

Ella tried to hide the look of panic on her face, desperate to keep the truth hidden. *"You are wrong."*

"Don't worry. Your secret is safe with me," the midwife said soothingly.

"I don't know what you mean. I have no secrets. I am an ordinary woman," Ella insisted with a shake of her blonde head.

"As you say, ma'am. You should rest now. That little one will be keeping you up all hours of the night. You'll need your sleep." The midwife chuckled.

"Thank you," Ella said quietly as the other woman left the room.

Adjusting her weary body in the bed, Ella gazed at her daughter as the baby suckled hungrily. It seemed the girl couldn't get her fill. Yes, she was strong. That would be necessary.

"My little Maja, I wish I could give you a better world. Life won't be easy for you, as it hasn't been easy for any of the women in our family. The best gift I can give you is

an ordinary life," Ella whispered as her eyes filled with tears.

Ella's husband, Aksel, was out to sea. He would be disappointed that he had missed the birth of his daughter, but it couldn't be helped. As a fisherman's wife, Ella understood it came with the territory. She had worried about giving birth alone, and she'd been grateful for the help of the local midwife. The couple had few connections, and Ella's distrusting nature made friendships especially difficult.

Aksel and Ella had settled in Vardø the previous year. Aksel decided the coastal village was a convenient place to put down roots. For Ella, it was a bit of a homecoming. Vardø was the village of her great-grandmother, Helga, who had fled during the witch panic of 1621. Helga had longed for her homeland, so she'd passed down stories to her daughter, who passed them down to the next generation, and so on.

Ella had always known she would end up in Vardø, but she'd been careful to keep her connection to the town a secret, even from her husband. What had happened to so many others would not happen to her.

Maja popped her mouth from Ella's breast and focused on her mother's face. A small trickle of milk ran from the corner of the baby's mouth, and Ella wiped it with the edge of her shift. Maja's eyes twinkled with an otherworldly knowledge, and in that instant, Ella's fears were confirmed. Maja had the gift.

Ella had spent the entirety of her pregnancy praying the

gift would end with her. She wanted nothing more than for her daughter to be normal. Ella's mother, Nora, had cherished her gift, begging Ella to embrace her own, and in some ways she had. But Ella was pragmatic enough to understand that their differences made them targets, especially in Vardø. She feared for Maja's safety.

The last witch trial in Vardø had been many years ago, but it had happened within Ella's lifetime. That fact alone terrified her to her very core. She had been careful to keep her power under wraps since coming to Vardø, but it was a dangerous game. In that moment, looking at her obviously magical daughter, Ella knew she would do anything she could to discourage Maja's gifts.

"Rest, my little one," Ella whispered.

She waved her fingers over the baby's eyes without making contact or touching her in any way. She didn't need to; the familiar tingle in her fingertips found its intended target. Maja's eyes closed immediately, and the infant nodded off to sleep.

Gingerly easing her exhausted, pain-drenched body from the bed, Ella made her way slowly across the room. Sinking to her knees in front of an old wooden box, she carefully lifted the lid. Tucked inside was a small leather-bound book with an Ansuz rune symbol carved into its cover. Tentatively tracing her hands across the book, Ella felt the familiar vibration of energy pulsing against her skin.

"My only purpose is to keep you safe, Maja," Ella said quietly, her voice floating like a flower on the breeze.

Removing the book from the box, she opened it to the next blank page. Tears streamed down her face as she made the only decision she could.

"The story ends with us. Maja can never know the truth."

FOUR

"Thank you, ma'am." Runa smiled as she handed the shopping bag across the counter to the customer. "I hope you'll come again soon."

"You can count on it. I'm telling all my friends about your store, as well. Your inventory is exquisite, much better than anything else we have in Departure Cove," the woman answered.

"I'm so glad to hear it. See you soon," Runa added as the woman made her way out the front door.

As soon as the store was empty, Runa turned to the teenager standing next to her. "Did everything about that transaction make sense to you, Emily?"

"I think so. You're really good at explaining things."

Runa had hired Emily, a senior at Departure Cove High School, the previous day. So far, the girl was a quick study, and Runa felt confident about her choice. She hadn't expected to hire an employee so soon, but the store had been packed every day of opening week.

Runa quickly realized she couldn't handle things alone, so she'd placed a Help Wanted sign in the window. Emily answered the call. Runa would have to work around the girl's school schedule, but she'd liked her so much she was willing to give it a try.

"Would you mind folding the shirts on that table, Emily? Remember how I showed you?"

"Sure. I remember," the girl replied as she walked in that direction.

As Emily set to work, the front door opened. Runa was surprised to see Chase Everwine walk into the store. She hadn't seen him since opening day—not that she was keeping track.

"Hello, Mr. Everwine," Runa greeted.

"I thought we agreed to be on a first-name basis the last time we talked, Runa," Chase reminded her with a playful shake of his finger.

"You're right. Hello, Chase," she corrected, warmth rushing into her cheeks.

"That's much better."

"What can I do for you? Or are you simply here to apologize again?" Runa teased.

"I suppose I deserve that." Chase gave her a dimpled grin

before continuing, "I'm looking for a gift for my mother's birthday."

"I'm sure we can find the perfect item. Tell me a little about your mother. What's she like?"

"She's a domineering, powerful woman who believes she's superior to most. Her greatest aspiration in life is having a full social calendar," Chase answered with a smirk.

"Well… that's… quite a description."

Runa wasn't sure what to think. She felt sorry for the man if that was the best he could say about his mother.

"I'm sure that sounds cold and heartless to you, but that's Camille Everwine in a nutshell." Chase shrugged.

"Do you know her favorite color?" Runa tried again.

"Green, like the color of money." Chase laughed.

"Okay, then."

Walking across the store toward a rack of clothing, Runa tried to hide her astonishment. She realized the relationship she had with her own mother was closer than most, but she couldn't imagine what it must be like for Chase to have such a jaded opinion of the woman who gave him life. She felt sorry for him.

Pulling a high-end emerald-green silk blouse from the rack, she held it up in front of Chase. "What do you think?"

"It's perfect. I can definitely see that on my mother," he answered. "You're very good at your job, Runa."

"Thank you. I try."

Chase's brown eyes locked on her blue ones, and Runa's cheeks went from warm to hot. He certainly elicited a physical reaction, but that didn't matter to her in the least. She refused to fall under the man's spell. He was undoubtedly charismatic and handsome, but she would not be charmed by Chase Everwine. She was sure he had a very long string of women trailing in his wake, and the last thing she wanted was to become one of them.

"My mom will love the gift, Runa." Chase's voice interrupted her thoughts.

"That's great to hear," she replied with a nod, reminding herself to keep her thoughts professional.

"And now that you've helped me with the first part of my dilemma, I'm hoping you can help me with the second," he continued.

"What would that be?"

"I came into your store for two things: a gift for my mother's birthday and a date to her party. So far, I have one of them," he hinted.

"Are you asking me out?" Her heart raced despite her warnings for it to slow down.

"I am. Would you accompany me to my mother's birthday party Friday night?"

"I can't do that, Chase," Runa declared with a decisive shake of her head.

"Why not?"

"I have to work Friday, and I have a million things to catch up on."

Runa gave the first excuse that came to mind. She wasn't sure why she was so hesitant to go out with him, but she was. She imagined he was quite the player, and she wasn't about to get caught in his trap.

"I noticed the store closes at six o'clock. The party isn't until eight. So technically you don't have to work at that time," Chase pointed out diplomatically.

"But—"

"Camille Everwine's annual birthday bash is considered the event of the season."

"So? Why does that matter to me?"

"Everyone who's anyone will be there. It's quite the coup to get an invitation," he explained.

"I appreciate the offer, really, but I'm not much of a party person," Runa replied as politely as she could. After all, she could refuse without being rude.

"Do I need to beg?"

"Beg? You can't be serious."

"I will beg if that's what it takes for you to agree to be my date," Chase said with a chuckle.

"I wouldn't have pegged you as the type who needed to grovel for companionship," Runa quipped.

"I've never begged for a date in my life, and yet here I am." Chase shrugged and gave her a sheepish grin.

"Chase—"

"I'm getting down on my knees," he warned, bending his legs in preparation.

Runa threw out her hand to stop him. "Why do you want me to go so badly, Chase?"

"I would like to say my motives are completely noble. I could tell you I'm looking out for your welfare, it'll be a good way for people to get to know you, and it'll be great for business," he started, straightening his body.

"But that wouldn't be the real reason, I presume?"

"No. The real reason is entirely selfish."

"And what's the real reason?" Runa raised her eyebrow in inquiry.

"Runa, I haven't been able to stop thinking about you since that day on the sidewalk. I'm intrigued, and I want to get to know you better," he finished.

Runa ducked her head in an attempt to hide her flushed cheeks. She made a quick mental checklist of the pros and cons of going on a date with Chase. The list of cons was surprisingly short. Not usually one to make spontaneous decisions, Runa decided to throw caution to the wind and take a chance.

Just as she was about to say yes, she felt the tingling, vibrating prickle that was becoming increasingly familiar. Her body quivered as energy passed over her in waves.

A voice she didn't recognize whispered in her ear, "Du er i fare."

"Did you hear that?" Runa asked, glancing around the room.

"Hear what?"

"I thought I heard something."

"It was the sound of me begging you to go out with me." Chase laughed jovially.

"Okay, I'll go," Runa blurted.

"You will?"

"Yes, I will." She flexed her fingers as the electricity left her body.

"Perfect. What time should I pick you up?"

"Just give me the address. I'll meet you there," Runa insisted.

"You're the sort of woman who likes to keep a man on his toes." He chuckled. "Very well, here's the invitation. The address is on it."

Chase reached into his pocket and handed her an envelope with an embossed wax seal in the shape of an *E*. Runa noticed the invitation smelled faintly of roses. Placing the envelope behind the cash register, she tried to forget about the strangeness of the moment or what she'd just agreed to. Instead, she rang up the sale and gift wrapped the green silk blouse for Camille Everwine.

"I'll see you Friday night at eight o'clock, Runa," Chase said as he grabbed the bag from her trembling hands. "Promise you won't change your mind."

"I promise," she said.

"Can I at least have your phone number? You know, in case you get lost or anything," he explained.

"Sure," she said, scribbling the number on the back of a business card.

"I will treasure it," he declared with a mock bow as he placed the card into his jacket pocket.

"You're something else, aren't you?" Runa said playfully.

"I am."

With a smile, Chase headed out the front door, his mother's package in tow.

As soon as the door closed behind him, Emily let out a squeal. Runa jumped, startled by the high-pitched sound that emanated from her new employee.

"I can't believe you're going on a date with Chase Everwine. Oh my goodness, Runa, that man is gorgeous," the teenager gushed.

"He's nice to look at, isn't he?" Runa replied, feigning an air of nonchalance.

The truth was, she'd never met a man like Chase. He had the air of old Hollywood glamor. He made her feel like she was the most important person in the room, and that was exciting and unexpected.

"That's the understatement of the year." Emily giggled. "Wait until I tell my friends about this."

"What do you know about him, Emily?"

"The Everwines are rich, and not just a little bit. They're like the kind of rich that makes them sort of royalty," Emily explained.

"Where did all their money come from?" Runa inquired.

"The Everwines have been in Departure Cove for hundreds of years. They're lumber barons or something like that. Everwine Manor, their house, is supposed to be an amazing mansion. I've never seen it myself, but I've heard about it," Emily continued.

"What do you know about Chase himself? Does he date a lot?"

"He never dates," the girl began. "Not since his wife."

"His wife?"

"Yeah, it was really sad. She disappeared about seven years ago. I was just a kid, but it was all anyone could talk about. Nobody knows what happened to her. Some people think she drowned. Chase searched for her for years before he finally accepted that she was gone," Emily said.

"That's terrible. Poor Chase." Her heart actually hurt for him.

"Yeah, as far as I know, he hasn't dated anyone since then. I don't think he ever got over her. Isn't that romantic?"

Ignoring Emily's teenage sentimentality, Runa stewed on the information, wondering how she had managed to catch Chase Everwine's attention. It was hard to picture him as a grieving widower, but apparently, that's what he was.

"I can't wait to hear all about the Everwine mansion," Emily bubbled excitedly. "Oh, by the way, some people in town think the house is haunted."

"That's nothing but superstition, Emily. There are no such things as ghosts and haunted houses," Runa reprimanded.

"We'll see if you feel the same way after visiting Everwine Manor," Emily warned.

Runa was heading back to the storage room when her phone buzzed. She took it out, a smile blooming across her face when she saw the text from Chase.

I'll be counting down the minutes until I see you again.

FIVE

R una slipped the black silk dress over her body, checking the results in her bedroom's full-length mirror. She'd purchased the garment as inventory for her shop, but on a whim, she'd decided it belonged in her own closet.

The light fabric hugged her shape perfectly, fitting her almost like a second skin. The small string of pearls accentuated the scooped neckline, giving her an overall air of sophistication. She'd worked her blonde hair into an exquisite French twist, her dangling pearl earrings completing the look.

"I suppose you're presentable enough for the party of the century," she said to her reflection as she slipped her feet into her black heels.

She glanced at the clock, her heart speeding up as she saw

it was almost seven thirty. She'd considered canceling at least ten times that day, but in the end decided against it. After all, she'd promised to go, and the thought of disappointing Chase didn't sit well with her, especially since he'd had two dozen red roses delivered to her shop earlier that afternoon.

He'd called to see if his driver could pick her up, but Runa refused. She had never been to Everwine Manor, and she barely knew Chase Everwine. Putting herself in such a vulnerable situation seemed unwise. Instead, she hoped to be prepared for the worst possible scenario, which meant driving her own vehicle.

Locking the front door behind her, Runa headed to her car. Sliding into the driver seat, she turned the key in the ignition, and her ancient Volvo rumbled to life. Typing the address into her phone, she discovered Everwine Manor was only twenty minutes away. Backing out of her driveway, she exited her neighborhood, drove down Main Street, and headed out of town.

The evening had grown dark, the winding road dimly lit. She had the fleeting thought that she should have driven the route at least once in daylight to give her some idea of her destination. But she hadn't, so there was nothing to do but drive.

Squinting, Runa finally saw the sign instructing her where to turn. Flipping on her signal, she veered off the main road onto the narrow one leading up the hill toward Everwine Manor. Slowing her car even more, she flicked on her bright lights in an effort to illuminate the encroaching blackness.

The road was deserted except for her car, a fact which seemed odd considering it was the only way to Everwine Manor. She had little time to ponder because it began to rain, huge drops pounding on her windshield and blurring her vision. Blinking rapidly in an attempt to see more clearly, Runa turned the wipers to their highest speed. The blades danced a sort of tango across the glass but did little to clear the deluge.

Slowing to nearly a crawl, she leaned in closer to the steering wheel. It had become impossible for her to see more than a few inches past the hood of her car. To make matters worse, her head was pounding and sudden waves of nausea rippled in her middle. It had all come out of nowhere. Between the lack of visibility and her sudden malaise, Runa thought it best to stop for a breather.

Noticing a spot to safely maneuver her car off the road, she eased the Volvo into Park and exhaled sharply. Her head was spinning like an out-of-control carousel. The rain, which had turned into a torrential downpour, pounded its fists on the hood of her car. The spot where she stopped was heavily wooded, the only light for miles around coming from her car's high beams. Looking at her phone, she squinted as the overly bright display illuminated the car. It was ten minutes before eight o'clock. She was going to be late.

Runa's stomach churned violently, and her head thudded

as the beams of her headlights grew blurry. She blinked, trying to clear her suddenly distorted vision, but it was no use. She grew disoriented, and before she could stop herself, she slumped in the seat as she passed out.

Without missing a beat, Runa's subconscious took over, playing a series of images like the reel of a silent movie. She saw a woman with blonde hair falling from a window high above the ground. Runa wondered if the woman had been pushed or if she had jumped. Strangely, she felt the woman's desperation deep inside her soul, almost as if she were the one falling.

The woman never hit the ground but instead continued to tumble. Down, down, down she went, on and on, free-falling into an abyss that seemed to have no end. Suddenly, the ground rose up beneath the woman. Runa let out a scream because she didn't want to witness her inevitable impact. Just as the woman was about to hit the ground, Runa jolted awake. Her eyes popped open, and strange words echoed into the stillness of the car.

"Du er i fare."

Panting, Runa straightened her body until she was once again sitting upright in the driver seat. Looking around to locate who had spoken the strange indecipherable sentence, she saw no one. She was alone in the car. The words began to fade, but Runa remembered she had heard them before.

"What is happening to me?" she whispered into the quiet, shivering uncontrollably.

Trying to make sense of the nonsensical, she winced at the scraping sound of windshield wipers on dry glass. The blades were going a mile a minute, but the rain had stopped. In fact, as Runa looked outside, she didn't see a drop of moisture anywhere on the ground. The leaves on the trees hadn't seen rain in several days. They were dry as a bone.

Turning the wipers off, she tried to untangle the web of confusion in her head. A rush of headlights drew her attention to the long line of cars heading up the hill toward Everwine Manor. The road, completely deserted before she passed out, now flowed in a seemingly endless stream of traffic.

Grabbing her phone, Runa checked the time. The display read ten minutes before eight o'clock, exactly the time she remembered it saying before she lost consciousness. How was it possible that no time at all had passed? It didn't make sense, and she was suddenly afraid. She wanted nothing more than to go home and bury herself beneath her blankets. Something strange was happening, and she had no clue what it was.

"Get a hold of yourself, Runa. You've been working too hard and you're stressed. That's all. There's a perfectly reasonable explanation for everything."

She took a deep breath, trying to convince herself of the simple fact.

Placing her shaking hands on the steering wheel, she maneuvered her car back onto the road. Taking her place at the end of the line of traffic, she aimed the Volvo up the hill toward Everwine Manor.

Runa turned up the volume on the radio in an attempt to drown out the strange words that echoed in her mind.

"Du er i fare."

She had no idea what the phrase meant, and she wasn't sure she wanted to.

SIX

Trying to control her racing heart, Runa followed the car in front of her, claiming a space in a cobblestone parking lot the size of a football field. She'd never been to a home that had its own parking lot. She estimated there were at least one hundred other cars parked alongside hers, her beat-up Volvo looking out of place next to the fancier models. The ancient vehicle didn't quite belong, kind of like Runa herself.

Pushing her feelings of inadequacy aside, she hopped out of her car and followed the line of guests as they meandered from the parking lot down a marble path winding through an expertly trimmed formal hedge garden. The sculpted shrubbery zigged and zagged, forming a sort of maze. Runa was glad she was following the crowd; on her own, she would have surely been lost.

The perfect symmetry of the towering hedgerows opened up to reveal the most opulent courtyard she had ever seen. A large fountain, interspersed with both cherubs and gargoyles, bubbled to life before her eyes. On the opposite side of the water feature, two men in tuxedos greeted the guests as they arrived.

As she waited in line, Runa took in her surroundings. The grounds were more opulent than anything she could have imagined.

"If the lawn is this magnificent, the house must truly be amazing, just like Emily said," she mumbled to herself, trying to calm her nerves. "I can't believe I'm here."

When it was Runa's turn to enter the party, the servants greeted her, placed a flute of champagne into her trembling hands, and directed her through the floral archway toward a large enclosed outdoor building teeming with guests. The glass ceiling of the structure, draped with gauzy white fabric, was twinkling with interwoven lights peeking through the delicate material.

The room's ambience was ethereal, making her feel like she was standing beneath a starlit sky. Four enormous chandeliers hung in each corner of the room. A black-and-white checkered dance floor was flanked on one side by a string quartet playing chamber music in the background.

Tables lined the perimeter of the room, each draped with elegant white linens and set with fine bone china dinnerware. Large flared vases overflowed with white plumeria and dangling green vines. Men in tuxedos mingled throughout the room, removing empty champagne flutes and replacing them with full ones. Everything was done so seamlessly it appeared to be a sort of choreographed dance.

Runa scanned the room for a familiar face but came up empty. Chase was nowhere to be seen, and she hated crowds. Her heart palpitated and her palms grew sweaty. She anxiously drummed her red fingernails on her champagne flute, debating how quickly she could make her exit before anyone discovered she was there.

She was just about to leave when she heard his voice.

"You're here."

Swallowing hard and trying to get her nerves in check, Runa turned and smiled at Chase, her eyes widening in shock and appreciation. He looked like he had walked off a movie set, sporting a black dinner jacket and matching trousers that fit him like a glove. His white shirt and black bow tie gave him an air of elegance and sophistication, and his perfect dimpled smile made her heart do jumping jacks in her chest.

"I was hoping you wouldn't change your mind," Chase said with a sparkle in his eyes. "You look absolutely gorgeous, by the way."

"Thank you. I almost stayed home," Runa admitted. "In fact, I was just about to run to my car and pretend I'd never come."

Chase leaned down and whispered into her ear, "Looks

like I got here just in time, then. I have no intention of letting you get away that easily."

Goose bumps erupted on Runa's flesh, and words failed her.

"Come with me and I'll introduce you to my parents."

Chase placed his hand on the small of her back and steered her through the crowded room. Runa allowed herself to be guided as she followed, almost in a trance. She was glad her legs remembered what they were supposed to do, because her brain had turned to mush. She was unable to form a coherent thought with Chase's proximity. He was completely intoxicating, and in that moment, she understood she could easily fall under his spell.

They came to a halt in front of the head table, and Runa glanced down at the champagne flute she was holding. A small drop of the liquid sloshed onto her hand, and she realized she was shaking. Chase must have noticed the tremor as well because he took the drink from her hands, placed it on the table, and clasped her clammy palm inside of his.

At the table before them, a beautiful golden-haired woman was perched beside a stunning dark-haired man. The man was in deep conversation with one of the servers, and the woman was working the clasp on a gigantic diamond tennis bracelet.

"Mother, Father, I would like to introduce you to my date." Chase cleared his throat in an effort to gain his parents' attention.

The woman stopped fiddling with her bracelet and stood to face them. "Of course, darling, I would love to meet—"

The elegant beauty stopped midsentence and covered her mouth with her perfectly manicured hand in an effort to stifle the loud strangling guttural sound escaping her lips.

Upon hearing the strange noise his wife made, Chase's father's head snapped in their direction. His tanned face drained of color as he looked back and forth between Chase and Runa.

"Who...? How...?" the man stammered, clearly at a loss for words.

Runa's eyes darted from Chase to his parents, a feeling of unease settling in her gut. Mother, father, and son stared at one another, their eyes speaking volumes, although no one uttered a word. They carried on a silent conversation which didn't include her; Runa was simply a bystander, an observer of the strange scene playing out before her eyes.

Chase's mother's hands flitted about like tiny butterflies, unable to find a landing place. His father shifted his weight from one foot to another, staring at Runa and shaking his head.

Finally, Chase broke the awkward tension.

"Runa, this is my mother, Camille, and my father, Easton," he said as he gestured toward his parents. "And this is Runa Brandon."

Easton seemed to remember his manners first and reached out to clasp Runa's hand tightly in his. He gazed at her with a look of blatant longing that made her feel strangely unsettled.

Without breaking eye contact, he brought her hand to his lips and kissed it tenderly.

"It is so nice to meet you, Runa. My, you are lovely." Easton's hungry eyes swept over her, lingering far longer than they should have. "My son has told us absolutely nothing about you, so you'll have to excuse our shock."

"Of course," Runa replied uncomfortably.

She slowly pulled her hand away from Easton, having to tug a bit harder than she intended. He seemed intent to hold on.

"Mother? Aren't you going to say hello?" Chase scolded.

"You've left me little choice in the matter, haven't you, Chase?" Camille retorted sharply.

"Mother, I'm warning you…," Chase began.

"What on earth do you think you're doing?" Camille snapped at her son.

"Enough," Chase warned through gritted teeth.

Taking a deep breath, Camille smoothed her shaking hands over her white dress. Turning her icy blue eyes toward Runa, she glared at the younger woman. The anger Runa saw behind those eyes made her take an involuntary step backward. She had no idea what she'd done, but obvious hatred emanated from Camille.

"You should not have come here," Camille practically spat.

"Mother," Chase warned again.

"You've brought this upon yourself, Chase. What were

you thinking, bringing her here? What will people say?" Camille shook her head in disdain.

"Who I spend my time with is no one's concern but mine," Chase replied.

Mother and son locked eyes in a battle of wills. After several moments of strained silence, Chase stepped away from his parents and turned toward Runa.

"Since my mother can't seem to remember her manners, Runa, we'll take our leave. I'll show you around the estate."

Without another word, Chase draped his arm across Runa's shoulders and steered her away from his parents.

SEVEN

Still reeling from the intense encounter with Mr. and Mrs. Everwine, Runa wiped beads of perspiration from her upper lip. She had no idea what happened, but clearly her presence greatly disturbed them.

Glancing at Chase, she noticed his face was a mask of indifference. He seemed completely unruffled by his parents' reactions to meeting her.

Needing some sort of explanation, Runa stopped walking.

"What was that about, Chase?"

She planted her body firmly in front of his, refusing to move until her question was answered.

"What do you mean?"

"The way your parents reacted. Why did they say those things?"

"Oh, that was nothing. My mother is a drama queen, and

my father is always over the top. Don't worry about them," Chase explained with a grin and a wave of his hand.

"Your mother looked like she wanted my head on a silver platter, Chase. I'm not sure how I'm supposed to ignore that," Runa replied indignantly.

"They don't matter."

"Your parents don't matter?"

"They have their lives and I have mine. Their opinions are inconsequential."

Runa searched Chase's face for clues but found none. Something told her she should simply thank him for the invitation and leave. It was clear there was more to the Everwines' reactions than met the eye, and getting involved with Chase was probably a bad idea. She should go home and forget she'd ever met him.

As if he could read her mind and sense her apprehension, Chase traced his fingertip across her cheek, wiping a wayward wisp of hair from her face. Her heart lurched inside her chest. She felt drawn to him in a way that was both exciting and terrifying. He was such a nice man. Maybe she should give him a chance. In that moment, against her best judgment, she pushed all thoughts of leaving aside.

"Forget about my parents. Come with me, Runa. I'll show you the rest of Everwine Manor."

He extended his open hand, and she placed hers inside without another moment's hesitation. All thoughts of anything besides Chase were whisked away on the breeze that ruffled the leaves of the weeping willow trees.

The pair wandered hand in hand down a winding path aglow with twinkling lights. Before Runa could prepare herself for the shock, Everwine Manor emerged into view. Resting upon a sheer cliff overlooking the Pacific Ocean, the mansion was both imposing and inviting. She caught her breath, unsure of whether she wanted to run away or inch closer. As her eyes adjusted, the house seemed to exhale, as if it had been waiting for her all along.

"It's beautiful," she breathed.

"It is," Chase replied.

"Tell me about it."

"Everwine Manor was built in 1898. It's surrounded by acres of forests overlooking the ocean. There's not another house for miles around."

Trying to memorize each nook and cranny of the exterior of the vast estate, Runa moved forward as if in a trance. Everwine Manor was a grand Victorian mansion interspersed with elements of both Queen Anne and Gothic Revival architecture. It was three stories tall, boasting cupolas, pointed frames and arches, wide porches, and a dizzying array of stained glass windows.

The steeply pitched roof was scattered with several gables, ornamental pillars, and various asymmetrical facades. A startlingly high tower with a large turret jutted from one side of the third floor, standing like a sentry above the house.

"It's huge. A person could get lost in there," Runa murmured.

"The sheer size is the only reason I'm able to live under the same roof as my parents," Chase quipped.

"How big is it?"

"The house is over twenty thousand square feet in area, with three floors, two separate wings, and twenty-five rooms. The tower itself rises a hundred feet above the ground," he explained.

Runa fixed her gaze upon the imposing turret at the top of the dangerously high tower. Something about the structure felt familiar, but she couldn't pinpoint why. It was circular in shape and boasted some of the most beautiful and intricately designed stained glass windows she'd ever seen.

As she watched, she thought she detected movement behind the windows, but it was so far away that she couldn't be certain.

"Would you like to see the inside?" Chase interrupted her thoughts.

"I'd love to. Can we go inside the tower?"

"No. The third floor has been closed off for years."

Runa followed Chase through the mammoth front door and stood in the grand entryway. Inlaid hardwood floors gleamed beneath her feet, and a sixteen-foot ceiling loomed above. Several glimmering chandeliers hung from the ceiling, bathing the area in soft light. She tried to conceal her shock and awe, but it was pointless. Everwine Manor was impressive, and it was absurd for her to pretend otherwise.

As she entered the hall, she noticed exquisite rooms to both her right and left. The first appeared to be a formal parlor. The polished table was set with a lovely china tea service, the ornate empty chairs beckoning, seemingly ready to entertain guests at a moment's notice.

A large maritime painting hung above the fireplace. The vivid depiction of the ocean caught Runa's attention. She could almost feel the icy coolness of the water upon her skin.

"That painting is lovely," she gushed.

"It's a Cleveland Rockwell. He did a lot of paintings of the area around the time Everwine Manor was built," Chase explained.

"I've always been drawn to the water."

"Well, you've come to the right place. The best view of the ocean is right outside."

Runa glanced in the opposite direction, toward the music room. Another large fireplace towered above a grand piano. A gigantic stained glass window decorated the far wall, and she drew closer to inspect its design as she absently traced her fingertips across the fabric of a plush velvet sofa.

Upon examination, Runa inhaled sharply. The colorful window depicted a blonde woman standing on the shore next to the crashing waves of the ocean. Peering intently at the glass, she realized the woman looked eerily like her.

"Who is the woman in the stained glass window, Chase?"

"I honestly have no idea," he replied nonchalantly, appearing not to notice the resemblance.

Runa inspected the window, finding it difficult to look away. As she tried to make sense of the uncanny similarities between herself and the woman, she felt a light touch upon her shoulder. Expecting to find Chase standing there, she was surprised to find him across the room sprawled over a velvet settee. He wasn't near enough to have touched her, yet they were the only ones in the room.

"Du er i fare," a woman's voice whispered in her ear.

They were the same words she'd heard before, but she still couldn't decipher their meaning. The sudden chiming of a grandfather clock caused Runa to nearly jump out of her skin.

"Feeling a little spooked?" Chase asked with a grin as he rose and came to stand next to her.

"Maybe a bit," she admitted sheepishly.

"The house has that effect on people."

"Don't get me wrong. It's gorgeous. It's just a lot to take in."

"You have nothing to fear here," Chase said, moving closer.

Runa turned to face him, her heart beating rapidly inside her chest. He took another step toward her, and she noticed the heat emanating from his body. Tilting her head up, she looked into his eyes, feeling a little dizzy. In one swift movement, he dipped his head toward hers. Their lips touched, and a jolt of electricity arced into her, the intensity of the kiss suddenly magnified.

The feel of his lips on hers was excitingly new, yet somehow familiar. It was as if she had always known him, as if some part of her had experienced this moment before. She knew it wasn't possible, and yet she couldn't deny the feeling.

"Wow…," she breathed when the kiss ended and they pulled apart.

"My sentiments exactly," Chase whispered, a knowing smile turning up the corners of the lips she'd just kissed.

"So… the window…," she said, breaking eye contact. She cleared her throat and tried to regain her sense of balance.

"Yes?"

"Well… don't you see it?"

"See what?"

"Forget it," she said with a wave of her hand.

If Chase didn't see the resemblance between her and the woman in the window, perhaps it wasn't actually there.

"What were you going to say, Runa?" he persisted.

"Well, this may sound odd, but I thought I recognized the woman in the design of the stained glass window," she began.

"That wouldn't be possible. I'm not sure if the artist based the design on a real woman or not, but even if he had, she wouldn't be alive. Those windows were crafted in the late 1800s."

Chase patted Runa on the arm and chuckled. She suddenly felt silly and naïve.

"I suppose you're right It's just that…."

"Yes?"

"The house feels… I don't know… familiar and… almost… alive."

"I assure you, Everwine Manor is nothing more than wood and glass." Chase grinned.

"It feels like more than that," she mumbled to herself.

Runa wasn't sure how to voice her feelings, but something about the atmosphere made her uneasy. It suddenly felt like the walls were closing in, like something was pursuing her and she needed to flee. Her stomach clenched with anxiety.

"Are you all right, Runa? You look pale."

"I'm not feeling well. I think I need to leave," she offered weakly.

"If you're ill, you have no business driving home alone. The roads out here are treacherous. Let me drive you, and I'll have my chauffeur pick me up at your house and bring me back."

"Chase, that's not necessary," she protested.

"Please. It's dark, and you don't look well. It's the least I can do after convincing you to come here," he insisted.

Not feeling up to an argument, Runa reluctantly agreed. Taking one last glance at the stained glass window, she allowed Chase to lead her to her car.

EIGHT

VARDØ, NORWAY, DECEMBER 1793

"Astrid, please come and help me prepare the lefse," Frida called.

"Coming, Mother," Astrid answered.

"Don't take all day. Your father will want his dinner soon," Frida scolded.

"Here I am."

Ten-year-old Astrid scrubbed her hands and joined her mother at the table. She started peeling potatoes while Frida prepared the flour. Mother and daughter worked side by side, both lost in silent contemplation.

As she worked, Astrid daydreamed. Cooking was a tedious chore, and the girl would prefer to do nearly anything else.

"I wish these potatoes would peel themselves," Astrid said as she dropped the knife and turned to her mother.

"Wouldn't that be nice?" Frida chuckled.

"I hate peeling them. It's such a waste of time. There must be an easier way." Astrid sighed.

"Less talk, more work, girl," her mother chided.

Turning back to the table, Astrid's eyes widened when she saw the potatoes lying on the table, fully peeled, skins stacked in a large pile. The girl's body tingled, and waves of electricity rippled down her spine. Mouth agape, she tried to ascertain how such a thing could have happened.

She raised her hands for inspection and noticed snaps of blue firing from her fingertips. Shoving them beneath her apron, she willed the sensation to go away. After several seconds, it did. Grabbing the knife, she pretended to peel so her mother wouldn't notice the job was already completed.

The self-peeling potato incident was one in a long line of strange events that had been happening to her. It seemed Astrid had somehow gained the uncanny ability to manifest her wishes into reality. Last week she'd said it would be nice if the cow could milk itself, and no sooner had the words been spoken than the milk bucket was filled. Astrid wasn't sure if she or the cow had been more shocked.

She hadn't breathed a word of it to anyone, especially not her mother. Frida had no patience for things that weren't practical. Her mother was a no-nonsense woman, and Astrid knew better than to share the mysterious and curious information. Besides, what would she say? There was no logical explanation for any of it.

"Would you look at that? You're quite fast at peeling pota-

toes, my girl." Frida raised one eyebrow as she observed how quickly Astrid had completed the chore.

"Well, you make me do it so often that I've become good at it," Astrid lied. "May I be excused since I'm finished?"

"I suppose so. Please carry that box of fabric up to the attic first, and then you may have some free time."

"Yes, Mother."

Astrid grabbed the small box and quickly made her way toward the stairs before her mother could change her mind. Taking the steps two at a time, the girl flopped onto the attic floor. She was glad to have a little space to think about the strange occurrences. Frida always said there was a rational explanation for everything, but she knew there was more to it. Some sort of magic was coursing through her body. She could feel it.

She shoved the small box into the corner and was just about to leave when another box caught her eye. Lifting the wooden lid, Astrid gasped. Tucked inside was a small leather-bound book with an Ansuz rune symbol carved into its cover. Tentatively tracing her hands across the book, she felt a vibration of energy pulse against her skin.

Curiosity got the better of her, and she removed the book from the box. Opening it, she flipped through the pages. Each had different handwriting, and as Astrid read, she began to piece together the information. It seemed to be a book of family history, each scribe relaying her generation's tale.

The women in the stories had power—some could read

minds, some controlled water and other elements, some were able to move objects with a thought, and others could even heal sickness. According to the book, the most special was the "generation of two," who possessed all of the gifts but would sacrifice something in return. Astrid didn't know what any of it meant, but she was intrigued.

She flipped to the front of the book. In curling script was the title, Daughters of the Sea. *Astrid's pulse quickened as she began to scour the pages. It seemed the women had been revered as healers in the community. For many generations they had been proud of their powers, writing story after story of the ways they used their special skills.*

As Astrid continued reading, she noticed things began to change. In the 1620s, a woman named Else was put to death for witchcraft, and her daughter, Helga, fled Vardø. Several generations later, her descendant returned to the village, but instead of pride for her gift, there was nothing but fear. That woman, Ella, decided it was best to hide her powers.

Astrid marveled at the treasure she'd found as she read aloud.

"1683, Vardø, Norway: This book carries the stories of generations of women in my family, some who have died because of the powers they were given. These gifts have become curses, and we must deny them if we are to stay safe. I will not write down my story. Instead, I will hide the book and give my daughter an ordinary life. That is the best I can do for her."

That was the last paragraph written in the book. Nothing followed but a list of names and dates.

Ella, 1663

Maja, 1683

Thea, 1704

Leah, 1727

Amalie, 1748

Frida, 1767

Astrid, 1783

Seeing her own name, as well as her mother's, on the list, Astrid began to connect the dots. These weren't random women—they were her ancestors. The book had remained a secret for over a hundred years. Although it had been passed down through the women, none after Ella had written their stories. Instead, they simply recorded their names.

As she cradled the book to her chest, something began to stir inside her. It was a slow burning sensation, creeping down her spine and radiating to her fingertips. In that moment, she understood. The things that were happening to her weren't strange at all. They were part of her birthright.

While the magic prickles tingled throughout her body, Astrid made a conscious choice in her young mind. She would be the keeper of the stories. She would write everything down so each woman who came after would know. She would be proud of her power and instill that pride in her own children someday. No longer would their powers remain hidden in the dark. Astrid would bring their gifts into the light.

NINE

"Runa, should I bring these shirts up front?" Emily surfaced from the back room. "It's the new shipment you've been waiting for."

"Yes, please. We'll use a couple in the window display and hang the rest over there." Runa pointed at a rack across the room.

"I'm on it," Emily replied.

"Thanks, Em."

Runa finished wiping down the jewelry case while Emily tackled the window display. She couldn't believe how helpful the girl was, a great worker, always ready to jump in and learn something new. She was the breath of fresh air that Runa needed.

"I've been waiting all afternoon to ask you, but I can't hold it in any longer. Tell me about your date. Was Everwine

Manor beautiful? Did Chase look handsome?" Emily gushed as she adjusted a shirt on the mannequin in the window.

"It was… an experience."

"What does that mean? You're going to need to elaborate, Runa."

Wrinkling her nose, Runa tried to think of a way to explain the evening to Emily. She'd barely slept the night before, playing it all over in her mind. The entire event had been unsettling. From her blackout experience on the way to the party, to the Everwines' strange reaction upon meeting her, and the eerie feeling when she stepped inside the house, nothing about it had been comfortable.

What was most disturbing, however, was the uncanny resemblance between herself and the woman in the stained glass windows of the mansion, not to mention the hand on her shoulder and the whisper of the strange phrase in her ear.

"I don't know exactly what to say, Emily. It was nothing like I expected," Runa began.

"In a good way?"

"Not really," Runa hedged. "The house was lovely, though, and Chase was wonderful."

"Are you going to see him again?"

"I'm not sure. I wasn't feeling very well, so he drove me home. He said he would call." She shrugged.

She didn't tell the girl that Chase had kissed her, or that the electricity she'd felt when his lips touched hers was magnificent. The connection between them was immediate and intense, and she still felt a bit light-headed when she thought of it. He'd been a perfect gentleman but had made it abundantly clear that he wanted to see her again. Her pulse quickened and her lips tingled as she remembered the kiss. If she was being honest with herself, she hadn't stopped thinking about Chase since that moment.

"What kind of man is Chase, Emily? I mean, clearly he's rich and handsome, but is he more than that?"

Discussing her personal life with her young employee was probably not the best choice, but Runa had no friends in Departure Cove. She needed someone to confide in, and Emily was there.

"You mean is he more than just a pretty face?" Emily giggled.

"Yes, something like that."

"Chase Everwine is rich, but he's also generous. He donates a ton of money every year to charities for women and children."

"Really? That's great."

"The children's wing of the hospital is named after him because he donated all of the money for it," Emily continued.

"Oh wow."

"And he volunteers as a mentor at the high school," she added.

"He does?"

"Yep, he does career coaching."

"He sounds like a really great guy," Runa replied thoughtfully.

"Chase is wealthy, gorgeous, kind, and generous."

"It seems like he is."

"I would definitely stay away from him if I were you," Emily said sarcastically.

"You're making fun of me?" Runa inquired, raising an eyebrow.

"Maybe a little bit. I don't think you should be so skeptical of him."

"I guess I'm a bit wary because I've had some bad experiences with men," Runa admitted with a shrug.

"You're so nice. Guys probably take advantage of that." Emily peered intently at Runa.

"I'm far too trusting, but it's something I've been working on. I always see the best in people, even when it's not there. It's gotten me in more than a few jams. Chase seems like the real deal, though."

"He's definitely one of the good guys. You don't have to worry about him. Does that mean you're going to go out with him again if he asks?" Emily raised one eyebrow in curiosity.

"Maybe. I guess we'll have to see if he asks, won't we?" Runa joked.

"Uh-oh. Don't look now, but Chase's mother is walking down the sidewalk," Emily said with a quick glance out the window. "Looks like she's headed this way, and she doesn't seem very happy."

"Great."

Runa gritted her teeth. The last thing she wanted was to deal with Camille Everwine. After her frigid reception the night before, she would prefer to never see the woman again.

"She's coming inside, Runa," Emily warned, her eyes wide with worry.

Before they could say another word, Camille shoved open the glass door, the bell jingling noisily. The click-clack of her high heels on the wooden floor echoed ominously throughout the room as she stomped toward Runa. The scent of the woman's rose petal perfume was cloying, causing Runa's insides to twist violently. Taking a deep breath, she prepared herself for the worst.

"Mrs. Everwine—"

"Let's skip the niceties, shall we? I'm sure you're smart enough to know I'm not here on a social visit," Camille sneered.

"I don't know—"

"Save it. All you need to do is listen to me. I'm here to tell you that if you don't stay away from my son, I will personally make your life a living hell. I don't know who you think you are, but a woman like you has no business with a man like my son," Camille spat.

"Mrs. Everwine—"

"A person of your breeding isn't fit to be a servant in my home, let alone date my son."

"You don't even know me," Runa replied defensively, offended by the woman's judgment.

"Asta Brandon is your mother. That's all I need to know. She was a gold digger. Apparently the apple doesn't fall far from the tree."

Camille raised her chin haughtily, looking at Runa as if she were a speck of dirt on her designer shoes.

"You can say what you like about me, Mrs. Everwine, but you will not come into my place of business and talk about my mother." Runa, who hated confrontations, felt her blood pressure rise.

"You're so pathetic. Do you have any idea how much my son loved his wife? No one, especially not you, could hold a candle to her. She was cultured, raised in an exemplary family. She was all the things you'll never be. You cannot live up to her memory, and you'd do well to remember it. Stay away from my son."

With that, Camille Everwine turned on her heel and stormed out of the boutique, leaving a startled Runa and Emily in her wake.

"Are you okay, Runa?" Emily ran across the room and hugged her boss tightly.

"I… I don't know what her problem is…."

"Did something happen at the party?" Emily asked.

"You could say that. She wasn't exactly excited to see me there. I still have no idea why," Runa admitted.

"She said she knew your mother. Doesn't sound like they

were friends," Emily mused.

"No, it certainly doesn't."

The buzz of Runa's cell phone in her pocket startled her, and she grabbed it. Her heart fell as she looked at the display. It was Chase. She considered ignoring his call, then decided she needed to put an end to things once and for all. She couldn't handle the drama of his mother in her life, no matter how attracted she was to the man.

"Hello, Chase," she said as she answered.

"I've been thinking of you since last night. Are you feeling better today?"

Chase's voice reached through the phone, reeling her in like a fish on a line. She was drawn to him, and she wanted to know him better. The thought both angered and saddened her because it wasn't possible. His mother had seen to that.

"Not especially," she replied icily.

"I'm sorry you're not feeling well. Maybe I can bring you dinner tonight after work? We wouldn't have to go out," he offered.

"That's not a good idea, Chase," she answered, sorry to have to say the words.

"Maybe tomorrow, then?"

"I don't think so." Her heart actually ached when she thought about never seeing him again.

"Is something wrong, Runa?"

"It's best if we don't see each other, Chase. At all." Tears fell from her eyes, and she wiped them away with the back of her hand.

"Why—"

"Please don't call me again."

Without another word, she hung up the phone and dropped it into her pocket as she gave in to the sobs that racked her body.

TEN

VARDØ, NORWAY, 1883

Mille paced back and forth across her bedroom floor as her husband watched, a worried crease crinkling his forehead. She cradled her enlarged abdomen as the pain radiated through her midsection, gaining in intensity. Gazing out the window, Mille saw the rainbow of the northern lights dancing across the sky. She closed her eyes and tried to feel the colors inside her soul. She had always been connected to them, and seeing their glow calmed her tumultuous spirit.

"Is it time?" Mathias asked.

"Not quite," Mille answered as calmly as she was able.

"But soon?"

"Yes. Soon, my love."

"Shall I get the book?"

"Yes," Mille replied. "I would like you to read it to me once more."

Mathias rose quickly, and Mille heard the attic stairs creak as they bore the weight of her husband's large frame. She felt the quickening as her daughters tried their best to move inside of their cramped living quarters. The girls were anxious to make their entrance into the world, and she knew they would arrive before the night was over.

For nine months Mille had been anticipating the birth of her twins. Mathias never questioned how she knew she was carrying more than one daughter; he simply accepted it as fact. He had known Mille her entire life, and to his credit, he always acknowledged that his wife was blessed with special gifts beyond his understanding.

Mille had a reputation as the village healer, and the couple's home was often filled with neighbors in need of help. Whether it was a special tincture she'd concocted to heal a sickness or someone seeking wisdom and advice, her neighbors held her in the highest regard.

She had an affinity for wind, and she warned the village fishermen accordingly. Mille's wind knots were legendary, and sailors visited her before charting their courses. Her potent charms were believed to be the most powerful, and her ability to call upon the wind was revered. She knew her daughters would be even more special than she was. She could feel it. She couldn't wait to teach them about their gifts.

A sharp pain gripped Mille's belly, and she doubled

over in an effort to find some relief. She let out a gasp and made her way to the closest chair. Mathias rushed into the room and dropped to his knees in front of his wife.

"Is it time?"

"Almost. Where's the book?"

"Here," Mathias said as he placed the leather-bound pages into her hands.

As she reached for it, she was gripped by another pain.

"What should I do?" Mathias asked anxiously.

"Read it to me," Mille answered as she closed her eyes.

Mathias's shaking hands leafed through the book as he began to read the familiar words to his wife, just as he had every day for the past nine months, although he didn't understand why. He'd spoken about Mille's ancestors so many times that he had their stories memorized.

"Tuva, born in 1803, could foretell the future in her dreams. Selma, born in 1825, could move any object with the power of her mind. Malin, your mother, born in 1843, was a healer who could keep sickness at bay with her knowledge of plants and herbs," he recited.

"They were powerful women," Mille said between labored breaths.

"Just as you are," Mathias replied.

She let out a loud wail and gripped her abdomen.

"Is it time?" he asked again.

"Yes, it's time. Help me to bed," Mille instructed.

"Should I call the midwife?" Mathias's face was a tumultuous sea of worry.

"Need I remind you that I am *the midwife?"*

Mille's face twisted with pain as she spoke.

"Yes you are. But perhaps another woman would be better suited to help you—"

"We'll do this alone. Everything will be fine. I've seen it," she replied with certainty.

"But if anything should go wrong—"

"Nothing will. I promise."

Mathias lifted his wife's slight frame and carried her to their bed. Her white-blonde hair fell across her sweaty face, and he brushed it away. Mille had insisted they would deliver their babies alone, and although he had agreed, he was having second thoughts now that the moment had arrived.

She had delivered too many babies to count, and she was confident in her ability to talk her husband through the ordeal. As long as the book was close by, everything would be fine.

"Where's the book?"

"Here, my love," Mathias replied as he held it before her.

"Place it under the pillow beneath my head."

Mathias did as Mille instructed, although the strange act made little sense to a man as practical and logical as he.

"Now open the windows so I can invite the breeze inside."

"The breeze? Mille, it's freezing out there. Are you sure?"

"I'm certain. The villagers call me the Wind Witch after all, don't they?"

Mille did her best to smile at the moniker as her body was seized by another pain.

"That they do. You're the Wind Witch of Vardø."

Mathias unlatched the windows, opening them wide as the chilling arctic wind billowed into the room. The gust of air howled and nipped at the skin on his face as it whizzed past, snuffing out the candles as well as the fire in the hearth. Startled, he attempted to relight the flame, but it was no use. The wind rushed through the room, whipping and blowing everything in its path.

"Mille—"

"As You will... som du vil... as You will... som du vil...."

Mille chanted and prayed in the darkness, her strained, haunting voice causing the hairs on her husband's arms to rise. Mathias stumbled across the room and perched on the bed at his wife's side. Gripping her hand in his, he watched as her face twisted with pain. She clenched her teeth and squeezed him with a force he didn't know she possessed.

Suddenly she stopped praying and her eyes popped open, locking onto his with a ferocity that took his breath away. She stared at him, unblinking, as if in a trance. A giant gust of wind blew into the room, powerful enough that it nearly knocked him over.

Opening her mouth wide, Mille sucked in a deep breath, and with it, she swallowed up all the wind in the room. Mathias watched in disbelief as his wife held the air inside her body for a split second and then blew it out.

A hurricane-force gale erupted from Mille's lips, leaving her body and exiting the room with a whoosh. As it left, the windows slammed shut, the flames on the candles reignited, and the fire in the hearth relit. Simultaneously, her body gave its final push and her daughters entered the world, one right after the other. The book, which had been tucked beneath her pillow, was now lying across her chest as sparks of blue radiated from its cover.

As she sank into the bed with relief, Mille's eyes searched for Mathias's.

"Meet your daughters, Brynja and Sigrid," she whispered weakly.

"You were right all along," he breathed, awestruck by his wife's power.

"The generation of two. I have never felt such potent magic."

ELEVEN

Runa sighed as she unboxed her most recent shipment. She'd been in a funk, and no matter what she did, she couldn't snap out of it. The shop was thriving, bustling with customers, busier than she could have imagined. Emily was a stellar employee and an asset to the store. Runa finally felt welcomed into the Departure Cove community. On paper, everything was perfect, and she knew she should be happy and content.

But she wasn't.

As much as she hated to admit the truth, the reason for her dissatisfaction was Chase Everwine. Although the friction with his mother was a hurdle she didn't want to jump, Runa couldn't help but wish they could have given things a chance. There was magnetism between them, an undeniable connection, and if given the opportunity, she believed that spark could have ignited into a full-blown flame.

It had been two weeks since she'd told Chase to leave her alone, and she'd second-guessed her decision every day since. She couldn't stop thinking about him, partially because he kept dreaming up new ways to change her mind.

He'd sent a dozen roses to the shop on three separate occasions, followed by expensive chocolates. One evening she'd arrived home and found he'd had dinner delivered with a note that simply said *I'm thinking of you.* He'd respected her wishes about not calling, but he had texted her several times, each message sweeter and more sentimental than the last. His various gestures let Runa know he hadn't given up on them.

Emily told her over and over that she should ignore his mother and listen to her heart, but she wasn't sure. Runa couldn't handle Camille Everwine's obvious hatred and disapproval, especially when she had done nothing to deserve the woman's vitriol.

"Do you want me to change out the mannequins in the front of the store? We have those new dresses that would look great on display," Emily suggested.

"That's a good idea. Let's do it," Runa agreed.

The two women were lost in creative concentration when the bell on the front door jingled, signaling a customer. Runa glanced up from her work, her heart skipping a beat when she saw Chase. Her lips grew warm as the memory of their kiss surfaced in her mind.

As much as she would prefer to hide and let Emily send him away, she knew she couldn't. She needed to handle the situation. Taking a deep breath, she approached him.

"Hello, Chase. What can I do for you?"

She straightened her spine and tried to keep her voice as chilly and unwelcoming as possible. It was more difficult than she imagined it would be.

"Runa, it's been two weeks since I've seen you. I couldn't wait any longer." The sadness on his face tugged at her heart-strings.

"Chase—"

"You said not to call, and I haven't. But you didn't say I couldn't come into the shop," Chase said sheepishly. "I had to see you."

Runa cleared her throat and tried to ignore the nagging voice in her brain telling her she was being too harsh on him. After all, Chase's mother was the problem, not him. Was it right to blame him for his mother's actions?

"I suppose I should have been more specific about you not calling." Runa did her best not to meet his eyes, knowing her resolve would crumble if she did.

"Did you get the flowers? And the dinner? And the chocolates?"

"I did. Thank you, but none of that was necessary." She kept her eyes focused on the floor.

"But it was. I wanted you to know I was thinking of you," Chase said helplessly.

The desperation in his voice made Runa's heart melt. She felt the veneer of her hard shell begin to crack open. She tilted her head up and looked at him, the sincerity on his face causing her heart to constrict.

"Look, I appreciate all of it, but this thing between us—whatever it is—can't happen," she insisted, trying to make herself immune to his charms. It didn't work.

"I know why you're saying that."

"What are you talking about?"

"I know my mother came to see you, to warn you to stay away from me," Chase stated.

"How could you possibly know that?"

"She told me. She was proud of herself for 'fixing' the situation," he retorted, a flash of anger in his eyes.

"She said some hurtful things to me, Chase," Runa admitted.

"I'm sure she did. Hurting people is her specialty. But forget whatever she said to you. As I've told you before, my parents' opinions matter little to me."

"That may be true, but if you and I are together, your mother's path will undoubtedly cross with mine. I can't live my life on the defensive," she argued, trying to make him understand.

"You won't have to defend yourself. I'll do it for you. I've warned my mother to stay in her place. And if she is ever a problem, you must come to me right away. I'll take care of it," he explained.

"I don't think it's going to be that simple. Your mother's feelings are intense. That won't go away." Runa shivered as the image of Camille's angry face surfaced in her brain.

"Perhaps. But she will keep her opinions to herself. Or else." Chase grinned, but there was an edge to his words.

"Or else what?" Runa inquired, curiosity getting the better of her.

"Just leave my mother to me."

"I'm not sure it's going to work."

"I'm sure enough for both of us." Chase grabbed her hand and squeezed it, pleading silently.

Runa's heart begged her to lower her guard and give him a chance. She knew her feelings for him were strong, and from the look in his eyes, he felt the same way about her. She didn't know how or why, but something about Chase pulled her to him. She was tired of resisting.

"Okay," she whispered, giving in.

"What does that mean?" he asked, a tinge of hope in his voice.

"It means we can give things a try."

A giant smile bloomed across her face as she spoke the words she'd wanted to say for weeks.

Chase sighed with relief and pulled her close to him in a crushing hug. He held her tightly, running his hands across her back in rhythmic strokes that soothed her frayed nerves. Being in his arms felt right, and although she couldn't explain it, maybe she didn't need to.

"You have no idea how happy you've made me," Chase whispered. "You're like a dream come true."

Runa beamed as she allowed herself to be fully engulfed in his embrace. She didn't understand her intense emotions, or why she was so certain she belonged with Chase. All she knew was she'd been lucky enough to catch his attention, and she wasn't going to blow it. She'd made terrible choices in the past in regards to men, but her dreams of a perfect life in Departure Cove were coming true. She was going to listen to her heart and forget about the rest.

"So we'll have dinner tonight? I'll pick you up at seven?" Chase offered, still holding on to her.

"I'll be ready," she replied, feeling completely content for the first time in ages.

Chase pulled away and tilted her face up toward his. He simply looked at her for a couple seconds, seemingly drinking her in. Leaning down, Chase cupped his hand behind Runa's head, gently pulling her face to his and lightly brushing his lips on hers. The kiss lingered, igniting a spark inside, filling her with anticipation. When he pulled away, it felt too soon.

"See you tonight," he whispered before he turned to leave.

Runa watched him go, mentally calculating the hours until she would see him again.

"I knew it. I knew the two of you belonged together," Emily gushed as soon as the door closed behind him.

"He's really something, isn't he?" Runa agreed, still a bit breathless.

"He's a good catch, Runa. Every woman in town is going to be jealous of you."

Still reeling from the kiss, Runa tried to bring herself back to reality by working on her inventory in the back room. She was going through her list when her phone rang. Glancing at the display, she smiled when she saw it was her mother.

"Hey, Mom," she answered happily.

"Hey, baby. Tell me," Asta stated, not wasting a second on small talk.

"What do you mean? Tell you what?"

"Something's up," Asta said knowingly.

"How do you know?"

"Your aura is red."

"Mom, you know I don't buy into that stuff," Runa replied with a roll of her eyes.

"That's your choice, but the fact remains."

"Fine. Enlighten me. What does a red aura mean?"

"Red auras signify love, passion, energy," Asta began.

"I suppose that makes sense."

"It can also be the warning of danger," Asta continued.

"Well… the first part is accurate," Runa hinted.

"What are you not telling me, Runa?"

"I've met someone, and he's wonderful."

"And?" Asta prompted.

"And his name is Chase Everwine—"

"Everwine?" Asta drew in a sharp breath. "No, Runa. You must stop this very minute."

"Mom—"

"Listen to me. The Everwines cannot be trusted."

"That's funny. Camille Everwine said the same thing about you," Runa said flatly.

"That woman—"

"Look, clearly you had some type of history with them, but that's in the past. You don't even know Chase. The fact that you had issues with his parents has nothing to do with him, or with me."

"Runa—"

"Tell me why you don't trust them. Give me a solid reason," Runa demanded, suddenly feeling very defensive.

"Well…."

"Go on. If it's so imperative that I stay away from Chase, you need to tell me why."

"I… I… can't…," Asta fumbled.

"That's what I thought. Since you can't back up your opinion with any facts, I don't want to hear another word about it."

"Runa—"

"I mean it," Runa insisted.

"All right. I don't want to upset you," Asta soothed.

"Then be happy for me. That's all I need," Runa pleaded.

"I'm not sure I can do that," Asta answered sadly.

"Then we're going to have a problem, Mom," Runa said quietly.

TWELVE

VARDØ, NORWAY, 1897

"Sigrid, are you all right?"

Fourteen-year-old Brynja ran into her twin sister's bedroom as she heard the loud fit of coughing. Concerned, she placed her hand on Sigrid's back, wincing at how thin her sister had become.

"It's happening," the girl wheezed.

Sigrid turned her too-pale face and held out the white cloth that was splattered with red bloodstains. Her body trembled, and her bony clavicle protruded through her nightgown. Sigrid's weight loss had been steady and relentless, and in the past few months, it had stolen any excess flesh from the girl's bones.

"No, Sigrid, no. It can't be." Brynja shook her head violently in denial.

"First Mama, then Papa, and now me," Sigrid whispered as tears rolled down her sunken cheeks.

"It won't take you. I won't let it." Brynja stamped her foot in anger.

"There's nothing to be done. It's consumption. We've tried all of our remedies, used all our power," Sigrid replied.

"There must be something else. I can't lose you. I wish it would take me instead," Brynja wailed.

She grabbed her sister and pulled her close, crushing her frail body within her desperate embrace. Sigrid winced and Brynja released her grip.

"Brynja, I am going to die. I've seen it. I saw it months ago, right after we lost Papa," Sigrid admitted.

"Why didn't you tell me?"

"I couldn't bear it. I hoped I was wrong."

"Mama always said we were powerful, stronger than any force she'd ever seen."

"We are," Sigrid replied calmly.

"She called us the generation of two." Brynja's angry voice rose as she paced the room.

"And so we are. But she also said a sacrifice was necessary."

"And you're the sacrifice?" Brynja railed.

"Something must be given up to have the power," Sigrid reminded her.

"What does it matter if we can't make you well?" Brynja yelled.

"Our power isn't given to us for ourselves, sister. It's given to us so that we may help others," Sigrid answered serenely.

The twins had always been opposite sides of the same coin. Where Brynja was spirit and fire, Sigrid was calmness and tranquility. Never had it been more obvious than in that moment.

"Well, I don't want the power. If I'm not strong enough to help you, what good is it?"

Brynja's anger turned to desperation as she sank to the floor and began to sob.

Sigrid, unable to handle the sight of her twin so distraught, knelt beside her and held her as tightly as her frail arms would allow.

"You know the good our power can do. Mama taught us our history. It isn't for us to control. We're simply the vessels. God directs it."

"But how will I survive without you? How can I live without my breath?" Brynja raised her head and looked into her sister's identical blue eyes.

"I'm part of you, and I always will be."

"The very best part."

"And I'll always be with you, but you will go on, long after I'm gone." Sigrid smiled.

"What will I do?" Brynja sobbed.

"You'll tell our story. You'll continue our legacy."

"I can't do it without you."

"But you will. I've seen that as well. My story ends here,

but yours will take you far away, across the sea, into a new land," Sigrid explained.

Sigrid reached beside her and grabbed the large leather-bound book from the table. She placed it into her sister's hands and clasped her own on top. Blue streaks of light emanated from the book and traveled through their skin, crackling and illuminating, filling the room with magic.

THIRTEEN

"Mom, you're here! I'm so excited to see you," Runa gushed as she opened her front door and pulled her mother into a giant hug.

"Hey, baby. I'm glad to finally be able to hug you." Asta gathered Runa's body closely to hers.

It had been more than three months since Asta had seen her daughter, and things in Runa's life had changed dramatically. Although it was difficult for her to leave Portland, Asta felt she had little choice in the matter. There were things she needed to discuss with Runa, and that was best done in person.

"Come in. Let's get you settled. I have the guest room ready for you," Runa babbled on excitedly as she led her mother inside and closed the door.

"You've really made this little house of yours into a home, haven't you? It has nice ambience. Good energy. Very welcoming," Asta complimented her daughter as she took in the view.

"It's great. I love it here. I feel like I've finally found my place, you know?"

"Yes, it would seem so…."

"What's wrong, Mom? I know something is bothering you. That's why you're here, right?" Runa raised her eyebrow perceptively.

"I'm just here to visit with my daughter for a few days. I missed you. Is that so wrong?" Asta strategically avoided Runa's eyes as she spoke the half-truth.

"Of course not. I've missed you, too, but I can't help feeling there's more to this visit than you're letting on," Runa answered.

"I just want to check out your new life. I don't really feel like a part of it, and that's new for me. I want to spend some time with you," Asta soothed.

"Well, in that case, I'm glad you're here."

The women deposited Asta's luggage in the guest room and made their way downstairs, where they seated themselves at the kitchen table.

"How are things at the shop?" Asta inquired, glancing around the homey kitchen.

"Things are amazing. It's been busy every single day. I'm constantly ordering more pieces, which is great. I've even hired an employee to help me out," Runa shared.

"That's great news, honey. I'm so proud of you. You've really taken control of your life."

"I'm going to make us some tea." Runa rose and went to the cupboard.

Asta watched her daughter measure out the tea leaves and place the kettle on the stove to boil. Runa seemed different, guarded, changed. On the surface, things appeared to be going well, but her motherly instinct told her there was cause for concern.

Asta had been having strong visions of Runa in trouble, but the messages were jumbled, and she couldn't make sense of them. Still, change was in the air. She could feel it. Runa was involved with the Everwines, and Asta had to tread lightly in that department. She couldn't afford to create an irreparable rift between her and her daughter. Not now, when there was so much at stake.

"The shop sounds like it's doing well," Asta began. "How is everything else?"

"By everything else, do you mean Chase?" Runa turned her head toward her mother and gave her a knowing look.

"Perhaps. How are things with Chase?" Asta's heart rate sped up considerably as she dove into the murky waters.

"He's wonderful. Truly. I've never been happier. The past three months with him have been the best of my life. He's so considerate, and he always puts me first, which is a change from any of my other relationships. He also doesn't try to control me."

"It sounds like things are getting serious," Asta hedged.

"Well…," Runa hesitated, knowing what she needed to say, yet dreading her mother's reaction.

"Well what?" Asta probed.

Runa poured the tea into the pot, carried it to the table, and plopped into the chair across from her mother. She took a deep breath as she watched the steam roll from the pot, taking a moment to formulate her answer.

"Well, you could say things are serious. As a matter of fact, I'm glad you're here." Runa reached across the table and clasped her mother's hands in her own. "There's something I need to tell you."

"What is it?"

"Last night, Chase asked me to marry him. And I said yes."

Asta's head spun with the unexpected information. Her breath came in rapid spurts, and she yanked her hands away from Runa's, gripping the edge of the table as her body grew stiff. The room began to twist, and her vision clouded with red. She tried to find her daughter, but Runa was surrounded by a solid red wall, and Asta had no idea how to get around it. She opened her mouth to speak, but rather than what she wanted to say, strange words that she didn't understand flowed from her lips instead.

"Du er i fare. Du er i fare. Du er i fare."

RUNA GASPED as her mother spoke the strange phrase, the same one she'd heard numerous times since arriving in Departure Cove.

"Mom, what does that mean? What are you saying?"

Asta didn't answer. She stared blankly ahead, as if in a trance.

Runa sprang from her chair and knelt before her mother, shaking the woman's shoulders in an effort to bring her back to reality.

"Du er i fare," Asta whispered again.

"Mom—"

As suddenly as the strange behavior began, it stopped. Asta's vision cleared, she straightened her body in her chair, shook her head, and glanced around the room in confusion.

"What happened?"

"I have no idea. Are you okay?"

"Yes, I think so."

Runa slowly took her seat once again.

"Why did you say that? What does it mean?"

"I don't remember saying anything," Asta replied, her forehead wrinkling with confusion.

"You kept saying a phrase over and over again, but the words weren't in English."

"Runa, I don't know any other languages."

"I've heard the phrase before. Several times, in fact," Runa continued. "Du er i fare."

"I wish I could be more helpful, but I have no clue what

that means." Asta shrugged. "All I remember is seeing a red aura all around you after you told me—"

"That Chase and I are getting married?" Runa finished.

"Yes. Runa, won't you please reconsider?"

"No. I won't. I love Chase, and he loves me. We are getting married, and that's final."

"How can you know you're doing the right thing? You just met him. Your relationship has moved so quickly. Give yourselves time to get to know each other," Asta pleaded.

"I know everything I need to know. Chase loves me. He practically worships the ground I walk on. What more could I possibly want?"

"Honesty, transparency…," Asta began, her eyes filling with tears.

"Here we go again." Runa stood from her chair and began to pace. "What makes you think he hasn't been honest and transparent?"

"Because I know the family he was raised in. People live what they learn." Asta sighed, wiping her eyes. "Some legacies are too difficult to overcome."

"What does that even mean, Mom? You talk in circles without ever giving solid answers."

"The Everwines are a powerful, controlling family. People are simply a means to an end with them. Relationships are disposable in their eyes. Is that solid enough for you?"

"No!" Runa exploded.

The women didn't speak for several minutes, each trying to corral their runaway thoughts.

Finally, Runa took a deep breath and sat down once again. "Look, I know something happened between you and them."

Asta reached across the table and gripped her daughter's hands in hers.

"Yes, I have a history with the Everwines. There's a lot of bad blood."

"Won't you please tell me what happened? Help me understand," Runa begged.

"I grew up in Departure Cove. We all went to the same school."

"Were you friends?"

"For a while. Until things grew… tricky."

"What happened then?"

"I became dispensable," Asta remarked coldly.

"Can you tell me more?" Runa begged. "Give me something else to go on."

"No. I wish I could, but I can't. It's for your own good."

"But why?"

"I have my reasons. It's best if we leave it at that."

"I thought honesty and transparency meant so much to you." Runa leveled her gaze at her mother as her words filled the quiet room.

"Runa…."

"Fine. Don't tell me. But Chase and I *are* getting married, and you're going to have to find a way to come to terms with that." Runa crossed her arms over her chest in defiance.

"You are my daughter, and I will give my life to protect you. I hope it doesn't come to that, but I'll do what's necessary," Asta replied cryptically.

FOURTEEN

The next afternoon, Asta and Runa took a stroll around town in an effort to avoid conversation. They spent the previous evening dancing around the elephant in the room, neither woman anxious to circle back to the subject of the Everwines. They were at an impasse.

Runa hated the divide that existed between her and her mother, but she didn't see any way to bridge it. She was marrying Chase, and Asta didn't approve of her decision. Rather than argue, it seemed best not to discuss the matter at all.

"What's this place? I've never seen it before," Asta mused as she glanced inside the window of a curious-looking shop.

"Talisman. It looks like a hippie shop. That's right up your alley. Let's go inside."

"Great idea," Asta agreed as they opened the door.

The smell of patchouli wafted through the air as the women entered the dim candlelit storefront. Various crystals, small vials of essential oils, and a plethora of glass jars packed with fragrant herbs lined the shelves. Runa tentatively ran her finger across the edge of a Tibetan singing bowl, and the sound echoed in the quiet room.

"This is amazing." Asta nodded in appreciation.

"Hello there," a voice called from the back room.

A door closed as a woman approached them. She was about Asta's age, with wild brown curly hair. The woman had the most astute green eyes Runa had ever seen, the kind that could look at a person and know everything about them in an instant. They were equally enchanting and unnerving.

"Welcome to Talisman. I'm Tawney, the owner," the woman greeted.

"Tawney Berg? Are you kidding me?" Asta raised her hand to her mouth in shock. "I haven't seen you in years!"

"Oh my goodness. Asta Brandon? I can't believe it's you," Tawney gushed as she grabbed Asta and pulled her into a huge hug.

Runa watched with surprise as the women babbled on about how long it had been since they'd seen each other. After a few moments, they seemed to remember she was standing there.

"Tawney, this is my daughter, Runa. She moved to Departure Cove a few months ago. She opened a boutique around the block," Asta explained.

"Runa's, yes, I've seen it. You have some beautiful things in your window. I've been meaning to stop by," Tawney replied.

"You should," Runa urged. "So how do the two of you know each other?"

"Oh, Tawney and I go way back. And I do mean *way* back." Asta chuckled as she grabbed the other woman's hand.

"Your mother and I were inseparable from kindergarten all the way to graduation." Tawney shook her head as a look of sadness swept over her lovely face.

"Yes, we lost touch after I left town, didn't we?"

"We did, although I never understood why. We were so close, and then you just… well… disappeared after—"

"That's one of my biggest regrets about my past," Asta interrupted as her hands fluttered nervously toward her throat. "Perhaps we can make amends. What do you say?"

"Of course we can. The past is in the past. All things happen for a reason, don't they?"

Tawney's astute eyes met Asta's, and the women stared at each other, seemingly sharing a lifetime of unspoken messages. After a couple minutes, they nodded, confirmation of a silent agreement to something Runa didn't understand.

"So, how are you enjoying our little town, Runa?" Tawney asked.

"I love it so far. The people have been quite welcoming," Runa replied, a blush creeping into her cheeks as she thought of Chase.

"You'll be settling down here?" Tawney's all-seeing eyes bored into Runa, reading and understanding things she shouldn't.

Runa squirmed under the scrutiny. "Yes. I'm getting married soon, so I'll be staying."

"Married? To someone local?" Tawney raised her eyebrow quizzically.

"As a matter of fact, yes. I'm engaged to Chase Everwine," Runa replied.

"Everwine?" Tawney's eyes met Asta's, and once again, the women seemed to communicate without saying a word.

"Yes." Runa stiffened her spine. "Let me guess, you don't care for the Everwines either?"

"I make a habit of keeping my opinions to myself. I'm a firm believer that people always show their true colors in the end." Tawney shrugged noncommittally.

"You two really are a pair, aren't you?" Runa asked, irritation filling her words.

"What do you mean?" Tawney asked.

"Never mind."

"All I will say, Runa, is that you need to listen to your instincts. Don't ignore them. They're there for a reason."

Tawney touched Runa's shoulder, and as she did, her eyes lit up like light bulbs. She stared at Runa for a couple moments without looking away. Runa squirmed nervously.

"What is it? Why are you staring at me like that, Tawney?"

"May I hold your hands for a moment, Runa?"

Runa shifted from one foot to another. She wasn't sure why, but Tawney made her feel unsettled, as if the woman knew too much.

"I know it's an odd request, but I feel compelled to do it. I always follow my intuition," Tawney explained.

Not wanting to be rude, Runa pushed her uneasiness aside.

"I suppose," she agreed as she joined her hands with Tawney's.

Runa watched as Tawney closed her eyes. Her hold on Runa's hands tightened, and her forehead creased as a look of concern passed over her lovely face. Runa's heart pounded as Tawney continued squeezing her hands.

After what seemed like a lifetime, Tawney's eyes fluttered open and she released her grip. Glancing back and forth between Asta and Runa, Tawney paused a few moments before speaking.

"Runa, do you believe in magic?"

"No." Runa chuckled, rolling her eyes. "That's my mom's department."

"Whether or not you believe doesn't change its existence. You have magic in your blood, Runa."

"I don't think so, Tawney." Runa waved her hand, shooing away the woman's words.

"But you've experienced things you can't explain." Tawney spoke the words as a fact, not a question.

"I'm not sure what you mean." Runa tried to avoid the woman's eyes but found she couldn't look away.

"I know strange things have been happening to you since your arrival."

"How could you possibly know that?"

"I saw it when I held your hands," Tawney answered nonchalantly.

"You saw it?"

"I see things. I'm a very observant woman. I'm a bit like your mother but in my own way."

"No wonder the two of you are friends." Runa shook her head as she tried to figure out how to extricate herself from the uncomfortable situation.

"I can see you're anxious to leave, Runa, but before you go, may I give you a gift?"

"A gift? Why would you want to give me a gift?"

"You are the daughter of my oldest and dearest friend. Consider it an engagement gift."

Tawney smiled mysteriously as she turned on her heels and walked across the room toward a glass case filled with crystals. She grabbed one and returned to where Runa was standing. Tawney held her palm out flat, revealing a necklace, glinting as the facets of the crystal picked up flecks of light.

"It's beautiful," Runa breathed as she ran her finger across the jewelry.

"It's a black tourmaline," Tawney explained.

"For protection," Asta chimed in as her eyes locked on to Tawney's.

"Protection from what?" Runa asked.

"I've told you for months now that your aura is red," Asta said quietly.

"Mom—"

"Your mother is right, Runa. I don't see auras, but the picture I saw when I held your hands told me you're going to need all the protection you can get," Tawney replied, her eyes holding Runa captive.

"If the two of you are conspiring to scare me out of marrying Chase, it's not going to work," Runa warned, looking away.

"That's not what this is about," Tawney answered as she hooked the necklace around Runa's neck.

"Good. Because I'm marrying him," Runa said stubbornly.

"Chase is part of the picture I saw, but I'm not sure what role he plays, if any," Tawney admitted.

"I don't buy into this, but just out of curiosity, will you tell me what you saw?"

"The pictures I see aren't always clear. I get snippets of a scenario but not the entire thing."

"Okay, then tell me the snippets," Runa demanded.

"Are you sure you want to know? Sometimes it's best not to," Tawney warned.

"Yes, I want to know."

"Tell her, Tawney. Maybe it'll help," Asta suggested.

"Very well. I wasn't able to see any faces, but I saw a blonde woman. She was crying. She was locked in a prison, and she wanted very badly to be free. But her path made freedom impossible."

"And you're saying the blonde woman is me?"

"I'm saying there was a blonde woman and I couldn't see her face. Nothing more, nothing less," Tawney answered evenly.

Runa fiddled with the black tourmaline necklace. Was it her imagination, or did the crystal feel hot beneath her touch?

"Thank you for the necklace, Tawney. It was nice to meet you. Should we go now, Mom?" Runa was suddenly anxious to leave.

"Of course," Asta agreed. She turned toward Tawney and embraced her. "This time we won't lose touch."

"We certainly won't. We're going to need each other," Tawney answered enigmatically.

Ignoring the undercurrent of mystery between the women, Runa cleared her throat. "I'll see you again soon, Tawney. I hope you'll consider coming to my wedding. I'll be sure to bring over the invitation as soon as they arrive."

"I'll be there. You can count on it. Our paths are connected now."

Tawney's all-seeing eyes locked on to Runa's, and a shiver slithered down Runa's spine. Glancing at her hands, Runa saw the strange flecks of blue light emanating from her fingertips. Shoving her hands into her pockets, she made her way out the door.

FIFTEEN

VARDØ, NORWAY, 1898

"Brynja, will you join me in my study, please?"

"Of course," she called. "I'll be right there."

Fifteen-year-old Brynja walked quickly down the hallway toward Captain Ingebjorg's office. Taking a deep breath, she went inside.

"Sit down, my dear," Captain Ingebjorg instructed.

"Of course, sir," Brynja answered as she sank slowly into the richly upholstered armchair.

"You've lived with us for six months, Brynja. I've told you that 'sir' is a bit formal." The kind man chuckled.

"I'm sorry, sir—I mean Captain Ingebjorg," Brynja corrected.

"Perhaps in time you'll feel more comfortable." He smiled.

"You and your wife have been so kind, taking me in after

my parents and my sister....” Her voice trailed off as tears filled her eyes.

“Your mother was a highly respected woman in our village. Her knowledge of the wind saved my ships on more than one occasion. It has been our honor to take you in and care for you,” he answered.

“I know I’ll never be able to repay your kindness.” Brynja wiped her eyes and tried to compose herself.

“Perhaps there is a way.”

“I am indebted to you, sir, and I will help you however I can.”

“I’ve observed that you have a great many abilities. Did your mother teach you?”

“My mother taught me from as far back as I can remember. My sister and I spent our lives honing our craft. Mother always said we were much more powerful than she ever was. I’m not sure whether I believe that or not.” Brynja shrugged.

“You have knowledge of wind knots?” Captain Ingebjorg steepled his fingers and leaned forward.

“I have constructed many.”

“Do you have an affinity for the wind as your mother had?”

“I can call upon the wind and communicate with it. I can feel it before it ever arrives,” Brynja explained.

“What else can you do?”

“I can make tinctures to heal sickness, but mostly I heal with the touch of my hands. I see colors surrounding people,

and those colors tell me the path that person will walk. I have visions, often very vivid, that foretell the future. I can control objects with my mind. I understand many languages that I have never spoken, which makes it easy for me to communicate. These are just a few of the things I can do."

"Your mother couldn't do all of that." Captain Ingebjorg's eyes widened with surprise.

"No, she couldn't. I think that's why she believed me to be more powerful."

"Well, your abilities are truly extraordinary, my dear," he replied.

"Thank you. Is that what you wished to speak with me about?"

"Indeed. I'm setting off on a long voyage, and I'm in need of your service."

"How can I help?"

"Mrs. Ingebjorg and I are leaving Vardø. This is to be a long journey to a place I've never been. I'm worried for the safety of my wife and my crew."

"You would like for me to make a wind knot?" Brynja asked.

"More than that, my dear. I'm asking you to accompany us on our voyage. Your knowledge and abilities will ensure our safety."

"What is the name of the place?" Brynja's forehead crinkled.

"Oregon. It's in America."

Her eyes widened. *"I've dreamed of that name."*

"What do you mean?"

"Ever since Sigrid died, I've been dreaming of a place called Oregon. I've seen it so vividly and have felt compelled to go there, but I had no idea it would ever come to pass. I didn't even know if it was a real place."

"I assure you, it's very real. Many Norwegians have settled there. Seafaring is a big industry, especially where we're heading," Captain Ingebjorg explained.

"I've seen the town in great detail," Brynja confessed. *"I dream about it every night."*

"Then perhaps you should tell me the name of the town where we're headed." Captain Ingebjorg chuckled with delight at his young ward.

"Departure Cove."

"You are indeed a wonder, my dear. That is the name of the place." The captain nodded and smiled widely. Brynja's inexplicable knowledge of the town was the confirmation he needed.

"Sigrid was right. My path will lead me on a journey to a faraway place," Brynja said quietly.

Captain Ingebjorg rose from his desk and stood in front of Brynja. Crouching down to her level, he clasped her tiny hands inside his large calloused and weather-beaten ones.

"So you'll join us on the ship? You'll speak to the wind on our behalf?"

She nodded solemnly. *"I will. I believe it's my destiny."*

SIXTEEN

"September 21 is the day we're getting married, Mother." Chase ran frustrated hands through his hair and sighed loudly.

"Summer weddings are best. Mark my words, you'll regret having a wedding in September."

Camille's voice lashed like a whip, and Runa wished she could hide under the large table in the Everwines' opulent drawing room. Chase and his mother had been fleshing out wedding details for what seemed like years.

Runa tried to be compliant and go along with whatever Camille wanted in an effort to keep the peace. Chase, on the other hand, had definite opinions on their wedding, most of which did not align with Camille's.

"Once again, Mother, this is not your wedding. Runa and I

will be married on September 21," Chase retorted. "It's the first day of fall. I've always loved autumn."

"I don't think you understand the consequences of such a choice. That date is less than a month away. Do you have any idea how long it takes to plan a proper wedding? Why such a rush?" Camille tapped her red nails on the table in irritation. Suddenly, a strange look washed over her face. "She's pregnant, isn't she?"

"What? No!" Runa interjected, her face flushing with embarrassment.

"Mother!" Chase admonished.

"Well, it's a legitimate question. You barely know the girl, and now you want to be married in less than a month. What am I supposed to think?" Camille insisted.

"You're supposed to think that I've found the woman I love and I can't wait to begin my life with her. You're supposed to be happy for me. That's what mothers do, I hear. Not that I would know." Chase glared at Camille.

Runa's stomach flipped. She hated conflict, and it was difficult to listen to Chase and Camille go at one another, especially since they were fighting about her. Honestly, she understood Camille's concern. Their wedding was rushed. They hadn't been together very long. Of course she had reason to be suspicious. But Chase wanted her, and she loved him. She loved him with a fierceness she didn't even fully understand. Perhaps she was caught up in the romance and whirlwind of it all, but she was happy, and all she wanted was to be Chase's wife. The sooner the better.

"Fine," Camille said after a couple minutes of uncomfortable silence. "But you do know that most people plan their weddings at least a year in advance. Everyone will think the girl is pregnant."

"I don't care what most people do, or what they think. Our wedding will be in three weeks, and it will happen with or without your help."

"But, Chase—"

"I've only included you in this discussion to be polite, but if you continue to be impossible, I will rescind the invitation and take care of the details myself." Chase straightened his backbone and glared at his mother.

"But what about caterers, florists, wedding planners—"

"You have connections, Mother, and wealth beyond measure. Surely you can use those things to your advantage. Or are you not up to the task?"

Runa watched as the woman latched on to the challenge, hook, line, and sinker. Chase certainly knew how to bend Camille to his will.

"Of course I'm up to the task. Don't be silly. If a wedding in three weeks is what you want, then that's what you'll get."

Camille patted her son's hand indulgently, and Chase smiled smugly.

"I need to marry this lovely woman before she changes her

mind. I can't let her get away," Chase joked as he winked at Runa.

"No, that would be too much to ask for, wouldn't it?" Camille replied with a cold glance at her future daughter-in-law.

Chase shot an angry look at his mother before turning to Runa to bring her back into the conversation. "This is what we want, right, Runa?"

"Of course. Really anything is okay with me. I don't want to be a bother," Runa replied quietly.

Camille skewered Runa with her icy eyes. "A bother indeed," she whispered under her breath.

"What did you say, Mother?" Chase challenged.

"Not a thing. A September wedding will be just fine. Where do you intend to have it?"

"Here, at Everwine Manor."

"Logical. That takes care of the venue, then," Camille agreed.

"We haven't discussed all of the details, but I'm sure Runa has some ideas she would like to share. It is her wedding, after all," Chase added.

Mother and son turned toward Runa, and she gulped, pushing down the feeling of nausea she'd been fighting since the beginning of the tense discussion. She was terrified of Camille, and although Chase kept his mother at an even keel, Runa knew the woman despised her. The last thing she wanted was to share ideas about the wedding. She simply wanted to disappear into the background and let the two of them fight it out. Better yet, she wished she and Chase could just elope.

"The details aren't important to me. I'm just happy to be marrying you, Chase," Runa replied quietly.

"Of course you are," Camille retorted. "Why wouldn't—"

Chase glared at his mother, and she didn't finish her sentence.

"Are you sure, darling? I know you must have ideas, preferences. Don't most girls have their weddings planned out from birth? I want to make our special day everything you've always dreamed of." Chase clasped Runa's hand in his.

"Really, Chase, I'm sure anything your mother wants will be just fine with me. I'm not much of an event planner, and Camille, you clearly have a knack for it." Runa smiled at the other woman in an effort to crack the veneer.

"It is amazing how much you look like her, yet the two of you couldn't be more different," Chase said under his breath.

"Chase!" Camille rebuked, causing her son's head to snap in her direction. The two shared a silent message that Runa didn't understand.

"Who do I look like, Chase?"

Runa was confused and unsettled by her fiancé's strange statement and his mother's reaction to it.

"No one, my love. I was speaking out of turn," Chase answered as he squeezed Runa's hand tightly. "No one matters but you."

"Clearly you were talking about someone." Runa pulled her hand away and crossed her arms defiantly.

"He was talking about his cousin, for goodness' sake. You slightly resemble the girl, but she's certainly much more well-bred," Camille said haughtily as she exchanged another perplexing glance with her son.

"Yes, my cousin," Chase agreed. "Now, tell me what you want for the wedding. The sky's the limit. You name it and it's yours."

"All I want is to pick out my dress. The rest doesn't matter to me." Runa smiled, trying to push the overwhelming sense of conflict and unease into the background.

"Ridiculous girl," Camille retorted with a roll of her eyes.

"Camille, I would be pleased to let you plan the wedding. Really. You have impeccable taste, and I trust you'll come up with something far superior to anything I could arrange." Runa hesitantly met Camille's glare.

She wanted nothing more than for Chase's mother to accept her, but that seemed unlikely. Perhaps if Camille had creative control over the wedding, they could manage to peacefully coexist. Maybe Camille felt threatened by the thought of another woman in the family. If Runa could convince her that she had no intention of usurping her place, perhaps the animosity would go away. It seemed worth a try.

"Very well," Camille wrinkled her nose at Runa with distaste. "Since you're unwilling to pitch in and help with your own wedding, I'll take care of it. Someone obviously has to. We have our reputation to consider, after all."

Pushing her chair away from the table, Camille stalked out of the room.

Sinking into her own chair like a deflated balloon, Runa buried her face in her hands.

"That's not what I meant at all. I'm not unwilling to help. I thought being in charge was what she wanted. I can't seem to do anything right."

Chase pulled her close to him and stroked her back reassuringly. "Don't worry about her. I love you more than anything, and I can't wait to marry you. That's all that matters."

"I know. I love you, too, Chase," Runa replied.

"Besides, Mother is positively elated that she'll have complete control now."

She looked up at him with a raised brow. "That's what elated looks like?"

"I know my mother. You gave her exactly what she wanted."

Runa sighed. "I guess we'll see, won't we?"

SEVENTEEN

DEPARTURE COVE, OREGON, 1898

"I want it to be the grandest house anyone has ever seen," Thomas Calais said as he patted the shoulder of Amos Winsome, his friend and builder.

"Your house will be a wonder. These designs are like nothing I've seen before." Amos scanned the drawings Thomas had received from his architect the previous week.

"You can do it?" Thomas inquired.

"Of course I can do it," Amos insisted. "You know my team is the best around."

"When will you break ground?"

"The day after tomorrow. Building will begin then."

"I know it's a struggle with the weather around here."

"We work regardless of the conditions. Your project is in good hands. Don't worry, my friend," Amos assured Thomas with a pat on the back.

As Amos perused the blueprints, Thomas gazed out at his plot of land. The location was breathtaking. It had cost him a pretty penny, but the end result would be well worth the price. It was the perfect spot for his home.

At just twenty-eight years old, Thomas Calais was a wealthy man, having inherited his family's fortune on top of amassing his own. He'd spent his life on the sea, and she had served him well. Thomas started out helping his father, eventually taking over as captain after his death. Before long, he had become a bar pilot on the Columbia River. His chosen career was a hazardous one, but he was compensated well for his efforts.

The treacherous Columbia River Bar, one of the most dangerous stretches of navigable water in the world, was so deadly that visiting sea captains had to step aside when crossing it and place their vessels in the hands of the bar pilots, who would escort them and their ships safely across the passage. The adrenaline rush Thomas experienced when crossing the bar was almost payment enough.

He walked to the edge of the property and peered down the cliff toward the sea. The view was unparalleled. When the house was completed, he would be able to gaze out of every window and see his beloved ocean.

As Thomas looked far below toward the shore, he noticed a woman walking. Her pale silky blonde hair lifted in the breeze and floated, suspended in midair. As he watched, the woman knelt on the sand. She opened a purse and arranged *several small items in a strange configuration, then bowed her head and sat quite still. He was mesmerized and couldn't look away.*

After a while, the woman rose slowly. She drew a circle in the sand that encompassed her body and the objects she had placed on the ground. Then she lifted her arms toward the sky and moved her body hypnotically, swaying from side to side. Once she had finished, she stood and walked away into the fog that suddenly descended like a thick blanket.

Thomas craned his neck as he tried to spy her figure in the distance, but she had disappeared into the fog. Something about the woman's hair caught his attention. It was such a lovely flaxen color, and the pale strands gripped him with a sense of recognition that he didn't understand. He had seen the woman before, but he couldn't remember where.

Closing his eyes, he tried to pull the memory from somewhere in the recesses of his brain. He fumbled through various scenarios until he landed on the right one. Several months ago, he had piloted a vessel across the bar belonging to a man from Norway named Captain Ingebjorg. He had seen that woman on the ship. Captain Ingebjorg told Thomas she was his ward. He had called her a wind witch.

Being a maritime man, Thomas was well aware of the various superstitions associated with the sea. His father hadn't been a big believer, but Thomas always had a curiosity for the supernatural. He'd observed seafaring rituals on his own sailing vessels in an effort to keep his crew safe. The fact that Captain Ingebjorg had his own wind witch intrigued Thomas.

It couldn't be a coincidence that he saw the woman again at the very spot where his future home would sit. Perhaps he was tied to her in some cosmic way that he couldn't understand. He was a man of the sea, and she was a wind witch. Their paths seemed destined to cross.

EIGHTEEN

"I'm glad you're here, Mom. You, too, Tawney." Runa squeezed Asta's hand tightly and smiled at Tawney.

"There's no place else I could be." Asta smiled, but Runa didn't miss the sorrow behind her mother's eyes.

"We're here for you. You'll be married tomorrow, on Mabon," Tawney added.

"Mabon?"

"The autumnal equinox, the turning of the wheel. We give thanks for summer and pay tribute to the coming darkness."

"Sounds like a lot of hocus-pocus to me. No offense, Tawney." Runa chuckled.

"None taken."

"Well, I'm just glad to have you both here. It's my rehearsal dinner, but other than Chase and his parents, I don't know anyone."

Runa flicked her eyes nervously, scanning the large crowd. The past three weeks had flown by, filled with dress fittings, invitations, and general wedding preparations. She'd had no clue how much went into planning a wedding fit for an Everwine. The fact that they'd done it in three weeks was nothing short of miraculous.

Camille had truly taken over, and Runa was glad. Chase kept her in the loop, but she was content to stay out of it as much as she could. At this point in the game, she would be relieved when it was all over. All she cared about was becoming Chase's wife.

"The Everwines don't do anything halfway, do they?" Tawney raised an eyebrow as she surveyed the opulence of Everwine Manor.

"No, they certainly don't," Runa replied.

Camille had turned the vast lawn of the estate into an outdoor wonderland. Twinkling lights adorned each tree, and the yard was filled with every kind of flower imaginable. The dinner itself would be held in the grand banquet hall, but champagne and hors d'oeuvres were being served outside.

The air was crisp, and a feeling of fall had settled in Departure Cove. The rain was holding off, and Runa was optimistic it would continue into the next day for the wedding. It was surreal to think that in less than twenty-four hours she would be Chase's wife, a member of the Everwine family. It had all happened so quickly that she'd had little time to ponder it.

She wanted to be Mrs. Everwine more than she'd ever wanted anything, although she understood why the speed with which they'd proceeded gave everyone reason for concern. Runa couldn't explain why she felt compelled to marry Chase so quickly, but she did. The force of it was so strong she couldn't resist, as if their union was somehow decided long before they met, and she didn't have a say in the matter. Some part of her recognized something in Chase that she couldn't deny. It was as if their very cells recognized each other, as crazy as it sounded, and their fates were somehow knitted together.

Chase was perfect. He had never so much as raised a finger to harm her. The red flags she'd experienced in her other relationships weren't there with him. She was lucky, far more than she deserved. Chase was a good man, and he told her every day how much he loved her, and how lucky he was to find her.

Maybe Chase had a few eccentricities, like the way she often caught him looking at her, examining her closely as if he couldn't quite believe she was real. His quirks simply meant he was human. On a couple occasions, he'd made statements about not letting her get away, and while they had made the skin on the back of her neck prickle, she came to understand that was just his way of conveying how much he loved her. Their love was intense, defying logic, so it was only natural.

Runa had heard Chase cry out in his sleep a few times, screaming strange words about betrayal and obsession that she didn't understand. He never remembered the nightmares when he awakened, and she didn't bring them up. He didn't like to dwell on dark things, saying their future was so bright they shouldn't think about the shadows. The last thing she wanted was to upset him. Besides, in the grand scheme of things, these little incidents meant nothing. All that mattered was their love.

As for dreams, she'd been having strange ones herself, always of the woman falling from the window. It had become a nightly occurrence, playing through her subconscious mind like a movie reel on loop. The odd words rang in her head, "Du er i fare." She had no idea what they meant, or even what language they were. She'd attempted to google the phrase, but having no clue as to the spelling, she'd come up empty.

The previous night, there had been a new addition to her dream. She'd been wandering along the shore below Everwine Manor, searching through the fog for something. A woman's voice whispered the strange phrase, and she glanced down at the sand below her feet. Lying there was a very old leather-bound book, an odd blue light emanating from its cover. As she opened it to look inside, she'd awakened, startled to find she was drenched with sweat.

Runa told herself it was all just pre-wedding jitters. Everything would be fine once the wedding was over and she was married to Chase.

Trying her best to push the thoughts aside, she glanced up to see him coming toward them.

"Hello, Asta, Tawney." Chase flashed his dimpled grin, taking his place by Runa's side. "Darling, may I steal you away? People want to meet the woman who has captured my heart."

"Of course," Runa answered with a smile. "Mom, Tawney, I'll find you both in a bit."

Chase led her through the crowd of people, introducing her to a dozen new faces along the way. She noticed that several of Chase's friends looked at her as if she were some sort of oddity. A couple of them appeared as if they wanted to ask questions, but Chase always maintained control of the conversation. Runa decided his friends' fascination with her was simply because she was a newcomer, an outsider. Chase had plucked her from obscurity and invited her into his world, and that made her interesting.

She did her best to smile and be polite, but the anxious flutter in her stomach reminded her how much she hated social events. She told herself that all she had to do was get through the engagement party and the wedding; then she and Chase could get on with the rest of their lives together, out of the spotlight.

After what seemed like a lifetime of mind-numbing small talk and hand shaking, Runa managed to pull herself away from Chase and the sea of strangers. Needing a few moments to breathe, she went off in search of Asta and Tawney. Scanning the crowd, she spotted Tawney chatting with someone, but Asta wasn't with her.

Runa continued walking, and before she knew it, she had left the crowd and found herself behind Everwine Manor. She wandered through trellises trailing with fragrant flowers, through immaculate gardens, and finally ended up face-to-face with the grandest rose garden maze she had ever seen. The multihued roses climbed and crawled over a large wrought iron fence, creating a barrier of beautiful color.

As Runa leaned in to smell the intoxicating flowers, she heard voices from the other side, their familiarity stopping her in her tracks. It was her mother and Easton Everwine, Chase's father. Feeling like a voyeur, she listened, unable to curtail her invasive behavior.

"I swear you haven't changed a bit, Easton. You still think you own everything and everyone," Asta hissed.

"That's because I do." Easton chuckled.

"You don't own me." Asta's angry voice floated through the roses.

"Darling, don't be that way. You know how I feel about you," Easton cooed.

"You still can't take rejection, can you?" Asta spat bitterly. "What would your wife think?"

"Don't be a prude, Asta. It'll be like the good old days."

"I've spent my entire adult life trying to forget those days. There was nothing good about them."

"Come now, don't say that. You, me, Garrett Brewster, and our whole gang, we had some good times, didn't we?"

"Do not speak Garrett's name to me," Asta demanded, the strain in her voice obvious.

"I never understood the two of you," Easton replied, a hint of sadness in his voice.

"No, you didn't. That was part of the problem," Asta quipped. "You've clearly had too much to drink, Easton, so I'm going to end this conversation."

"Oh, I'm just getting started."

"Let go of me this minute, or I swear you'll regret it."

Runa listened with bated breath. She was fully prepared to march into the rose garden and rescue her mother, but she quickly discovered that wasn't necessary. She heard the sound of a slap, then Easton's gasp, followed by his laughter. Runa backed against the wall of flowers, trying to hide herself, as Asta stomped out the other side and ran back toward the crowd. A couple seconds later, Easton emerged, hand on his cheek before straightening his tie and smoothing his jacket.

Once she was alone again, Runa's heart pounded inside her chest. She had no clue what to make of the overheard conversation or the fact that her mother had just slapped Chase's father. She knew her mother had a past with the Everwines, but it sounded like it was even more twisted than she'd imagined. Had Easton been in love with Asta? Had the feelings been mutual? Who was Garrett Brewster? His name had clearly upset her mother.

When the coast was clear, Runa ran through the gardens, across the lawn, and back to the crowd. Scanning the faces quickly, she spotted her mother standing with Tawney. The two were in deep conversation, and the looks on their faces spoke volumes. She approached and the two stopped talking.

"Mom, what's going on?"

"I'm just enjoying your party." Asta plastered a fake smile on her face and tried to make her daughter believe her lie.

"Don't lie to me."

"Runa!"

"I'm not a child, so stop treating me like one. Something is clearly wrong."

"Fine. Do you want to know what's wrong? I can't bear the thought of you marrying into this family. Please reconsider."

Asta's eyes glistened with tears. She'd dropped the words like a hand grenade and now waited expectantly for the explosion.

"You know I can't do that, Mom. I love Chase. I'm marrying him tomorrow."

Runa looked away from her mother, crossing her arms defiantly.

"Then your fate is sealed."

NINETEEN

The next morning, Runa and Asta rode in silence as the battered Volvo wound its way up the hill toward Everwine Manor. The women had spoken little since the previous night. They were having difficulty reconciling their differences regarding Runa's impending nuptials, so it seemed best not to speak at all rather than say something either of them would regret.

Runa yawned as she steered the car through the hairpin turns. She'd slept fitfully, the dark circles beneath her eyes a telltale sign of her exhaustion. She couldn't forget what her mother had said about her fate being sealed. The words prickled beneath her skin, irritating her like a biting mosquito.

She had always trusted Asta's opinions implicitly, but her mother had clearly misjudged Chase. He loved her very much, and she loved him with a ferocity she couldn't explain. They just needed to get through the wedding and move on. Once they were married and Asta realized how wrong she'd been, everything would be fine.

Glancing at Asta in the passenger seat, Runa could see the worry written all over her face. She would give anything to lighten her mother's load.

As if sensing Runa's thoughts, Asta turned toward her daughter.

"Are you sure you've remembered everything?"

"I checked and double-checked. I have my makeup, my hair supplies—"

"Your dress?"

"Yes, I took it there last week. It's hanging in the closet of the room where I'll be getting ready."

"That dress is lovely. It really captures your personality."

Runa sighed dreamily. "I can't wait to put it on. When I saw it, I knew it had to be mine. It's understated and simple, but the classic lines just spoke to me."

"You've never been one for frills and glamour."

"You know me so well."

"Yes I do."

Asta's words were innocent enough, but Runa heard everything that wasn't said. Her mother did know her. She had been Runa's biggest defender and champion for all of her life. They weren't only mother and daughter—they were the best of friends. Runa hated the rift she felt between them, and she vowed that as soon as life calmed down, she would do whatever she could to repair it.

The women pulled into the driveway of the vast estate. Putting the car in Park, Runa looked up at the house. Everwine Manor was the most beautiful thing she'd ever seen, and she'd felt an immediate connection, almost as if she were tethered to its foundation by an invisible thread. She couldn't explain it, but the feeling vibrated in every cell of her body.

In spite of the connection, or perhaps because of it, she also feared the house. It seemed ridiculous to be afraid of a building made of wood and glass, yet she was. The feelings surrounding her future home warred inside her, pushing and pulling in equal measure.

"Let's go in," Runa said to her mother, and they grabbed their belongings.

A maid, who introduced herself as Maisie, greeted them at the front door. Runa had never seen her, and she wondered how many people worked at the estate. She was uncertain how she felt about being constantly surrounded by strangers, but she supposed that was part of living in a mansion.

Grabbing the items from Runa's hands, Maisie advised the women to follow her.

"We must move quickly, ma'am. We don't want Mr. Everwine to see his bride before the wedding. That would be bad luck," she admonished.

She led the women up the grand staircase to the second floor. The sound of their shoes on the immaculately shined hardwood floors echoed as they ventured down the vast hall-way. They passed far too many rooms to count before finally arriving at the one which would serve as the bridal suite. Maisie ushered them into the room and shut the door quickly.

"I believe everything is in order here. I've been assigned specifically to you, so if there's anything at all you need, please let me know."

"You've been assigned to help me for the wedding?" Runa asked.

"No, ma'am, I'm your personal maid."

"For how long?"

"From now until… well… whenever, I suppose."

Maisie flitted about the room, smoothing the covers on the four-poster bed and running a finger across the top of an antique chest of drawers. She straightened the freshly cut roses in the Waterford crystal vase on the dressing table before adjusting her own apron over her black dress.

Runa was unsure how to respond. She'd never had a personal maid, and she didn't know what to do with one.

"Thank you, Maisie. I'm sure everything is perfect."

"Oh, it is. Everything has to be perfect here, ma'am."

"Well." Runa cleared her throat uncomfortably. "My mother and I will let you know if we need anything."

"There's an intercom system next to the door. Everything is labeled, so just give me a ring when you need me," Maisie replied as she prepared to exit.

"Oh, I almost forgot. There is one thing. I assume my dress

is in the closet? I put it there last week."

"Indeed. I saw it there this morning when I was dusting." Maisie crossed the room to the closet and flung open the door. "It's right—"

The maid's abrupt halt and sharp intake of breath caused both Runa and Asta to rush to her side. Runa stared in horror at the empty rack. Her wedding dress wasn't there. In fact, there was nothing at all inside the closet.

"My dress...."

Runa's hands flew to her mouth and her heart began to pound.

Her dress was gone.

"It was there. I saw it. I swear it was there," Maisie muttered nervously.

"All right, let's all just take a deep breath. I'm sure there's a logical explanation. There are about a hundred rooms in this house. It probably just got moved into another one by mistake." Asta tried her best to defuse the situation.

"Yes, that must be it. I'm going to talk to the rest of the staff and to Mr. Everwine. You aren't to worry, Miss Brandon. We'll find your dress!" Maisie ran from the room.

Runa collapsed onto the bed. It was supposed to be her perfect day, and instead it was going to end in disaster. The newspapers had declared the Everwine wedding the "event of the year." Everyone who was anyone was going to be there. Runa couldn't marry Chase in her sweatpants and hoodie.

"Mom, this cannot be happening," Runa said desperately.

"I should have known this was all just too good to be true."

"Sweetie, it's going to be fine. They'll find your dress. I'm sure it just got moved," Asta soothed.

"I hope you're right."

"Let's let the staff do a search while we get you ready. We'll fix your hair and makeup, and by the time we're finished, I'm sure they'll have returned with your dress in tow."

Asta pulled Runa to her feet and led her to the dressing table. Once Runa was seated on the finely upholstered stool at the vanity, Asta went across the room and reached into her bag. She pulled out a candle jar and grabbed a lighter.

"I have the perfect thing." She held up the jar for Runa's inspection.

"You made it?"

"Of course I did. I had a feeling we were going to need it." Asta flicked the lighter, and the flame licked the wick and began to burn. "From the feel of the energy in this place, I should have brought my smudge sticks. Maybe next time."

Runa didn't recognize the scent of the burning candle, but she was sure it had some sort of mystical meaning, as everything did with her mother.

"What's the scent?"

"Cypress. It uplifts vibrations. It'll make you feel grounded and safe," Asta explained as she grabbed the brush and gently pulled it through Runa's hair.

"It's nice." Runa breathed deeply, trying to push away her

anxious thoughts. "You always know just what to do."

"Not always," Asta remarked quietly.

The women readied themselves for the wedding, each lost in thought. Runa finished applying her makeup as Asta twisted and piled her daughter's hair into an exquisite updo. The completed look was breathtaking.

"My hair is perfect. Now I just need my dress." Runa sighed.

Both women turned at a knock on the door.

"Come in," Asta called.

Maisie hurried into the room, wringing her hands and biting her lip. "Miss Brandon, the entire staff looked everywhere. We've inspected every single room in this house. I hate to be the one to tell you this, but your dress is nowhere to be found."

"I hung my dress in that closet last week." Runa pointed angrily in that direction.

"I know, ma'am, and I saw your dress in that closet just this morning. I have no explanation." Maisie fretted with her apron strings.

"What am I going to do? This is not happening." Runa lowered her face into her hands and tried to push away the encroaching tears.

"Maisie, will you ask Chase to come here, please? I need a word with him." Asta spoke with authority.

"I'm afraid that's not possible. The groom can't see the bride before the wedding. It's bad luck," Maisie countered.

"We're well past bad luck. If we don't get a handle on this catastrophe, there won't be a wedding at all. Now please get Chase," Asta commanded.

The maid, wise enough not to argue, turned abruptly and scampered from the room. Mother and daughter waited in silence for several moments before they heard Chase's heavy footsteps coming down the hall.

"You wait here. I'll handle this," Asta instructed.

Runa, far beyond her wit's end, simply nodded.

CLOSING THE DOOR BEHIND HER, Asta stepped into the hallway to meet Chase. From the look on his pale face, she knew he was already aware of the issue.

"Asta, I have no idea how something like this could have happened." Chase ran his hands through his hair in frustration.

"How is it possible that Runa's dress just disappeared into thin air? That doesn't make sense."

"I don't know. I've asked everyone. The staff have torn this place apart. I've looked for it, too. It's nowhere."

"Have you asked your mother where it is?" Asta raised an eyebrow and looked Chase in the eyes.

His mouth gaped. "My mother? You think she had something to do with this?"

"I don't know. I haven't seen her at all today, which strikes me as odd, don't you agree?"

"She's seeing to the wedding details. You don't really think my mother would sabotage Runa like that, do you?"

"Do you want me to answer that honestly, Chase?" Asta put one hand on her hip and waited for the answer.

"No, I suppose I don't."

"Well, regardless of the reason, Runa has no wedding dress, and she's walking down the aisle in less than an hour. We're now in damage control mode," Asta replied.

"Runa must be beside herself with worry. She was so excited to wear that dress. Should I go in and talk to her?" Chase asked.

"Haven't you heard it's bad luck for the groom to see the bride before the wedding?" Asta asked sarcastically. "That maid of yours has been saying that since we arrived."

"I guess we don't need any more of that."

"Listen, Chase, I've made no secret about the fact that I believe my daughter is making a huge mistake by marrying you. That being said, the last thing I want is to see her upset, so you and I are going to fix this. I don't know how, but we are."

"I have an idea," Chase replied as a smile bloomed across his face.

"Go on," Asta encouraged.

"You know this is a very old house. Generations of people have lived here. They've been married here," Chase began.

"And how does that help Runa?"

"Well, a lot of clothes have been kept over the years. One

of the bedrooms has wardrobes filled with old gowns. I'm not sure there's anything appropriate, but we could look. I know it's a long shot, but maybe we could find something?"

"I don't know, Chase. Runa is going to be devastated if she can't get married in a dress she loves."

"I know. Her gown was the only detail that mattered to her," Chase said sadly. "I can't bear to see her disappointed."

"Well, it's worth a try. Let's go see what we can find."

Chase opened the door to the bridal suite and said gently, "Darling, I love you. And I'm going to fix this. I promise."

"I don't see how, Chase," Runa cried.

"Trust me," he answered.

"I do. I trust you with my life," she replied.

"I'll be back soon," he assured her. "Everything is going to be fine."

Chase closed the door, and he and Asta walked swiftly down the hallway, around the corner, and down another corridor. Turning the glass doorknob, Chase flicked on the light and entered the room. Asta followed.

It was another opulent bedroom suite, lined on all sides with large armoires. Asta counted, shocked to discover there were fifteen of them in the mammoth room.

"Are all of these armoires filled with clothes?" she asked.

"Yes. The maids organized them several years ago. The tags are labeled. They're arranged in order of time period, with the newest ones closest to the door and the oldest ones against that wall." Chase motioned across the room.

"We don't have much time. I suppose we should divide and conquer," Asta recommended.

"Great thinking. I'm sure Runa would prefer a more modern gown, so I'll start with the ones closest to the door," Chase declared.

Asta realized Chase didn't understand his future bride at all. She knew her daughter had a penchant for vintage elegance, but clearly he didn't. She was well aware that the couple didn't know each other well enough to get married, and she hated being right.

"I'll look through the older ones." Asta sighed.

The two worked in silence for several minutes. Asta marveled at how well kept the gowns were. The wardrobe she was perusing held garments from as far back as the late 1800s, yet they still looked brand-new.

She was so caught up in the past that she was startled when Chase spoke.

"I think I've found the perfect one."

He presented an ultra-modern gown, probably worn within the last ten years. It was floor length, adorned from top to bottom with glittering sequins, and the bustle in the back was pinned with what appeared to be a mile-long train. It was flashy, eye-catching, and over-the-top. The gown was everything Runa despised. The fact that Chase believed it to be perfect underscored how little he knew about the woman he was marrying.

"I don't know, Chase. That dress isn't really Runa's style."

"I can picture her in it so clearly...."

A strange look came over his face. He caressed the gown lovingly, tracing his fingertips across the sequins.

A chill ran down Asta's spine as she watched her future son-in-law clearly caught up in a vivid memory. She didn't understand, but it made her uncomfortable.

"That's not my daughter's dress, Chase. It's not right for her at all."

Turning back to the armoire, Asta continued her search. Her fingertips grazed the fabric of a gown, and a bolt of electricity arced from the dress into her body. For a second, all she could see was blue. The aura surrounded the dress, and she immediately understood.

The color blue, signifying truth and healing powers, called out to her. Asta knew the gown was meant for Runa even before she pulled it from the rack. Once she looked at it, she was even more convinced. It might as well have been custom-made for her daughter.

It was quite old. Asta read the label inside and saw it was dated 1900. The floor-length vintage lace wedding gown had flowing sleeves and crystal buttons leading down the back before ending in a small train. It was made of ivory crepe silk, and the Chantilly lace overlay accentuated the empire-style waistline and bateau neckline. It had small bits of tasteful beading, yet its understated elegance was classic and simple.

"This is the dress. We must take it to Runa immediately,"

Asta instructed as she lovingly draped the gown across her arms and headed for the door.

"Are you sure? It's so old. This one is much more... special." Chase gestured toward the gown he was still holding.

"I'm her mother, and I know far better than you the kind of gown she wants. And since someone in your household has lost my daughter's dress, this is the one she'll wear."

"Look, Asta, I know you don't want me to marry Runa, but I need you to understand that I love her very much. I want to make her happy," Chase said, meeting Asta's eyes.

"Then you'd better do it. Or you'll have me to answer to."

With a curt nod, Asta pushed past Chase and headed toward the bridal suite. She didn't wait for him to follow. Turning the knob, Asta entered the room confidently, locking the door behind her before Chase could attempt to join them.

***.

"I've found your dress," Asta announced, turning to approach Runa.

"You found it?"

Runa jumped from the stool, excited that it'd been found, but confusion overwhelmed her instead when she saw the gown in Asta's hands wasn't her own.

"That's not my dress," she protested.

"It's the dress you were always meant to wear."

"What are you talking about, Mom?"

Asta presented the gown for her daughter to see. Runa's hands shook as she tentatively ran her fingertips across the lace. As she caressed the vintage fabric, specks of blue light emanated from her hands. She didn't know if her mother saw it, and she didn't care. Nothing had ever felt more perfect than touching the fabric of that dress.

"What if it doesn't fit me?" Runa murmured.

"It will," Asta decreed.

Runa shimmied out of her sweatpants and hoodie and grabbed the garment from her mother. Asta unfastened several of the crystal buttons and slipped the gown over Runa's head. As it fell into place, Runa sighed contentedly. The dress whispered to her, clinging to her frame as if it were part of her skin.

Asta buttoned it and smoothed down the lace in the back. "Look at yourself," she instructed.

Runa walked across the room and looked into the mirror. She thought she'd found the perfect wedding dress before, but that garment paled in comparison to the one she was wearing. Her eyes filled with tears. No dress had ever fit a woman so well.

As she gazed in the mirror, the image shifted a bit. Runa was seeing herself, but then she wasn't. It was nearly her, but not completely.

She reached out to touch the image, and the reflection in the mirror reached back. Blue light flickered between outstretched fingertips. The woman in the mirror whispered, "*Så det.* So be it."

TWENTY

"I now pronounce you husband and wife," the minister declared loudly. "You may kiss your bride."

Chase gave Runa a satisfied grin before wrapping his arms around her and making her forget everything but him. She was Mrs. Everwine. They had really done it, and nothing else mattered.

The crowd erupted in shouts of congratulations and hearty clapping. It all seemed like a lovely dream.

Camille had outdone herself with the wedding details, and Runa believed no ceremony had ever been more beautiful. Everything went off without a hitch, except Chase's slight pause over her name when he said his vows. Was it her imagination, or had his lips momentarily formed an F sound rather than an R?

No one seemed to notice, of course, except Camille. She

had cleared her throat loudly, sending Chase an icy glare. Runa felt badly for him. She'd smiled encouragingly, assuring him everything was all right. He'd been so nervous. Camille shouldn't have made such a fuss.

Clasping her husband's hand inside her own, Runa squinted at the barrage of camera flashes. She felt like a celebrity being hounded by the paparazzi. She reminded herself that it would all be over soon, and then she and Chase could settle into normal married life.

"Are you happy, Mrs. Everwine?" Chase whispered in her ear.

"I am," Runa replied with a smile and squeeze of his hand. "I love you."

"And I love you. You've made me the happiest man alive," Chase said as he kissed her again.

The reception in the ballroom continued well into the evening. She did her best to be social, but all Runa wanted was to find a quiet place to be alone. Chase was occupied with their guests, so she quickly made her escape, her high heels clicking on the hardwood floors of Everwine Manor.

Leaving the grand banquet hall behind, Runa found the deserted conservatory. Alone, surrounded by plants and flowers, she felt as if she could finally breathe. The glass walls sparkled in the moonlight as she took a seat on a cushioned iron bench in the corner. She glanced at her reflection in the window, her face filled with stress and anxiety.

She wasn't used to being the center of attention, and

having strangers pelt her with requests for photos and small talk for hours was nearly more than she could bear. Runa was exhausted. The weeks leading up to the wedding, as well as the stress of the ceremony itself, had nearly drained her. If she weren't afraid of being perceived as rude and socially awkward, she would run up to the bridal suite, crawl beneath the covers, and drift off to sleep. She just needed a little peace and quiet in order to recharge her battery.

Lost in her thoughts, Runa jumped when she heard the sound of high heels echoing on the tile floor. Her heart sank inside her chest when she saw it was Camille. Standing quickly and smoothing her wedding gown, Runa greeted her mother-in-law.

"Hello, Camille."

"What are you doing in here?" Her voice lashed out like a whip.

"I was just taking a moment to breathe. Social gatherings drain me." Runa shrugged.

"Unbelievable. You are obviously not cut out to be an Everwine. I don't know what my son was thinking. You clearly have no breeding or social grace."

Camille tapped the toe of one sparkly high heel on the tile floor, the sound causing Runa to wince.

"I… I just needed a moment… alone," she stammered.

Camille inched closer to her, leaning in until Runa could feel the woman's warm breath on her face. Runa took an involuntary step backward.

"Listen to my words very closely, Runa. Let them sink in. You may have married into the Everwine family, but you will never be one of us. You don't belong here. My son has obviously taken leave of his senses, but I can see right through you."

Overcome with the warring emotions of anger and disbelief, Runa bit back her tears. She needed to get away from Camille.

She turned to walk away, but Camille stuck her glittery-heeled foot directly in her path.

Perhaps if she'd been prepared, Runa might have caught herself. But she wasn't. Camille spun Runa off balance in every possible way. Toppling, her body crashed onto the tiled floor. She hit the ground with a thud, screaming out in pain as her knees came in contact with the unyielding ground.

"Oh, you must be more careful, my dear. There are a million possible ways to have an accident in a house this size."

Camille smiled wickedly as she sauntered out of the conservatory, leaving Runa behind without a second glance.

Runa gasped, not quite able to wrap her brain around what just happened. Camille had purposely tripped her. Then she threatened her.

Hot tears rolled down Runa's cheeks, in part because of the pain but mostly because of the situation. Chase's mother had always hated her, that much was clear, but now she feared the woman might be outright dangerous.

Runa pulled herself to her feet, wincing as pain shot

through her knees. Hobbling to the bench, she gave in to the sobs she could no longer hold at bay.

That was how Asta and Tawney found her.

"Runa, what's going on?" Asta's worried voice echoed throughout the room as she ran across the conservatory floor, kneeling in front of her daughter.

"Why are you crying?" Tawney sank onto the bench beside Runa, tenderly brushing away strands of hair from Runa's damp face.

"I… I… fell," Runa replied.

"Just now?" Asta inquired.

"I tripped on the leg of the table and hit my knees on the tile. You know how clumsy I am." Runa tried to laugh it off. "It really hurt."

"Are you sure that's what happened?"

Runa avoided her mother's perceptive gaze, knowing if she looked at her, she would be forced to spill the truth. She wasn't about to do that. There was no way she could tell Asta that Camille had threatened her. Not on her wedding day. That would only fuel Asta's fire and turn her even further against Chase.

"Yes. I'm fine, really," Runa lied.

"You poor thing." Tawney reached out and squeezed Runa's hand.

As she grasped it, a strange look came over her face, catching Runa's attention.

"What's wrong, Tawney?"

"I'm not sure. There's something… a picture…."

"What do you see?" Asta asked worriedly.

"I see a woman… the same blonde woman I saw before. I can't see her face. Wait, now she's turning around," Tawney said.

"What's the woman doing?" Asta prompted.

"She's walking along the beach. The moon is full. She has driftwood… shells… feathers. She's drawing a circle in the sand… salting it… enclosing herself inside of it. She's crying."

"Do you know the woman?" Runa was intrigued.

"She… looks… like… you."

TWENTY-ONE

DEPARTURE COVE, OREGON, 1899

T homas Calais closed the mammoth front door behind him and clomped down the front steps of his house. After a month of living in his dream home, he wasn't as happy as he thought he'd be. Throughout the building phase, he'd felt something was missing. He kept telling himself he'd feel differently once he moved in, but he didn't.

He had furnished his opulent home with only the best decorations and trappings, carefully choosing each exquisite piece of furniture, selecting the artwork with care. He wanted his home to not only strike awe but to be welcoming as well.

Although the house was the grandest around, Thomas wanted it to feel like a home, not a museum. On the surface, he had succeeded, but in spite of the lavish décor, it felt empty.

The place needed something, although for the life of him he didn't know what that was.

Lighting his pipe, he wandered down the rough-hewn path leading from his home to the beach. It wasn't an easy walk, as his house sat on a sheer rocky cliff above the ocean. He'd spent weeks clearing out the vegetation enough to traverse it. Eventually he hoped to build a staircase, but for now, he walked the path. He was hearty, physically fit, and hungry for adventure. It was nothing he couldn't handle.

Thomas pulled his wool coat closer to his body as the wind blew off the Pacific Ocean, nipping at him. Puffing on his pipe, he continued his descent toward the shore. He'd walked the trail every day for a month, becoming quite acclimated to the route. Tiny drops of sea mist stuck to his full dark beard and clung to his wavy black hair. He squinted, shielding his green eyes against the precipitation, pulling his fisherman's cap a bit lower.

Reaching flat land, he angled his body toward the shoreline, making his way across the sand. In his mind, there was nothing better than being near his beloved sea. He felt more at home on the water than on land, so much so that his father often teased him about being half fish. The sea made sense to him. He understood it. It was constantly changing yet always the same.

Lost in a daydream, Thomas didn't notice that he wasn't alone on the shore. Had he realized it sooner, he might have been prepared for the shock of electricity that nearly brought him to his knees. It'd been almost a year since he'd last seen her, but the thrumming excitement coursing through his body was familiar. It was the woman he'd first seen on the ship, then again performing the strange ritual on the shore. She was the Norwegian captain's wind witch.

She was several feet away, her back turned to him. He stopped walking, maintaining a comfortable distance between them so as not to disturb her work. Thomas knew he should make his presence known, yet he remained silent. He didn't know what the woman was doing, but he was mesmerized by her every move.

He watched as she reached into a pouch and pulled out a vial filled with a powdery substance. Bowing her head, she paused a moment before sprinkling it around herself in a circle. When she turned toward him, Thomas expected his presence might startle her, but he was mistaken. The woman's face showed no surprise. She smiled enigmatically, as if she'd always known he was there.

Moving toward her, he returned her smile. When he was close enough to be heard above the roar of the ocean, he greeted her.

"Hello."

"Hallo," she replied.

"Do you speak English?"

"Yes. But I prefer my native tongue."

"Norwegian?"

"Ja," she said with a grin. "Snakker du norsk?"

"A little." Thomas chuckled. "I also prefer my native tongue."

"I understand many languages, so we may converse in whichever one you choose."

"That's helpful." He fumbled for what to say next. "What's your name?"

"I'm Brynja."

"Do people call you Brynn?"

"You may call me that if you like."

"I'm Thomas Calais."

"Yes, I know."

"How do you know?"

"I know a great many things. But if I told you how, you wouldn't believe me," she answered.

"Can you be sure? You haven't even tried."

Thomas could have asked a million questions in rapid succession, but he paused, anxious for her answers.

"I've known you for some time, Thomas. I dreamed of your face long before I ever arrived at your shore."

"You dreamed of me?" His heart pounded inside his chest.

"Every night for over a year. I've been waiting for you."

Brynja reached into her pouch and pulled out something that looked like a stick of rolled-up leaves.

"How is that possible?"

"Anything is possible."

Brynja lit a match, placing the flame next to the end of the stick. Smoke began to curl, but it didn't catch on fire.

"Do you believe in fate, Thomas?"

"I... I don't know. I suppose," he stammered.

"What would you say if I told you that fate brought me to you?" She stared at him, never flinching, never looking away.

Thomas swallowed hard, his Adam's apple bobbing up and down. His throat had gone dry, and he couldn't speak.

"What if I told you that I sailed thousands of miles across the sea from my own country because I saw your face, Thomas?"

Her blue eyes met his green ones, and time stood still. He wasn't used to being caught off guard. Not many things took him by surprise, but Brynja and her fantastical story did. He didn't know what to say, so he said nothing.

Brynja closed her eyes, and her lips began to move. Thomas couldn't understand her words, but she seemed to be saying some sort of prayer. The smoking stick of leaves smoldered as she waved it in the air. The strange scent wafted on the breeze and stuck to his nostrils.

Opening her eyes, Brynja looked at Thomas. Without saying a word, she took his hand inside her own, her eyes never leaving his. Then she dropped his hand, sank to her knees, and drew a second circle in the sand, this one surrounding them both.

Standing, she reached in her pouch and pulled out a vial of oil. She placed a single drop on the tip of her finger and touched it to Thomas's forehead, drawing a symbol he didn't recognize. He didn't move or speak, afraid to disrupt the strange crackling energy in the air. He didn't understand what was going on, but it felt right, as if he were always meant to be in that space at that moment.

When she completed her ritual, Brynja exhaled deeply, handing the smoldering stick of leaves to Thomas. He held it awkwardly, inhaling the scent, a feeling of complete contentment and peace washing over him.

"What is this?"

"The scent is angelica. It's used to bring blessings and purification to a new home. It wards off evil and encourages a harmonious home life," Brynja explained.

Thomas stared at her blankly.

"Isn't that what you were seeking, Thomas?"

"How could you know that?"

"You might be frightened if I told you."

"I could never be afraid of you, Brynn."

"I like when you call me that." She smiled.

Unrelenting, Thomas persisted with his questioning.

"How did you know I was seeking harmony in my home?"

Brynja gazed at him, a strange look on her lovely face. She sighed deeply, appearing to contemplate her words before speaking.

"I've stood on this shore every day for almost a year. I've watched as your grand home was constructed. I've prayed for your happiness and safety."

"You have?"

"Yes. But there's something else, Thomas."

"What is it?"

"I've also felt your loneliness. Your desire for connection and companionship has weighed on me. I've said prayers for you. I've performed rituals for you. But the feeling consumed me. Today I've learned the answer."

"And what is the answer?"

"I feel your emptiness because it mirrors my own. Last night I dreamed I was living in your home. It was the first time in years I hadn't felt lonely. That's when I knew."

"Knew what?"

"I knew our paths were destined to cross and our futures were meant to collide. We're two branches of the same tree. Together our roots will be strong and deep."

Thomas couldn't believe what he was hearing, but in that moment, everything made sense.

"Brynn, I need you to come with me. There's something I have to show you."

"Of course I'll come with you."

She knelt and collected her ritual objects, placing them back in her pouch. With a nod, she followed him without question.

When they reached the path leading up the cliff, Thomas paused. He was accustomed to the difficult climb, but she wasn't.

"Maybe this isn't the best idea. The walk isn't easy."

"Don't worry about me, Thomas. I'm sturdy and strong," Brynja assured him.

He grasped her hand, and the two climbed the path together. He was surprised at how well she kept up. She was younger than he, although he couldn't be sure how much. He didn't ask her age because it didn't seem to matter. Her eyes contained a depth of wisdom far beyond her years.

When they reached the top, she wasn't even out of breath. Glancing at the beautiful home up close, Brynja smiled.

"It's even lovelier than in my dreams."

"Come with me."

Thomas led her through the front door and into the immaculate entryway. Brynja looked around at the lovely parlor with its perfectly chosen furniture ready to seat visitors at a moment's notice.

"Your home is exquisite, Thomas."

"There's something I want to show you."

He led her into the music room, where a large fireplace towered above a grand piano. A gigantic stained glass window decorated the far wall, and she drew closer to inspect its design as she absently traced her fingertips across the fabric of a plush velvet sofa.

Brynja inhaled sharply when she examined the colorful window depicting a blonde woman standing on the shore next to the crashing waves of the ocean. Peering intently at it for a moment, she then turned her head toward Thomas. A smile bloomed across her beautiful face.

"Is that me?"

"It is. When I had the window designed, I was working

from an image in my mind of a woman I had only seen twice. Until today I didn't understand why I was compelled to permanently etch that woman's face into my home, but now I know."

"What do you know?"

"You were always meant to be here," Thomas murmured.

"Perhaps you also have a bit of magic in your blood. You speak like a man who does." Brynja chuckled.

"So where does this leave us? What does it all mean?"

"It means some things are decided long before we even understand. Across thousands of miles of ocean, we have found each other."

Thomas cleared his throat awkwardly. "Would you like some tea?"

"Yes." Brynja laughed. "I believe I would."

They found their seats in the parlor. Thomas rang a bell and started a fire in the hearth. Before long, a maid brought them tea. As they sipped their warm drinks, they chatted easily, as if they had always known each other.

"Houses like this usually have a name. What do you call your home?" Brynja inquired.

"I've been mulling it over since I moved in. I had no idea until today."

"What have you come up with?"

"I believe I'll call it Angelica House," Thomas replied.

"Angelica House?"

"Yes, the fragrance in your ritual. You said angelica

brings blessings and purification to a home. What name could be better than that?"

"I brought that angelica from Norway for my ceremonies. It's important. I don't know what I'll do when it's gone."

"We'll plant all the angelica you desire. Any flower or herb you want, we'll find a way to grow it here. I've built a conservatory. You may do with it what you will. It's yours," he said excitedly.

"You don't fear my ways? I've been told that people in America don't embrace beliefs that are different."

"That may be true, but I'm not like most people," Thomas answered truthfully.

"No you're not."

"Will you answer something for me? My opinion of you will be no different regardless of what you say."

"Of course, Thomas. You may ask me anything."

"Captain Ingebjorg called you a wind witch. Is that true?"

"I am a great many things. Some call me a klok kvinne, *a wise woman. My power is something few can understand or define. Captain Ingebjorg called me a wind witch, but I'm much more than that."*

Brynja stood from her chair and crossed the room to look out the window toward the sea. Thomas followed, placing his hand on her shoulder.

"Go on, Brynn," he encouraged.

She sighed before continuing. "Gifts have been given to me, passed down through the women in my family line."

"Gifts?"

"Or curses. Opinions vary on what they are. Throughout history we've been hunted, persecuted, burned, and cast out of communities. Some women have feared the gift, hidden it, locked it away, but I was taught to embrace it, to help others."

Brynja paused and looked at Thomas's face, seeming to measure her words to see how much she should reveal.

"In my brief time in your country, I've come to understand that people don't appreciate my sort of gifts. So between you and me, Thomas, yes, I'm everything you believe. But outside of these walls, I'm just an ordinary woman with a keen sense of herbs and flowers," Brynja explained.

"I understand. Your secret is safe with me."

Thomas took her hand in his and lifted it to his lips.

"But that's where you're wrong, Thomas. A secret such as this is never safe."

TWENTY-TWO

As Runa lay in bed, the early morning light filtered through the heavy drapes of the bedroom. Rolling from her side to her back, she winced in pain as she bent her knees. She could feel the bruises from her fall the night before.

She hadn't told Chase what happened with his mother, and she didn't intend to. They'd both been completely exhausted from the wedding and had fallen asleep right away. Hiding it had been easier than she'd anticipated.

Glancing beside her, the shape of Chase's head was still imprinted in the fluffy pillow. Other than that, his side of the bed looked barely slept in. She'd known he had to leave early for work, but the reality of waking up alone in a strange room the morning after her wedding hit Runa a bit harder than she'd expected. She bit back tears.

They had talked about it, of course. Chase had work obligations, in place far longer than he'd even known Runa. He couldn't get out of the appointments, scheduled months in advance. Chase was a busy man, and his work was demanding and time-consuming.

Besides, Runa didn't want to leave her shop. The idea of closing her boutique to go on a honeymoon seemed irresponsible. It hadn't been open long enough to warrant a closure, and she couldn't risk losing customers who had just begun to frequent her establishment.

Chase and Runa agreed their work must take precedence. They had responsibilities and commitments to keep. They had discussed it at length, deciding to put their honeymoon on hold indefinitely. The important thing, they'd both agreed, was that they get married and begin their lives together right away. The honeymoon could come later. She'd been perfectly fine with that decision, yet the reality of waking up alone in Everwine Manor felt empty and depressing.

"Snap out of it, Runa. You're Mrs. Everwine. That's what you wanted," she chided herself. "And now you need to get ready for work."

Rolling out of the giant canopy bed, she stretched her body, trying to ease some of the residual tension from the day before. She walked across the room and opened the drapes, letting the morning sun creep into the dark room. Glancing outside, she saw large waves undulating on the surface of the ocean. She couldn't believe the view from her window. Of course, there didn't seem to be a poor view from anywhere inside Everwine Manor.

Turning from the window, Runa was surprised to see a silver tray on the table across the room. She lifted the lid on the large platter, and steam rolled off the eggs and bacon. She touched the carafe and realized the coffee was still hot.

It must have been brought in while she was sleeping. The thought of someone in her room while she slept sent a shiver down her spine. Even though it was more than likely placed there by a servant, whose job it was to do so, it still made her uncomfortable. It felt like an invasion of privacy.

A light knock on the door caused her to jump.

"Mrs. Everwine?"

Runa recognized Maisie's voice, but before she could even manage an answer, the door swung open and the jittery maid entered the room. Startled, Runa pulled her silk robe around her body and tried to smooth her tousled hair.

"Can I help you, Maisie?"

"I'm here to see to your morning schedule."

"My morning schedule?"

"Yes, ma'am."

Maisie crossed the room and lifted the lid on the silver platter. She frowned when she saw it hadn't been eaten. "You don't like your breakfast?"

"I… I do. I mean, I'm sure it's delicious. I haven't tried it yet," Runa fumbled.

Maisie gave her a quick once-over and wrinkled her nose

in apparent confusion. "You look like you just got out of bed, ma'am."

"I did."

"Oh. Mr. Everwine left the house hours ago."

"Yes. Chase has to be at work much earlier than I do. I slept in a bit. I suppose I was tired from all the festivities."

Runa didn't know why she felt compelled to explain herself, but she did.

"Very well, ma'am. Shall I help you dress now?"

Maisie spoke the words as if they were the most normal ones in the world. Runa, however, was shocked.

"Help me dress?"

"Yes, ma'am."

"Uh, well, I think I can manage that on my own," she replied, a bit shocked.

"Are you dismissing me, Mrs. Everwine?"

The irritation in Maisie's voice was obvious. She made no attempt to disguise her distaste.

"I'm not exactly dismissing you, Maisie. It's just that I've been dressing myself for most of my life, and I don't intend to stop now. I really don't require your assistance in that area."

"Very well," Maisie huffed. "Please let me know what you do require. Until then, I will leave you to your own dressing."

Straightening her spine, Maisie gave Runa a scathing look before scurrying from the room without another word.

Runa, reeling from the awkward encounter, tried to gather her wits. Apparently there was far more involved in being

Mrs. Everwine than she'd imagined. Unfortunately, she didn't know how to do any of it, and she'd therefore begun her first morning as Chase's wife by offending the maid.

Feeling guilty and embarrassed, Runa went to the door and opened it, glancing down the long hallway in search of Maisie. She intended to apologize, but the woman was nowhere to be seen. In fact, the entire hall was deserted.

Closing the door behind her, Runa sighed. There didn't seem to be another soul in the east wing, where she and Chase had set up their living quarters. He assured her it was the best way to guarantee their privacy, as Easton and Camille occupied rooms in the west wing. As with most things, she'd deferred to his advice, seeing as she had no idea about the operations of an estate like Everwine Manor.

Feeling completely and utterly alone, Runa did her best not to let the tears fall, knowing if they began, they might never stop. Glancing at the clock across the room, she saw it was nearly nine, which meant she had better get ready for work or risk being late.

Flipping on the light in the closet, she stepped inside. The space was larger than her entire house. There was even a large settee in the middle, presumably in case dressing grew exhausting and sitting became necessary.

She scanned the racks of clothing. The servants had moved all of her belongings from her house to Everwine Manor the previous day, and seeing her clothes hanging in the same space as Chase's was jarring. Everything was new and different, and being alone to process it all suddenly felt like a terrible idea.

Running her fingertips across Chase's shirts, Runa pulled one close and inhaled, smiling when she realized it smelled like him. Curious, she examined his clothing, familiarizing herself with his side of the closet. She counted his shoes, lined up like soldiers at attention, marveling at the fact that he had fifty pairs. Pulling open one of the drawers, she saw a plethora of neckties, one after another, in every color of the rainbow. She thought her wardrobe was extensive, but it paled in comparison to her husband's.

Walking to her side of the closet, she pulled a black dress from the hanger and draped it across the settee. Opening the top drawer, she searched for the perfect necklace to accentuate the deep neckline. The servants had certainly done an amazing job organizing all of her belongings, but it would take her a while to figure out where everything was.

The necklace wasn't in the top drawer, so she opened the next one. Smiling when she saw it, Runa grabbed it and placed it next to her dress. She was about to close the drawer when something in the back corner caught her eye. Stooping down to get a better look, she saw what appeared to be a photograph sticking out from behind the drawer.

Grabbing the corner that was visible, she gave the photo a tug, careful not to rip it. Curious, she glanced at the picture, blinking twice, certain her eyes were playing tricks on her.

Shocked, she sank slowly onto the settee, suddenly very glad it was there.

With trembling hands, she held up the photo, forcing herself to take another look. The photograph was taken on the deck of a ship, the bright sun glittering off the waves in the distance. Chase was smiling, carefree, happier than Runa had ever seen him.

His arm was draped casually across the slender shoulders of the woman who stood next to him. He wasn't looking at the camera but at his companion, and his expression spoke a thousand words. He gazed at the woman with such love, longing, and admiration that seeing it caused Runa physical pain. The woman, however, wasn't looking at him but directly at the camera.

She searched the woman's face in an effort to understand, trying to catch the breath that had been stolen away. The face in the photo was nearly identical to Runa's—her eyes the same color of blue, her face the same structure, her body the same shape. The only difference was their hair. Where Runa's was long and lush, the woman in the photo sported a short pixie cut. Besides that small difference, the woman could be Runa.

Confused and suddenly afraid, she debated what she should do. Her need to know clashed with her desire to pretend she'd never seen it. In the end, she slid the photo in her sock drawer, far beneath the pile, choosing to forget it existed. Then she dressed for work.

TWENTY-THREE

DEPARTURE COVE, OREGON, 1900

"*Are you happy, Mrs. Calais?*"

Thomas kissed Brynja's hand and inhaled her scent, lavender and lemongrass. The two sat on the enormous porch of Angelica House, sipping their afternoon tea and watching the waves crash in the distance. They'd been married for three months, and every moment had been pure bliss. Thomas had told her more than once that he had a hard time remembering his existence before making her his wife, and she felt the same way. Their souls were knitted together.

"Of course I'm happy. I couldn't ask for more," Brynja answered with a smile. "And yet...."

She turned her face toward her husband's and graced him with an enigmatic smile, the one that said she knew far more than he would ever understand.

"And yet what, my love?"

"I couldn't ask for more, and yet it seems we shall have it."

"Why is it that your every word is a puzzle?" Thomas chuckled. "It's almost as if you take pleasure in my constant confusion."

"Me?"

"Yes, you."

Brynja feigned shock but quickly dissolved in a fit of laughter. She loved keeping her dear husband guessing. He was such a good sport about it, after all.

She smiled and stood from her chair. Standing in front of Thomas, she took his hand and gently placed it on her stomach. As their eyes met, she tilted her head.

"You're—"

"I am. We're going to have a baby, Thomas," Brynja answered.

"You're sure?" he whispered.

"Very sure." She placed her hand on top of his, still resting on her abdomen.

A faint blue light emanated from her fingertips, gone as quickly as it had come.

"You've made me the happiest man alive. You know that, right?" Thomas whispered.

"Our daughter will always know our love."

"It's a girl? How can you know so soon?"

"I've always known I would have a daughter," Brynja

replied confidently. *"Her name will be Ingrid, and magic will be in her blood."*

Tears filled Thomas's eyes as he stood, wrapping his arms around his wife and pulling her body close to his. They had brought each other such happiness that they dared not hope for more, and yet they were to have it. Their family would be complete.

"Tell me we'll always be this happy, Brynn," Thomas said quietly as he smoothed his wife's hair.

Brynja sighed and pulled away, gazing intently at her husband before speaking. A dark look passed over her beautiful face, and the tiniest bit of nagging worry crept into Thomas's eyes.

"I cannot promise you that, my love. We must soak up all the happiness we can while it's in front of us."

"Have you seen something?"

Looking away from Thomas's desperate eyes, Brynja cushioned the truth.

"All I can see when I look at you is love, Thomas. Let's not worry about tomorrow. Today is here, and nothing else matters."

TWENTY-FOUR

"I understand, Chase. I'll see you when you get home."

"I love you, darling. And I'm sorry," Chase apologized once again.

"I love you too."

Runa hung up her phone and dropped it on the table. She fought the tears that threatened to spill, fully aware they were from frustration, not sadness. It was the fourth night in a row that Chase would be coming home late. They had been married only a month, and in that time, she could count on one hand the evenings they'd eaten dinner together.

She kept telling herself everything was fine. She'd known what she was getting into when she married Chase. He was a busy man, and running the Everwine empire was tireless work. He deserved a supportive wife, not a needy one. She was trying to be that, but the transition to living at Everwine

Manor had been more difficult than she'd imagined. The jarring change was compounded by the fact that she'd been navigating it alone.

Camille never failed to communicate her displeasure at Runa's presence, so it had become Runa's motivation to avoid her whenever possible. Most nights she had Maisie bring the dinner tray to her room, where she ate alone. Boredom and loneliness were better companions than her vengeful mother-in-law.

Asta checked in on her a few times a week, but Runa was careful not to reveal too much. She'd grown adept at concealing her feelings, although she knew her mother was far more astute than she let on. The only solace Runa found in her new home was the rose garden maze, where she'd grown accustomed to taking a nightly stroll. It was the one thing she loved about living in the mansion.

Slipping quietly from her room, she descended the back stairway, primarily used by the servants, and exited through the kitchen. Once outside, she breathed a sigh of relief. It was twilight, the soft glowing sky whispering its goodbye to the sun. In the half light, it was easier to forget her worries and focus on the beauty around her, abundant at Everwine Manor. The waves crashed below the cliff, and Runa made her way to the rose garden maze.

Most nights she simply sat there, processing her thoughts, but that night she decided to amble through the walls of colorful flowers. As she walked, she wondered how many other Everwine women had traversed the path before her. Had they been happy? Had Everwine Manor welcomed them with open arms? She hoped the women before her had been loved well.

As she rounded a corner deep inside the maze, she jumped, startled to find Easton Everwine sitting on a wrought iron bench in front of her. The shock was all Runa's, as he didn't seem at all surprised to see her. In fact, the disconcerting smile spreading across his handsome face made her believe he was waiting for her.

"Hello, my dear. It's a lovely night for a walk," Easton declared with a wink.

Caught off guard, Runa didn't know how to respond. She stepped to the side, wincing as a thorn pricked her shoulder. Ignoring the pain, she offered her father-in-law a shaky smile.

"I-I'm sorry to disturb you. I thought I was alone."

"Almost. It's just you and me."

"Well, I was about to head inside, so I'll see you later."

Nervous, Runa turned to leave.

Before she knew what was happening, Easton sprang from the bench, wedging his body between her and the exit. Feeling like a cornered animal, her breath came quickly and her heart beat rapidly.

"You just got here, my dear. There's no need for you to leave so quickly," he purred, the corners of his mouth curling into a devilish grin.

Telling herself not to panic, Runa took a shaky breath, trying to exhale the fear.

"I have to get up early for work tomorrow, so if you'll excuse me...."

She tried to move past Easton, but he sidestepped her, blocking her once again. She raised her eyes toward his face, momentarily distracted by the resemblance between Easton and Chase. If she ever wondered what her husband would look like in his late forties, she need look no further than his father.

"It's early, my dear. You don't need to rush off."

With Easton in front of her and the hedge of roses behind, Runa had no means of escape. He took two steps toward her, and she took two steps back. Her ragged breath seemed inordinately loud in the quiet of the labyrinth.

Just when she believed the situation couldn't get worse, Easton brought his hand to her face, lightly caressing her cheek with his fingertips. She shivered reflexively, and his grin bloomed. She tried to avoid his stare but couldn't look away.

Suddenly, his face changed. His eyes glazed over and he leered hungrily at her body. He leaned toward her, his lips moving swiftly toward their target—her mouth. Horrified, Runa moved her head slightly, and they grazed her cheek instead. He was undeterred.

"Playing hard to get, I see. You were always that way, Asta. You know how to drive a man wild." Easton chuckled and tried to grab her shoulders.

The fact that he called her by her mother's name stopped Runa dead in her tracks. Confusion warred with fear, causing her to find her voice.

"Easton, I'm Runa. Chase's wife."

He stared through her, not quite seeing her.

"I don't know why you can't let things be the way they were before, Asta."

As he spoke, his face crumpled and his eyes filled with tears. He took a step away from her, and Runa sprang into action. Without thinking twice, she shoved him and ran. Tears coursed down her cheeks. She struggled to catch her breath as her feet pounded through the maze. Every twist and turn looked exactly like the last, and she fought down the fear that she would never find her way out.

When she finally emerged, Everwine Manor swam into view. She ran as quickly as her aching legs would carry her, through the kitchen entrance, up the back staircase, and down the winding corridors to the east wing. Flinging open the door to her room, she practically fell inside, locking the door tightly behind her. Frantic with fear and confusion, she collapsed on the floor, sobbing and sucking in gulping breaths. She cried until her tears ran dry and exhaustion took over.

She didn't know how much time had passed, but when she heard footsteps in the room, she sprang to her feet, terrified Easton had come after her. Runa's eyes worked to adjust to the darkness around her as her breath came out in a ragged hiss.

"Runa?"

Chase's familiar voice brought her back to reality. Barreling across the room toward her husband, she hurled herself into the safety of his arms.

"Chase—"

She didn't have the capacity to say more, so she buried her face in his chest and sobbed. Chase swept her up in his arms, carried her across the room, and gently deposited her on their bed. Flicking on the bedside lamp, he grabbed a tissue and handed it to her. Wiping her face obediently, she tried to gain her composure.

"Darling, what is it? The door was locked. It's a good thing I have a key."

"It's nothing." Runa was unable to speak the truth.

"Runa, you were on the floor, completely terrified. I would say that's something."

"I… I can't…."

"I'm your husband. I love you. You can tell me anything."

"You're not going to like it."

"I don't like coming home to find my wife afraid in our room. Tell me."

Runa swallowed hard and tried to formulate an explanation.

"It's your father."

"What about my father?"

The muscles in Chase's jaw clenched, and he fisted his hands.

"He was inappropriate."

"How so?"

"He… well… he tried… to kiss me. He blocked me in the rose garden and wouldn't let me pass."

Chase recoiled. "What?"

"It's true. And he called me by my mother's name."

His face progressed through several emotions as he processed the information. Runa held her breath, bracing herself for his certain anger toward Easton. Chase didn't move for a couple minutes. He said nothing at all. Runa began to believe he hadn't heard her.

When he did respond, it was nothing like she'd anticipated.

"Well, that's my father for you." Chase laughed heartily. "You never know what he's going to do next."

Betrayal and disbelief pounded in Runa's brain.

"You're laughing? You think this is funny?"

"I'm sure it wasn't funny at the time, at least not to you. And I'm sorry he scared you. I'll have a talk with him. But you mustn't think anything of it, darling. My father will do anything for shock value. I think you misunderstood his intentions."

"I didn't misunderstand anything."

"Runa—"

"You don't believe me."

"It's not that, sweetheart. Clearly you're upset, and I'm sorry for that. All I'm saying is you've misinterpreted his meaning. My father is harmless," Chase explained, rubbing her shoulders gently.

"He's harmless?" Runa shook her head numbly. "Just like your mother, right?"

"My mother? What did she do?"

"Nothing. I'm sure it's all just one big misunderstanding on my part."

Without another word, Runa shrugged his hands away and climbed under the covers, still fully clothed. Turning her back to her husband, she closed her eyes, doing her best to calm her racing mind.

"Runa—"

"I'm tired, Chase. I'm going to sleep now."

TWENTY-FIVE
DEPARTURE COVE, OREGON, 1902

"*Isn't she lovely? Just like her mother.*"

Thomas stepped back and admired his two-year-old daughter as she spun, giggling as her skirt flounced. He'd purchased the fanciest, frilliest dress he could find, and he seemed quite satisfied with himself.

"*You spoil her.*"

Brynja chuckled as she kissed him on the cheek.

"*It's a sad day indeed when a father can't spoil his daughter. Do you like your dress, Ingrid?*"

The little girl bobbed her head, her blonde ringlets bouncing happily. Her blue eyes glistened as she clapped her chubby hands. Thomas smiled at his wife, then his daughter. Both of the women in his life had him wrapped around their little fingers.

"Of course you may spoil your daughter. Far be it from me to suggest otherwise."

Brynja shook her head and feigned irritation, but they both knew it was a ruse. She found it impossible to remain angry with the man who had completely captured her heart.

"In case you were worried that I forgot about you"—*Thomas reached into his breast pocket and pulled out a small box*—*"I've brought something else."*

Her eyes widened as she lifted the lid, seeing the lovely gold rose brooch with a diamond center inside.

"It's beautiful."

"I'm glad you like it. It reminded me of your rose garden, which is going to be a wonder once it grows."

"Yes, it will." Brynja hugged Thomas tightly. "Thank you."

"I love buying gifts for you and Ingrid. You may call it spoiling if you like, but I will continue to do so." He grinned.

"I know you will."

"That's not all I did in town today. I also had a meeting, Brynn."

"I know."

Brynja's heart squeezed inside her chest. She knew what Thomas was going to say before the words were spoken. She would beg him to reconsider, but in the end, he wouldn't listen.

"How do you know I had a meeting?"

"After all this time, Thomas, do you really need to ask?"

He shook his head. "I suppose I don't."

"Tell me about your meeting."

Thomas sat on the velvet couch, and Brynja sank into the armchair opposite him. Ingrid, blissfully unaware of the drama between her parents, played with her blocks in the corner.

"I'm going to sea. There's a shipment that needs to be delivered to San Francisco, and I'll be the captain."

"Thomas—"

"No one has more experience with the waters of that area than I do," he explained.

"Please don't go, Thomas."

"It's a course I've sailed plenty of times, Brynn. I'm the man to do it. I'll be there and back in no time."

"I'm begging you, please don't go," she persisted.

"Have you seen something that would convince me I shouldn't?"

"Nothing definite, but I've seen things which worry me greatly."

Brynja stood, then perched herself next to Thomas on the couch. She clutched his hand in hers, desperate to convey her concern.

"Tell me what you've seen, Brynn," he persisted.

"I've been having dreams."

"What does that mean?"

"You're in danger. I'm afraid you won't return."

"Have you seen anything for certain?"

Brynja paused for a moment, considering her answer. She

knew if she told Thomas she'd foreseen his death, he wouldn't go. But to tell him that would be an outright untruth, since she had seen no such thing. She detested dishonesty, and she couldn't bring herself to tell Thomas a bald-faced lie. It was more an overwhelming sense of doom, something she couldn't articulate.

"I have seen nothing for certain. It's just a feeling."

"Then we have our answer. If I were truly in danger, you would have seen it, my love. You always do," Thomas reasoned. "I'll leave tomorrow and be home before you know it."

"But, Thomas—"

"Yes, darling?"

"I love you."

Brynja was on the verge of falling apart. Terror squeezed her heart so tightly she could barely breathe.

More than anything in the world, she wanted to be wrong.

But somehow, she knew she wasn't.

TWENTY-SIX

Dejected, Runa sat in her room scooping bites of food into her mouth. Her dinner was delicious, but eating alone gave her no enjoyment. Her solitary evenings had become the norm, and as a result, she'd settled into a bleak existence where she went to work and came home to an empty room.

Camille and Easton were away on a tour of Europe. As a way to boost her spirits, Chase dangled the fact that they were alone in the house like a carrot in front of her face. He told her he would be home for dinner every night while they were away, but so far, it hadn't happened once. Runa wasn't even upset. She'd grown too numb to care.

Ever since the incident with Easton, she'd had little to say to Chase. The rift between them grew wider by the day. She was angered by the fact that he hadn't taken her seriously when she told him about his father. Instead, he'd made it seem as if she'd overreacted. Runa loved Chase more than anything, but it wasn't a stretch to say there was a chink in the armor.

Chase knew she was angry with him, and he had been even sweeter than usual. Earlier that day, she'd come home to a dozen red roses on her bedside table. Last week he brought home her favorite chocolates. The week before, he'd given her a new bracelet. She knew he was trying to apologize, but she was still bitter about the fact that he hadn't believed her.

She stabbed a green bean with the tines of her fork and jumped when her phone rang. She saw it was Chase and mentally prepared herself for the conversation which had become routine.

"Hello."

"Hello, darling. What are you doing?"

"Eating dinner. Alone."

"I'm sorry I missed it. Again. But I have good news. I've finished my meeting early, and I'll be home in an hour or so."

"Really?" She wasn't expecting that.

"Yes, really. Since you're eating now, I'll grab a quick bite at the office while I finish up some paperwork. When I get home, we can take a walk through the grounds or watch a movie. It will be just the two of us, all night long."

"That sounds really nice, Chase."

"It does, doesn't it? I'm sorry things have been so hectic. I feel like we saw more of each other before we were married."

"That's because we did," she answered matter-of-factly.

"I know. I'm going to do my best to change that."

"I hope so. It's been… lonely."

"I know, darling, and I'm sorry. I'll finish up and be home soon."

Runa hung up the phone, surprised by how much the thought of spending time with Chase raised her spirits. Maybe things would be fine after all. Settling into marriage was a transition, and they hadn't had time to do it well. They just needed to reconnect; then everything would be better.

Finishing her meal, she placed the lid on the tray and left it outside the door for Maisie. She had a bit of time before Chase would arrive, and she wanted to do something besides twiddle her thumbs. He had mentioned them taking a walk, so that was out. She could read a book, but her thoughts were too scattered to focus.

Remembering that Camille and Easton were gone, it seemed like a good time to explore the inside of Everwine Manor. She'd basically hibernated inside her own suite of rooms and was long overdue for familiarizing herself with the rest of the estate. With no one around but the servants, the timing was perfect.

Sliding her cell phone into the pocket of her sweater, Runa slipped into the silent hallway. The east wing was deserted, as usual. Creeping quietly down the mile-long corridor, she rounded several turns, finally opening the French doors connecting the wings. Closing them softly behind her, she climbed the small staircase leading to the west wing.

The evening had grown dark, and there were no lights on in the hallway. Reaching into her pocket, Runa grabbed her phone and turned on the flashlight. It faintly illuminated the darkness but also cast strange shadows along the walls and ceilings. Shivering, she found a light fixture on the wall and flipped it on quickly.

She wasn't sure where she was going or what she was looking for, and she was terrified of getting caught. She'd never been in the west wing of Everwine Manor, but her curiosity outweighed her fear. Runa continued on, her footsteps making virtually no sound as they sank into the plush carpet in the high-ceilinged hallway.

Peering at the intricately carved woodwork on the walls, she ran her fingertips across the molding, marveling at the craftsmanship exhibited in every inch of the home. Her eyes bulged at the various works of art hanging in the vast hall, some of which probably belonged in a museum. Obvious thought and care had gone into the selection of each piece.

When she came to the end of the hallway, she saw doors on both her left and her right. She turned the glass doorknob on the door to her right, opening it slowly. It creaked and groaned, echoing in the stillness. Runa wiped her sweaty palms on her pants, certain that at any moment a servant would come along and catch her snooping.

When the door opened a crack, she peered inside. It was mostly dark, but a light had been left on in the corner. It was a suite of rooms similar to her own but much more opulent. She decided it must belong to Camille and Easton, so she shut the door quietly, backing away as quickly as she could. She had no desire to go inside.

Turning around to the door on the left, Runa twisted the knob. It was dark, but she soon found a light switch next to the doorway. When the room was illuminated, she smiled. It was a beautiful sitting room, filled with some of the most exquisite decor she'd ever seen. Stepping inside, she ran her hands across the lovely floral wallpaper. She was excited to explore it, but her phone vibrated in her pocket.

"Hello," she said when she answered the call.

"Hello, darling," Chase greeted. "I just called to tell you I'm about ten minutes away."

"Oh, really?" She glanced at the time on her watch, startled to see it had been an hour since they'd spoken. "The time just flew by."

"You must be doing something interesting." He chuckled.

"Not really. Just waiting for you," she diverted.

"I'll be right there."

Saying goodbye, she dropped the phone back into her pocket. Her explorations would have to wait for another day. She didn't want Chase to catch her in the west wing.

Turning off the light, she left the room and shut the door behind her. She was about to go back the way she came when she noticed one more doorway at the end of the hall.

Runa knew she should ignore the impulse to check it out, but she simply wanted to take a quick look.

Walking to the end of the hallway, she opened the door. It was dark, with no visible light switch, so she turned on her phone's flashlight and shined it into the blackness.

She was shocked to find another staircase, quite large and twisting, leading upward as far as the eye could see, presumably to another section of the house. She guessed it must be the way to the attic. The rickety stairs were old, appearing quite precarious. The wallpaper on the landing was faded, ripped in several places, and the carpet was threadbare. The area was incongruently shabby in comparison to the opulence of the rest of the house.

Runa was so wrapped up in her discovery that she didn't hear footsteps behind her until it was too late.

Maisie cleared her throat loudly. "Are you looking for something, ma'am?"

The unexpected sound cut through the quiet like a knife. Unprepared, Runa let out a loud scream, gripping the doorway for stability. Maisie must have known she would startle Runa, as was evidenced by the satisfied smirk on the servant's face.

"Can I help you find something?" Maisie asked matter-of-factly.

"Oh, Maisie, you scared me half to death," Runa panted.

"I can see that."

"I-I was just—"

"Just what, ma'am?"

"I don't know. I guess I was lost," she offered weakly.

"I see. What were you looking for?"

Runa worked to gain control, trying to come up with a good reason for being in the west wing. Unfortunately, there wasn't one, so she said the first thing that came to her mind.

"What's up there?" She motioned toward the old staircase.

"The third floor."

Maisie didn't elaborate.

"What's on the third floor?"

"Nothing."

"There's nothing up there? It's empty?"

"Of course it's not empty, ma'am. But no one goes up there."

"Why?"

"It's been closed off for years. It isn't safe."

Something about Maisie's words sent a shiver down Runa's spine. It wasn't what she said but the underlying connotation. It felt like a warning, an undercurrent of meaning that wasn't spoken yet was perfectly understood.

"Du er i fare," a voice whispered in Runa's ear.

Suddenly the walls were closing in. She could almost hear the footsteps of the ghosts of the past traversing the old staircase.

She slammed the door and practically ran down the hallway, back toward the east wing.

"That's right, ma'am. You should stay away from there," Maisie called behind her. "The Everwines wouldn't like you poking around where you don't belong."

TWENTY-SEVEN

Breathless, Runa slammed her bedroom door shut with a thud. She ran to the bathroom sink and splashed cold water on her face. Patting it dry with a fluffy towel, she tried to gain command of her runaway thoughts.

"What just happened?" she whispered into the silence of the room.

Runa was scared out of her wits just thinking about the strange encounter at the entrance to the third floor. She'd undoubtedly heard footsteps traveling up and down, each stair creaking beneath the weight of some ghostly apparition. She'd certainly heard the woman's voice, as well as the strange phrase, the same one she'd heard several times. Maisie's reaction and warning to stay away made the hairs on her neck tingle.

Even as Runa's chest constricted and her heart ran laps inside, she knew she would eventually return to the third floor. There were secrets to be discovered, and nothing, neither her fear nor the warnings of the dour maid, could keep her away.

As she glanced at her shaking hands, the strange blue light flickered from her fingertips. She blinked twice, trying to make it disappear.

Holding her hands in front of the mirror, she looked closely. There was no denying the fact that her hands were glowing. She wiggled her fingers in front of her face, feeling a strange crackling electricity in the room. It wasn't the first time she'd experienced the phenomenon, and it was becoming harder to ignore.

"Runa, darling, I'm home," Chase called from the other room.

Glancing in the mirror, she pinched her cheeks to put some color back into her pale complexion. Dabbing her eyes, she convinced herself her inner turmoil didn't show on her face and went out to meet her husband.

"I'm glad you're home," she greeted him.

Runa rose on her tiptoes and brushed her lips across Chase's cheek in a welcoming kiss. She was about to pull away when he wrapped his arms around her tightly, crushing her body against his. Pushing her apprehension aside, she melted into him as he stroked her hair and deepened the kiss. He had a way of making her forget everything except how much she loved him.

"I'm glad to be home." Chase chuckled once they came up for air.

"That was nice." She swallowed hard, her body on fire. "It's been a while."

"It's been far too long, and I intend to rectify that very soon." He gave her a wink and clasped her hand inside his. "But for now, how about a walk?"

"A walk sounds great," Runa agreed, her mind racing ahead, thinking of what was to come.

Chase led her from their suite, down the stairs, and out the front door. It was a lovely evening, and the weather was unseasonably mild. The sun was about to set, yet it was warm enough to render jackets unnecessary.

The couple strolled across the front lawn hand in hand, taking in the surrounding beauty. They walked toward the edge of the yard, following the roar of the ocean. Gazing down the cliff, Runa smiled as she watched the mammoth waves crash against the rocks below. Sea spray floated on the breeze, tickling her nose and collecting in a fine mist upon her hair.

Closing her eyes, she reveled in the sound and smell of the ocean. She'd always felt a spiritual connection to the water, almost as if they belonged to each other. She'd often had dreams of herself commanding the waves and interpreting the wind. The dreams had become even more vivid since arriving at Everwine Manor. Of course, she realized how ridiculous that was, and she'd never told anyone. But it was an interesting thought to entertain.

"What are you thinking about, darling?" Chase squeezed her hand, interrupting her thoughts.

"Crazy, nonsensical things." She laughed. "Nothing important."

"Tell me," he persuaded. "Please? I love hearing what goes on in that pretty head of yours."

"You'll think I've lost my mind."

"Give me a try. You know you can trust me."

"Well, I was thinking about water. I've always felt a connection, even when I didn't live anywhere near it," she began.

"How so?"

"When I was younger, my favorite place to be was in a swimming pool or bathtub."

"Wow, you're taking me way back, aren't you?" Chase smiled.

"I remember the first time my mother brought me to the ocean. I was only five years old, but the memory is so vivid. The minute I saw the waves, I felt this intense rush inside me. I broke free of my mother's hand and ran as fast as I could into the surf. It was like I could hear the water speaking, telling me its secrets. My mother didn't stop me. She seemed to know I felt something. I remember her satisfied smile as I lifted my hands and tried to gather the sea mist in my fists."

"Go on," Chase encouraged.

"As I grew older, I had these intense dreams where I could control the water and the wind. I even tried to do it once."

"Do what?"

"Control the water."

"How did that go?"

"Well, it worked, actually. Or at least I thought it did at the time. Looking back now, I'm sure it was all just one big coincidence. I mean, a person can't really do that." Runa chuckled.

"And… uh… you only tried it once?"

Chase cleared his throat and swallowed hard. His face had grown quite pale, and beads of sweat pooled on his upper lip. He appeared to be bothered by her story. For a moment, he almost looked as if he was afraid of her.

"Yes, I only tried it once. I was a kid. It was a silly fantasy."

"A silly fantasy," he repeated.

Runa placed her hand on Chase's arm, and when she did, she noticed the blue light flickering beneath it again. Shoving her hands inside her pockets, she tried to decipher his strange reaction to her story.

"Are you okay, Chase?"

"Yes, of course I'm okay. Why wouldn't I be?" He smiled, planting a kiss on her forehead.

"I'm not sure."

"Shall we continue our walk?"

Runa nodded and fell into step beside her husband.

She glanced up at Everwine Manor. Watching the sun set behind the pitched roof made her think of her earlier discovery. She decided to ask Chase about it.

"I'm curious about something," she started. "What's on the third floor?"

"The third floor? Why in the world would you want to know that?"

Runa detected agitation in her husband's voice.

"No reason, Chase. I just wondered."

"That seems like a strange thing to wonder, don't you think?"

"Not really. I mean, I live here now, so it's only natural for me to be curious about my new home."

"I suppose so."

"So what's up there? I assume you've been on the third floor."

"Of course I have," Chase replied. "But it's been years."

"What's it like?"

He stopped walking and ran his hands through his hair, a gesture that signaled his frustration. Taking a deep breath, he stretched his neck from side to side, a look of tension upon his face. Runa was convinced he wasn't going to answer her question, but after several moments, he finally spoke.

"I used to play up there when I was a child. I would ride my tricycle up and down the halls. It's huge, larger than you can imagine. There are rows and rows of rooms. The staff used to live up there, but they haven't for years."

"Really? Why is that?"

"It's not safe."

Runa realized that Maisie had said the exact same words.

She knew she should drop the subject, but something forced her to continue.

"What's not safe about it?"

"The flooring needs to be fixed. The whole thing needs to be renovated."

"So why hasn't that been done?" she pushed, desperate for answers.

He narrowed his eyes at her. "Why the sudden curiosity about the third floor, Runa?"

"I'm a naturally curious person, I suppose."

She laughed in an attempt to lighten the suddenly tense mood.

Taking a deep breath, Chase looked her in the eyes. "A house of this size is tremendously expensive to maintain. Something always needs to be done. The only way to remain afloat is to prioritize. Fixing the third floor, which serves no purpose, has not been a priority."

"I see. I suppose that makes sense."

"Why wouldn't it make sense?" he snapped.

"Why are you lashing out at me, Chase? It was a simple question."

"You're right. I'm sorry." He sighed heavily and forced a smile. "You have every right to ask questions. I suppose I'm just tired."

"Perhaps we should go inside, then," Runa suggested, not wanting to spoil their rare time together.

"Yes, we should. I have plans to occupy your thoughts for the rest of the evening." He grinned mischievously.

Arm in arm, the two walked back across the lawn toward the main entrance to Everwine Manor. Glancing up at the roof, Runa spied the turret at the top of the immense tower. Circular in shape, the entire structure was encased in intricately designed stained glass windows. She'd always thought they were lovely, but at that moment, something seemed off.

Just as they were about to slip inside the front door, Runa thought she detected a faint light and swift movement behind one of the windows in the turret, but she couldn't be certain. The vivid colors and designs of the windows made it difficult to see if someone was behind them.

A shiver trailed down her spine. She felt like she was being watched. Not wanting to get into another tense conversation with Chase, she told herself it was just her imagination and went inside.

She and Chase spent the next couple of hours catching up on lost time. They were hungry for one another, their bodies conveying the love inside their hearts. When she finally collapsed onto her pillow and drifted off to sleep, the dreams began and continued on a loop throughout the night. She dreamed of a woman locked in a tower of stained glass windows.

The prisoner was desperate to escape, but no matter how hard she tried, freedom was beyond her grasp. The woman picked up a small silver mirror and gazed at her reflection. Blue light arced off her hands into the glass, and when the woman looked in the mirror, Runa saw her own face.

TWENTY-EIGHT

DEPARTURE COVE, OREGON, 1902

"*M*rs. Calais? Won't you please open up?*"
The desperate maid rapped on the door of Brynja's suite of rooms.

"Go away!" Brynja yelled.

"But, Mrs. Calais, you haven't eaten in two days," the maid pleaded.

"I'm not hungry," Brynja mumbled into her pillow.

"Ma'am, your daughter is asking for you. Miss Ingrid wants her mother," the servant said softly.

Her daughter's name was the thing that finally caught Brynja's attention. She'd locked herself in her room two days ago without a thought to anything other than the searing pain that ripped her heart in two. The maid's mention of her daughter reminded Brynja that she was a mother. Ingrid was young, and she needed her. The girl was all she had left of her beloved Thomas, after all.

When the messenger sent word to Angelica House saying Thomas's ship had gone down in an unexpected storm, Brynja had screamed, wailing so loudly that she'd eventually lost her voice. She'd curled herself into a ball on the floor of the sitting room, sobbing for hours.

Finally, exhaustion took over and she couldn't move. A servant eventually carried her upstairs to her room, where she'd been ever since. Selfishly, she realized, she hadn't given a second's thought to her child. The vast expanse of her own grief had taken over.

"Of course my daughter needs me," Brynja replied as she wiped her face and rose from her bed.

Padding softly across the room, she opened the door. Mrs. Stevens, the maid, gasped when she saw her mistress's face. Her cheeks were hollow, her eyes sunken. Dark circles outlined Brynja's lovely blue eyes, and her flaxen hair was matted to her face and knotted in several places.

"Oh, my poor dear," the servant gasped. "Let's get you cleaned up. You can't see Miss Ingrid looking like this."

Nodding numbly, she allowed Mrs. Stevens to lead her to her dressing table, where the maid set about making her mistress presentable. Brynja could barely form a coherent thought, and tears streamed down her face. All she could think of was her beloved Thomas and how she would never see him again.

If only he had listened. If only she had lied to him and told him she'd foreseen his death with certainty. If she could go back, she would lie to him a thousand times if it meant she could keep him alive.

When Mrs. Stevens had done all she could, she helped Brynja to her feet and led her into the adjoining sitting room where Ingrid was playing with her nanny. When the little girl spied her mother, she clapped her hands, ran to Brynja, and hugged her knees.

"Mama! Mama!"

Ingrid's voice cut through the fog inside her mother's brain, and Brynja knelt down and wrapped her arms tightly around the girl. She inhaled her sweet scent and muttered a prayer of thanks that at least she still had her. Ingrid was now her sole reason for existing.

Settling into the armchair, she watched as Ingrid jumped onto her rocking horse. The little girl was soon lost in her world of make-believe, where the bad things couldn't survive.

How Brynja wished she could go there.

Steeling herself for the answer, she asked, "Mrs. Stevens, what is the latest news? Have they found Thomas's body?"

"No, ma'am. They haven't. And it's unlikely they will. That storm came out of nowhere, they say, and the ship and crew were lost."

"What do you mean, the storm came out of nowhere?"

"Well, ma'am, folks are saying that it was... well... almost... supernatural," Mrs. Stevens replied shakily.

"A supernatural storm sank my husband's ship. That's what you're saying?"

"Yes, ma'am."

Brynja puzzled over the words in her mind. She'd always had such clear visions, and water was tied to her gifts. She and the ocean were one and the same. How had she not foreseen the danger to Thomas on the water? Why had she been unable to find the storm and calm it? Had her deep love for Thomas weakened her power? Had it made her blind? That had to be the answer. She was too focused on her own happiness and not properly attuned to her gifts.

"Is there anything else? Any other news, Mrs. Stevens?"

"Er... well... I don't think it's anything you need to hear," the maid sputtered.

"If there's news, I need to hear it," Brynja insisted.

"Very well, ma'am. Let me just say that anyone who knows you knows it's just a lot of nonsense, but the folks in town are saying things."

"What sort of things?"

"It's ridiculous, I'm telling you," Mrs. Stevens continued, "but they're saying you caused the storm."

"Me? Why on earth would I cause a storm to kill my own husband?"

Anger boiled inside of Brynja, and she sprang from her chair and paced back and forth across the room.

"That's why I said it's ridiculous, ma'am. It's not true. But people are saying it all the same. They say you're a witch and

you conjured up a storm to kill Thomas so you could have all his money," Mrs. Stevens explained in a rush.

Brynja gasped. "Who would start such a rumor?"

"I don't know, ma'am. You know how tongues wag. You're an intelligent woman, and your skills with plants and herbs have always made folks talk. The things you're able to grow here, in this climate, well, it makes people suspicious."

"That's absurd," Brynja insisted.

"Of course it is, ma'am. Folks in this town have small minds," the maid said with a click of her tongue.

Brynja's head spun with a thousand questions. How could anyone think she would harm Thomas? She'd rather harm herself. She would die a thousand deaths if it meant she could keep Thomas alive. First, she'd lost her parents, then her twin, and now her husband. The sacrifice was too high. What good were her powers if they couldn't protect those she loved?

She glanced across the room and watched as Ingrid giggled and rode her rocking horse. All that mattered now was protecting her daughter. But how could she make a home in this place for Ingrid? Without Thomas, Brynja had no hope of ever becoming a true part of the community. She would always be on the outskirts, the fringes, living in the shadows. Especially now, when they thought she had conjured up the very storm that stole him away.

The room began to spin, and Brynja's head pounded. Her knees grew shaky, and before she knew what was happening, she collapsed, hitting the floor with a thud.

TWENTY-NINE

Runa cleaned the glass display case in her boutique, a tedious task designed to keep her runaway mind in check. For the past few days, she'd had a difficult time quieting the voices in her head, the ones screaming that something was wrong. Her vivid dreams prevented her from resting, and she was exhausted. The doppelgänger woman seemed to whisper to her, even in the light of day.

She couldn't shake the fact that living at Everwine Manor had unearthed something deep inside, a sense of unrest, the feeling that she needed to find something, although she had no clue what that might be. Still, the agitation lingered, gaining in intensity as one day bled into the next.

Frustrated, Runa peered into her latte, as if the drink could somehow answer her questions. She took a sip and frowned, realizing the coffee had grown cold. As the thought entered her mind, a strange compulsion followed. Not understanding why, she fixed her gaze on the liquid and imagined it warming. Suddenly, small bubbles rolled in the mug, and steam floated from the surface.

Gasping, she grabbed the coffee and took a quick sip, wincing in pain as the latte burned her lips. Sputtering, she spit the coffee back into the mug before slamming it on the counter, splashes sloshing over the edge and puddling at the base of the mug.

"What? How?" Runa stammered.

"Did you say something, Runa?" Emily called from across the room.

"No. Nothing at all," Runa lied, continuing to stare at the mug.

"Do you want me to unpack the shipment in the back?" Emily offered.

"That would be great," she replied distractedly. "Hey, Em, do you think you could handle things here for a bit? I need to step out."

"Sure I can," Emily answered. "Is everything okay?"

Worry creased the young girl's forehead as she gazed suspiciously at her boss.

"Everything is fine. I just have an errand to run. I'll be back in a bit. Call if you need anything."

Glaring at the coffee mug one last time, Runa grabbed her purse and jacket and practically ran out the front door. Stepping outside, she breathed in the fresh air, trying to still her racing thoughts. Walking quickly down the sidewalk, she tried to convince herself that she wasn't losing her mind.

"You just boiled a cup of coffee with your mind, Runa," she whispered to herself. "You are way past crazy."

She wanted nothing more than to talk to her mother, but all Asta would do was worry or try to read her aura, neither of which she wanted. Instead, she decided to do the next best thing. Turning the corner, she stepped into Talisman.

"Hey there, sweetie," Tawney said with a smile as Runa approached the counter.

"Hi, Tawney," Runa replied with a grimace.

Frowning, Tawney stepped around the counter and pulled Runa into a tight hug, seeming to know that was exactly what she needed.

"Now that's from your mama, because it's just what she'd do if she were here," Tawney whispered into Runa's ear.

"You're right. She would," Runa mumbled as she allowed herself to be held.

Pulling away, Tawney scrutinized Runa's face for a moment. "You're wearing the black tourmaline?"

Runa reached beneath her blouse and pulled out the crystal necklace. "I promised my mom I would."

"Good. You need protection. I'm not sure why, but something tells me you do," Tawney answered. "Come, sit with me. I've brewed some herbal tea."

Obediently, Runa followed Tawney through the beaded curtain into the back room, where a large crystal sat in the center of a table. Tawney led Runa to two comfortable time-worn armchairs across the room. A small table between the chairs held two steaming mugs of herbal tea, ready and waiting. Tawney had expected her all along.

"So, what do you want to ask me?" Tawney began unceremoniously as she sank into the chair.

"How do you know I want to ask you something?" Runa hedged.

"Are you saying you didn't come here to ask me questions?"

Shaking her head slowly, Runa admitted, "You're right. I am looking for answers."

"I know," Tawney replied.

"All right, here goes. What do you know about the Everwines? I need to know everything."

"I'll reveal what I'm able to, but some of this story is not mine to tell."

"You're talking about the secrets my mother is keeping?"

"Your mother is my dearest friend, and I won't betray her confidence."

"I'll take what I can get, I suppose," Runa agreed.

Tawney closed her eyes for several moments, appearing to gather her thoughts before she began her tale.

"We all went to school together—your mother, Easton, Garrett, and me. Asta and I didn't really run with their crowd except for a brief time in high school."

"Who's Garrett?" Runa questioned, her heart beating rapidly.

Tawney swallowed hard as she avoided Runa's eyes. "Garrett Brewster. He was Easton's best friend."

"What else was he, Tawney? What aren't you saying?" She knew he was the key to unlocking the secrets of her mother's past.

Tawney sighed heavily. "Your mother and Garrett were in love."

"He's my father, isn't he?" Runa knew the answer to the question even before she asked it. Somehow she'd always known.

"Your mother should be the one to tell you this, Runa. Why don't you ask her?"

"I have asked her, Tawney. She can't talk about it. The sadness is so heavy she can't lift it. I need you to tell me."

"Very well." Tawney nodded. "Garrett Brewster is your father."

"Tell me everything you know about him," Runa pleaded.

"Garrett and Easton were best friends. When Garrett and your mother fell in love, it put a strain on his friendship with Easton."

"Why did it affect their friendship?"

"Because Easton was also in love with your mother, Runa. But it was more than that, really. Easton was obsessed with Asta. He followed her around like a lost puppy."

"He wasn't with Camille back then?"

"Oh, Camille wanted him. Being with Easton was a status symbol for a girl like Camille. But Easton only had eyes for Asta. Camille was green with envy," Tawney explained.

"That's why she hates my mother. And me," Runa deduced.

"That's certainly part of it."

"What happened then?"

"After we graduated, Easton and Garrett went into business together. Easton inherited his share of the lumber business, and he and Garrett decided to partner up on some new distribution idea they had. About that time, your mother found out she was pregnant," Tawney explained.

"What did Garrett do?"

"He wanted to marry Asta, and she felt the same way about him."

"Why didn't they get married?"

"Garrett's family was quite wealthy. His parents believed your mother wasn't good enough for their son. They threatened to disinherit him if he married Asta."

"And he listened to them?" Runa asked indignantly.

"Money causes people to do many things they wouldn't do otherwise." Tawney drummed her fingers on the arms of the chair.

"Is that why my mother left Departure Cove?"

"Easton found out that Asta was pregnant. Like I said, he was in love with her. He told Asta he would marry her and raise her child as his own. She refused, and Easton went crazy with rage." Tawney shuddered as a vivid memory replayed in her mind.

"Did he hurt her?" Runa asked nervously.

"I wasn't there, but whatever he said or did spooked Asta enough to make her run. Your mother packed up and left the next day. I didn't see her again until you both showed up here."

"So Easton married Camille. And what happened to my father?"

"Garrett was killed in an accident a few days after your mother left. No one really knew what happened. Easton found him on a jobsite. He was dead. I believe his death was eventually ruled a suicide, which might be plausible. Garrett was devastated when Asta left."

"But you don't believe it was a suicide, do you, Tawney?" Runa's heart pounded as she waited for the answer.

Tawney shook her head, her eyes on Runa. "No I don't. I've never believed Garrett killed himself."

"What do you think happened?"

"I wasn't there, so I can't be certain," Tawney hedged.

"But you must have a theory," Runa encouraged.

"Here's what I think. Easton Everwine is no one to trifle with. He was angry about your mother and jealous of his best friend. He was the one who found Garrett dead. I've always had my suspicions."

"Do you think Easton is capable of something like murder?"

As Runa posed the question, she had a flashback of the insanity behind Easton's eyes when he attacked her in the rose garden. She knew without a doubt it was entirely possible.

"I think the Everwines take what they want when they want it. They feel entitled."

Runa's stomach clenched, and she took a deep breath before asking the question she could barely bring herself to voice. "What about Chase? Do you think he's like his father, Tawney? Because I don't."

"I don't know. But I'm begging you to be careful, Runa."

Rising slowly, Runa nodded. She bent to hug Tawney before turning to leave.

She'd wanted to ask Tawney's opinion on her strange experiences, like blue light shooting from her fingertips, or the fact that she'd boiled liquid with her mind. But at that moment, all she could think about was Easton pursuing her, his hungry eyes raking over her body, and the fact that Chase hadn't believed a word of it.

Fingering the black tourmaline necklace, Runa waved goodbye to Tawney and headed back to the boutique.

THIRTY

After closing up the shop and driving home to Everwine Manor, Runa paced back and forth across the floor of her bedroom. Confusion and desperation warred within. She felt caged, imprisoned in a cell of her own making. She loved Chase with all her heart, didn't she? Wasn't that what she felt for him? Of course, she didn't have a lot of experience with healthy relationships. Was it possible that she'd mistaken infatuation for love? Things had moved quickly, but she had always felt sure of her love for Chase. She couldn't bring herself to believe he was dangerous.

But was she wrong? Did she truly love him? Did he love her? Or was she simply blinded by her intense feelings for him?

Easton seemed capable of anything. She'd experienced that firsthand. She'd also been on the receiving end of

Camille's evilness. Even though they were Chase's parents, that didn't mean he was like them. Chase was good. He was a philanthropist, a solid citizen. He would never hurt her.

Deep down, she believed that. Chase wasn't like his parents. She'd married him, not them. She hadn't made a mistake.

When she'd finally managed to calm her nerves, Runa decided she needed a distraction. Chase wasn't due home from work for a couple of hours, and Easton and Camille were still out of the country. Maisie had errands to run in town, and the rest of the staff was otherwise occupied. It was the perfect time to continue her exploration of Everwine Manor.

Closing the bedroom door behind her, she walked quickly down the hall, around the corner, down the next corridor, and into the west wing. She'd been planning her return since the day Maisie chased her away.

Opening the doorway to the sitting room, she ducked inside quickly, flipping on the light. She glanced around the room, her pulse quickening as she surveyed the opulence on full display.

The walls were lined with priceless oil paintings, several of landscapes and flowers as well as a few portraits. She scrutinized the portraits, looking into the lifelike paintings of people she didn't know. She assumed they were members of the Everwine family.

Frowning, she gazed into the eyes of a man whose face so closely resembled Chase's that it took her by surprise. Perhaps it was his grandfather. Although he was quite handsome, his countenance was cold. Runa traced her fingertip across the man's chiseled features, noticing his face would have been perfect if not for a giant red gash on his cheek. She wondered what accident may have befallen him. Whatever it was must have been bad.

Moving across the room, Runa saw an ornate easel covered with a large cloth. Curious, she lifted the cloth, a gasp escaping her lips as the portrait beneath was revealed. Inching closer, she could hardly believe her eyes.

Beneath the cover was a perfectly rendered painting of the woman from her dreams, wearing the same wedding dress Runa had worn. The woman was blonde, her flaxen hair the exact same shade as Runa's. Her identical blue eyes seemed to look directly into Runa's soul.

Glancing at the bottom corner, Runa noticed the portrait was dated 1900. Pulling her sweater closer to her body to fight off a sudden chill, she grabbed her phone and snapped a photo of the portrait. She needed concrete proof of what was in front of her eyes, because it was impossible to wrap her brain around it. The woman was the spitting image of Runa.

She felt connected to the woman in a way she couldn't explain.

As she stared at the portrait, something happened. Before her eyes, its subject came to life. The woman's eyes began to blink, and tears coursed down her cheeks. Her full red lips began to move, and strange words filled the room. The phrase began as a whisper but grew in intensity. Soon the portrait woman was screaming, "Du er i fare," the words echoing throughout the room.

Trembling, Runa collapsed into a nearby desk chair. Burying her face in her trembling hands, she told herself none of it was real. She took ten deep breaths, certain that when she opened her eyes, everything would be back to normal. But it wasn't. When she looked at the portrait, the woman was still crying, the odd words continuing to fall from her mouth.

Not knowing what else to do, Runa faced her fear head-on. Speaking directly to the woman in the portrait, she managed to find her voice.

"What do the words mean? I've heard them before, but I don't understand."

"Du er i fare," the portrait repeated.

"I don't know what that means," Runa protested.

Sudden movement on the desk before her caught her attention. Runa blinked twice as a feathered quill pen dipped itself into the inkwell and began to scrawl out a message on the paper in front of her. Aghast, Runa watched as the pen wrote the mysterious words over and over again across the page: "Du er i fare."

As quickly as it began, everything stopped. The portrait grew still, and the quill pen clattered onto the desk.

Glancing back and forth between the painting and the pen, Runa waited. Nothing else happened. The room was eerily quiet, the portrait silent.

For a moment, she was sure she'd imagined it all. But the paper filled with scribblings of the strange phrase remained. She couldn't deny the words were real.

Grabbing the paper, Runa folded it several times and shoved it into her pocket before she practically ran from the room, turning off the light and exiting as quickly as possible. The walls were closing in, making it impossible to breathe.

She was about to head back to the east wing when she heard a loud thump on the floor above. The sound came from the third-floor entryway. As she eased the creaking door open, her heart pounded. Someone or *something* was up there. She was as certain as she'd ever been.

Runa remained stock-still, listening intently for several moments, but she heard nothing. Shoving her trembling hand into her pocket to finger the paper, she ran back to her room.

She didn't know what the words meant, but she was going to find out.

THIRTY-ONE

Runa tossed and turned on her side of the bed, restlessly searching for a comfortable position to allow her tormented mind a moment's peace. Chase's warm body lay beside her, still and calm, breathing in the even pattern indicating deep sleep. She envied his ability to turn off his thoughts and sleep like a stone. For her, sleep had become elusive, always just beyond her grasp.

She hadn't told Chase about her encounter with the weeping portrait or the phantom quill pen, but she had brought up the sounds she'd heard on the third floor. He'd brushed off her words, reminding her that Everwine Manor was a centuries-old mansion where it was perfectly normal to hear creaking doors and groaning floorboards. Runa insisted the sounds she heard were different, more than just the house settling. She hadn't been prepared for her husband's reaction.

Chase's words still echoed in her mind: "You've been acting very strangely, Runa. I don't think you're adjusting well to your new life here. Perhaps you should talk to a professional about the issues you're having."

She hadn't spoken another word to him the rest of the night, and they'd both fallen silently into bed. Runa was hurt that Chase had accused her of being unstable and needing to talk to a therapist. It wasn't that she had anything against therapy; in fact, she'd been down that road before and found it beneficial. What bothered her was that her husband refused to take her seriously.

Runa flopped from her back to her side. Finally giving up on sleep, she rolled out of bed, padded softly to the window, and gazed outside at the swell of the ocean in the distance. The moonlight glittered on the water, causing the surface to glow like a crystal. The ocean spoke to her, singing, beckoning like a siren's call. Grabbing her jacket, she slipped it over her pajamas, slid her feet into her boots, and quietly headed outside.

She felt herself being pulled like a magnet toward the rose garden. She hadn't been back since that terrible night with Easton, but since he was away, it felt safe to return.

As she rambled through the maze of flowers, she began to relax. Under the cover of darkness, while the ocean serenaded her in the background, she let her mind spin in circles, giving herself permission to entertain the disconcerting thoughts she tried to suppress in the light of day.

Runa considered the cryptic phrase, "Du er i fare." Now

that she knew the spelling, she was too afraid to google it. Somehow, she understood that the answer would change everything, and she wasn't ready for that. She replayed the image of the weeping portrait and the quill pen. She thought of the footsteps she'd heard traversing the creaky steps leading to the third floor and Maisie's admonitions about it being unsafe. She remembered the woman in the portrait, her doppelgänger, wearing the same wedding gown Runa had worn to marry Chase, the one found at Everwine Manor when her own had gone missing.

She revisited the story Tawney had told about her father, his mysterious death, and the fact that Easton had loved her mother. Had he loved her enough to kill his best friend in a fit of jealous rage?

It was all too much. She didn't know what to do with any of it, and the load felt inordinately heavy for her to bear alone.

Wiping the tears that rolled freely down her cheeks, Runa reached into her coat pocket and pulled out a tissue.

After drying her face, she checked her cell phone. There was a notification of a missed call and voice mail from her mother. She must have missed it while she was talking to Chase.

She pressed Play and smiled as she heard Asta's warm voice, wrapping around her like a bear hug.

"Sweetie, I'm worried about you. I don't want to alarm you, but I've been having visions. I can't shake the fact that my premonitions are telling me you're in danger. Please call me tomorrow, Runa. I love you."

Sighing heavily, Runa dropped the phone back into her pocket. Most of the time she believed her mother's visions were nothing but a bunch of hocus-pocus, but she'd been having experiences she couldn't explain. Her logical mind had difficulty with the fact that nothing in her life made sense.

The strange warning dreams, the random blue light that flickered from her hands on a regular basis, and the fact that she could control elements with her mind—there was no logic to any of that. Asta's auras and premonitions didn't seem half as farfetched as they once had.

Runa vowed to call her mother the next morning and made her way back toward the house. She was emotionally exhausted, hoping to convince her weary body to sleep.

As she entered the house, she glanced at the turret on the third floor, where a faint, unmistakable light glittered behind the stained glass windows.

Runa watched closely. Was it her imagination, or were two distinct silhouettes peering back at her?

THIRTY-TWO

DEPARTURE COVE, OREGON, 1903

*B*rynja paced back and forth across the floor of Thomas's study. She'd intended to clear out some of his belongings but was unable to do so. Instead, she'd become a puddle of tears as she rifled through his paperwork. Tears had become all too common since his death.

Six months had passed since her life was irrevocably changed, yet for her, time seemed to stand still. She barely left the house, instead sending the servants into town for anything she needed. She and Ingrid were recluses, tucked away, hidden behind the walls of their self-imposed prison.

Folks in town continued to whisper about Brynja's role in the sinking of Thomas's ship. Her staff tried to keep the rumors from breaching the walls of Angelica House, but it was no use. She overheard snippets of conversations, enough to piece together the fact that everyone seemed to believe she was a witch who had cursed her husband and his crew to death.

It broke her heart that people thought she could hurt another soul, let alone the husband she loved more than her own life. She believed in helping, never harming. She still performed her rituals daily by the shore, begging for guidance, some sort of sign of what she should do. But despite her efforts, it seemed her powers had abandoned her, the empty words drifting into the wind, gaining no purchase. Brynja felt alone in a strange, unfamiliar world.

Glancing at her hands, she noticed the flicker of faint blue light emanating from her fingertips. The glow wasn't as strong as it once was, but it was there. Perhaps her powers remained and were simply dormant.

Only time would tell.

Brynja turned her head toward the door as she heard heavy footsteps in the hall, signaling the arrival of Mrs. Stevens.

"Mrs. Calais, you have a visitor."

"A visitor? Me?"

The maid's face mirrored the same look of surprise as her mistress's.

"Indeed, ma'am. I thought it was odd as well. We haven't had a visitor at the house in months."

"Who is it?"

"It's a man, Mrs. Calais," Mrs. Stevens replied with a furrowed brow.

"A man? I don't know any man who would care to visit me. Most people in Departure Cove are too afraid to come here. They fear I'll put a hex on them." Brynja scowled.

"They're daft, ma'am. There was never a kinder soul than you."

"Thank you, Mrs. Stevens. Please go see who the man is and what he wants. I'll wait for your answer," Brynja instructed.

Nodding, Mrs. Stevens rushed from the room.

Brynja collapsed into Thomas's desk chair, her heart thudding as she puzzled over who the visitor might be. Was she in danger? If the people in town truly believed she was a witch, what were they capable of? Witch hunts didn't happen like they once did, but she understood that frightened people could commit terrible deeds.

It didn't take long for Mrs. Stevens to return. Standing quickly and smoothing her dress, Brynja raised her chin, reminding herself she could handle anything that came her way.

"Well, Mrs. Stevens? Who is our guest?"

"Ma'am, he says he has a business proposition for you."

"A business proposition? For me?"

"Yes, ma'am." Mrs. Stevens nodded gravely, something in her face causing Brynja's pulse to quicken.

"Very well, I will see him. Send him in."

Mrs. Stevens gave her one lingering look before nodding and exiting the room. Not even a minute later, she was back, *the stranger following in her wake. Brynja pasted a cool smile on her face, steeling herself for whatever the man wanted. The maid ushered him into the study and promptly left the room.*

Brynja stared at the stranger in front of her, startled by the way her heart lurched in her chest and her brain screamed out in protest. The blue light flickering from her fingertips, dull only moments before, shot from her hands like lightning bolts as the man drew closer. She shoved them behind her back in an effort to hide the light.

"Mrs. Calais, you are too lovely for words." The man's smooth voice slithered like a snake into the room.

"And you, sir, are extremely bold. You show up at my home unannounced, offering no introduction, and your first words are empty compliments," Brynja snapped.

"The lady has a tongue to rival her beauty." The stranger chuckled.

"Who are you, and why are you here, sir?"

She forced herself to hold the man's penetrating gaze in spite of the fact that her hands were shaking behind her back.

"You may not know me, but I certainly know you. I've been watching you for some time, and it seems you and I may have something to offer each other."

"What could you possibly offer me?" Brynja practically spat. "If you've been watching me, as you say, you know I have no need of money."

"I'm not talking about money."

"Then what are you talking about, sir?"

"Protection. Stability. Status. A place in the community. A way to keep your daughter safe."

"What makes you think I need your help with any of that?"

"Surely you've heard what they're saying. Women like you can't be too careful," he warned.

"Women like me?"

"Witches," he answered nonchalantly.

Brynja swallowed hard. She felt like a small animal in a trap. If she moved the wrong way, it would be the end of her.

Pulling her bravery from somewhere deep within, she jutted her chin defiantly, refusing to allow the man to believe he had the upper hand.

"Sir, you come here, flinging about accusations, trying to persuade me that I need your protection, yet I don't even know your name."

"I do apologize. I truly believed everyone in town knew who I was. After all, I'm the richest lumber baron in the country."

"Wealth means nothing to me. Your name, sir?" Brynja raised one eyebrow at the man.

"Why, I'm Lucas Everwine."

THIRTY-THREE

Morning light flickered through the bedroom windows, waking Runa from her restless sleep. She glanced at the bedside clock, grimacing when she saw it was only six. Chase stirred beside her as his alarm began to buzz. He rolled out of bed, turned it off, and stalked across the room toward the bathroom, closing the door behind him.

Runa heard the shower running as she lay in bed pondering what she should say. They hadn't spoken since their argument the night before, when he'd told her she needed to talk to a therapist. Part of her thought she should just drop the subject, pretend it hadn't happened, and move on. The other part refused to sweep it under the rug. If they had any hope of getting past it, they should meet it head-on.

After several minutes, Chase emerged from the steam-filled bathroom, his towel slung haphazardly around his hips. Pain and longing flashed in Runa's belly. She was drawn to him like a magnet, and she wanted him desperately. She wished they could be happy, but it seemed they were too out of sync to find any common ground. Had everyone been right? Had she jumped headfirst into a rocky marriage? She thought Chase was different, but now she questioned everything.

She waited a few moments while he rummaged through his closet for clothes. After a short time, he emerged, fully dressed.

"Chase, can I talk to you?" Runa sat up in bed, leaning against the headboard and pulling the thick blankets to her chest.

"About what?"

The tone of his voice made it clear that he was upset. If she hadn't felt so strongly about their need to talk, she would have kept her mouth shut. Instead she pressed on.

"I want to talk about what I've seen since coming to Everwine Manor. What I've heard."

"Are you going to start in on that again?" Anger flashed in his eyes.

"Yes, Chase, I am. And I don't understand why everything I say has to turn into an argument."

"Because you're talking like a crazy woman, Runa," he retorted. "How do you expect me to react?"

"You keep saying that, yet you won't even listen to what I'm trying to tell you."

"I've been listening. I've heard you spin your tales about creaking floors and phantom footsteps on staircases. You even seem to believe my parents are trying to harm you."

"Because it's all true!" Runa insisted.

"It isn't!" Chase hurled back.

"It's all true, Chase. And there's more. Last night I saw a light in the turret on the third floor. You told me no one goes up there. You said it's not safe."

"What do you want from me?" Chase exploded. "I've given you everything a woman could possibly want, and you're still not satisfied."

"Chase—"

"Just leave things alone!" he roared.

Taken aback by Chase's anger, Runa was rendered speechless. She stared at him as he stomped back and forth across their bedroom floor, his face red and contorted with rage. He was barely recognizable.

"If you would just listen—"

"I'm through listening. Something is wrong with you. Go get some help and leave me alone!"

Without another word, Chase grabbed his phone and wallet before storming from the room, slamming the door behind him.

Runa sat in shocked silence, tears pouring down her face. In less than ten minutes, her life had gone from bad to worse.

Instinctively, she reached for her phone and dialed Tawney's number, heedless of the fact that it was still so early.

Tawney picked up on the first ring, as if she'd been waiting for the call.

"What is it, sweetie?" Her calm voice cut straight through the phone line.

"It's everything." Runa sobbed. "I need to see you."

"Of course. I'll come to you if that works," Tawney suggested.

"Okay. No one is here but me and the staff."

"Perfect. I'll be there in an hour."

Runa hung up the phone and cried, her body shaking with sobs she couldn't control. Her life was falling apart.

"I need answers, and I just keep getting more questions. I need to know what's going on."

As she spoke the words aloud, an image popped into her head. It was clear and exact, leaving no question about what she must do.

Rising from her bed, she walked across the room, went into the closet, and opened her drawer. Rifling through her socks, she dug all the way to the bottom. There it was, hidden from view but never from her thoughts.

Grabbing the photograph of the woman with Chase, Runa marveled once again at their similarities. The happy smile on Chase's face was like a knife to her heart. It pained her to admit that she'd never seen him that happy. He'd never looked at her the way he did at that woman.

Returning to her room, she placed the photograph on the table. Then she dug through her purse where she'd hidden the paper with the strange phrase. Sighing, she placed it on the table next to the picture. It was time for answers.

She went into the bathroom and quickly secured her hair in a bun, brushed her teeth, and pulled on some clothes. She barely gave herself a second glance. Nothing mattered except getting to the truth.

She grabbed her phone and sent Emily a quick text explaining she was closing the shop for the day because she didn't feel well. It wasn't even a lie. The queasiness in the pit of her stomach made her feel as if she were going to vomit.

Heading downstairs, Runa paced in the entryway as she waited for Tawney.

Prompt as always, Tawney parked in the circular driveway. Opening the front door, Runa burst into tears as soon as she saw her. Tawney hugged her tightly, whispering that everything was going to be all right. After wiping her face with a tissue, Runa led Tawney upstairs to her room.

Closing the door behind them, Runa offered Tawney a seat at the table. She sat in the chair opposite. Unable to manage small talk, Runa cut directly to the heart of the matter, shoving the photograph of the woman across the table toward Tawney.

"Do you know who that woman is with Chase?"

Gazing intently at the photograph, Tawney studied it for several moments. Her brow furrowed, but then a look of recognition spread across her face.

"Yes, that's Chase's first wife."

Runa felt like the rug had been pulled from beneath her. It

wasn't as if she hadn't guessed that the woman was Chase's wife, but the confirmation felt cruel and surreal.

"You're sure?"

"Yes, I'm certain. I saw them around town together all the time back then. They were always on the news for something or other. Her name was Freya."

"Freya…."

Runa wasn't sure why the woman's name sparked something in the back of her mind, but hearing it felt like a gut punch.

"It's been under my nose all this time and I didn't even see. I can't believe I never noticed it until right this moment," Tawney said.

"Noticed what?"

"The fact that Freya looks so much like you. If it weren't for her pixie cut, she could be you. It's disconcerting, and I'm frustrated with myself for not seeing it sooner."

"I don't understand any of this, Tawney. Is that why he married me? Because I look like her?"

"I don't know, sweetie."

Tears rolled down Runa's cheeks as she pondered her situation. It hurt her heart to consider that Chase may have married her simply because she resembled his first wife, but she couldn't deny that it made sense. She'd been told that he'd never gotten over his wife's disappearance. Maybe she was simply a look-alike replacement.

"There's something else I want to show you," Runa said as she slid the paper across the table.

Tawney picked up the paper and looked at the scrawled handwriting spelling out the strange phrase.

"What is this, Runa?"

"I don't know exactly," Runa hedged. "I found it somewhere."

"What do you want to know?"

"Do you know what language that is?"

"Yes I do. It's Norwegian."

"Norwegian? How do you know that?"

"I learned the language from my grandmother. That's part of what drew me and your mother together when we were kids, our shared Norwegian roots," Tawney explained.

"I had no idea we were Norwegian. Mom never talked about where our family came from."

"I don't think she knows much. Your grandmother was pretty tight-lipped. She rarely talked to your mother about anything. Asta knew she had Norwegian roots, though."

"You said you learned the language from your grandmother. Do you have any idea what those words mean?" Runa's heart pounded so loudly she was sure Tawney could hear it.

"Where did you get this, Runa?" Tawney held up the paper and frowned.

"I told you, I found it. Do you know what the words mean? Please, Tawney, I need to know," Runa begged.

"Yes, I know what it means. It says, 'You are in danger.'"

Runa's eyes widened. "You're sure that's what it says?"

"I'm positive. It's what I've been trying to tell you for months," Tawney explained.

"I know, Tawney. And I know you and Mom are worried. But please don't tell her any of this. I don't want to freak her out any more than she already is."

"I won't tell her, but you should," Tawney admonished.

Runa sighed. "Maybe you're right. Things aren't so great here right now." An idea popped into her head. "I think I'll take a trip to Portland. A bit of space might give me some perspective."

"Your mom would love to see you. You should surprise her," Tawney encouraged.

"I think I will. I'll leave today. Thank you so much for all you've done for me."

Runa rose from her chair and Tawney followed suit. Runa hugged her tightly, grateful that she'd become such a source of comfort.

"Go spend time with your mom. It'll do you both some good."

Tawney kissed Runa on the cheek. Runa walked her to the front door before returning to her room. Grabbing her suitcase from the closet, she packed enough clothes and toiletries to get her through a few days. She had no idea how long she'd be gone, but she wanted to be prepared.

She hated the way things were with Chase, but she needed

some space. She'd actually been afraid of him that morning. He'd been so angry. The way he screamed at her made her wonder what else he was capable of.

Not wanting another confrontation, she grabbed a sheet of paper and scribbled a note, telling him she was going to visit her mother and didn't know when she'd be back. Then she texted Emily and let her know the shop would remain closed for a few days.

When her bag was packed, she dragged it out into the hallway without a second glance at what she was leaving behind. As much as it pained her, she had to get away if she wanted to maintain even a shred of her sanity.

As she approached the staircase, she felt a sudden compulsion to visit the west wing. She knew she should ignore it but couldn't quiet the voice in her head searching for answers.

Leaving her suitcase at the top of the stairs, she crept down the hallway, around the corridors, and into the west wing. As she passed the doorway leading to Easton and Camille's room, she stopped abruptly. Her heart leaped inside her chest when she heard Camille's shrill voice from inside the room.

Apparently Chase hadn't bothered to tell her that his parents were back. Runa had believed she was alone. That meant Easton and Camille had been in the house for the entirety of Tawney's visit. Had they seen her break down on the front steps? Had they heard the things she'd said to Tawney? Did they hear Chase scream at her and storm out of the house?

She was about to turn and run from the west wing when the door to the Everwines' bedroom opened. Not wanting a confrontation with Camille, she sprinted down the hall and ducked inside the entryway to the third floor. The ancient door creaked on its hinges as it opened. She prayed Camille didn't hear.

Plastering herself against the shabbily papered wall, Runa tried to slow her breathing. She listened for sounds in the hallway, calming a bit when she heard Camille's voice begin to fade away, indicating her departure.

She waited a few minutes to make sure Camille didn't return, then decided it was time to grab her suitcase and get out of there. Knowing the Everwines were back made her want to leave Everwine Manor even more.

Just as she was about to turn the knob and open the door, she heard the creaking of floorboards above her head. The unmistakable sound of a door closing above the staircase reverberated in her ears, spurring her into action.

Runa scurried behind the stairwell in order to remain hidden. She crouched in the darkness, listening as heavy footsteps pressed on the groaning stairway above her head. She peeked from her hiding place, her eyes widening as Easton descended the stairs. He opened and shut the door quickly, leaving her behind as he returned to the hallway.

A million thoughts raced through her head. She remembered the sounds she'd heard before, the light she'd seen in the turret the previous night. Why did everyone keep saying no one went up to the third floor when that clearly wasn't the truth?

Ignoring the warning bells inside her mind, Runa decided she was going upstairs. Pausing at the bottom of the rickety staircase, she reminded herself that if the structure was strong enough to support Easton's weight, it could support hers. Before she second-guessed herself, she sprinted up the stairs.

Chase was correct when he said the third floor was immense. At the top of the stairway, one giant landing area led to five different hallways. Not sure where to begin, Runa stared down each one. It was dark, so much so that she could barely see her hand in front of her face. The shades were drawn over all of the windows in the landing area, so little outdoor light filtered through.

All at once she spotted a faint light peeking from beneath a door down one of the long hallways. As she walked toward it, Runa's heart pounded. Once she reached it, she tried to turn the doorknob but discovered it was locked. Rattling the knob, she tried to pry it open, to no avail. Placing her ear against the splintered wooden door, she waited quietly, listening intently. The hairs on the back of her arms stood on end as the sound of hushed voices floated through the door. Then she heard a child crying.

Spooked beyond reason, Runa ran from the third floor, down the rickety staircase, through the entryway, and out of the west wing. Grabbing her suitcase, she scurried down the stairs and out the front door. Sprinting to her car, she jumped inside, placed the key in the ignition, and sped out of the circular driveway and down the winding road leading away from the estate.

As she drove, she tried not to hyperventilate. She had no idea what was happening to her, but she had to get as far away from Everwine Manor as she could. Each moment she stayed caused her sanity to slip a bit further from her grasp.

Were the voices real? Had she actually heard a child crying on the third floor? What was Easton doing up there?

Maybe Everwine Manor was haunted.

Or maybe Chase was right and she was losing her mind.

THIRTY-FOUR

DEPARTURE COVE, OREGON, 1903

Mrs. Stevens arranged Brynja's flaxen hair into an expertly crafted French twist. Pulling her mistress to her feet, she slid a plain ivory dress over Brynja's slim body, grimacing as she noticed the bones jutting from her thin frame. A slip of a woman to begin with, months of not eating had taken a toll on Brynja. She was alarmingly thin, barely eating enough to stay alive.

"Are you sure this is what you want to do, ma'am? It's not too late to call it off," Mrs. Stevens probed.

"Of course I don't want to. I have to," Brynja answered woodenly. "There's no other choice."

"We always have a choice, ma'am."

"You're wrong. Women like me rarely have a choice," Brynja insisted.

Buttoning up the back of Brynja's wedding dress, Mrs.

Stevens frowned, marveling at the stark differences between this wedding and when Brynja married Thomas. There were no similarities to be found.

"You're sure, then? The minister is here and ready to proceed whenever you are."

Nodding numbly, Brynja followed Mrs. Stevens from her room, through the hall, and down the stairs toward the parlor. She caught a glimpse of her image in the large mirror in the hallway and barely recognized herself. Hollow eyes and sunken cheeks set in a ghostly pale face made her look like a stranger.

No one should be forced into the choice she'd had to make. She'd wrestled with the decision for weeks, finally realizing there had never been a choice at all. Lucas Everwine had guaranteed she would do exactly as he said or else. Their angry conversation the day before played over again in her mind.

"You understand, Brynja, that if you refuse me, you'll live to regret it," Lucas had said with a sneer.

"I already regret any dealings I've had with you, Lucas. You've tarnished my name, convinced the people of Departure Cove that I'm a danger to them, and threatened to fabricate proof of the fact that I had something to do with the sinking of Thomas's ship."

"Darling, how can you think I was a part of any of that? On the contrary, I've told everyone in town what an incredible woman you are."

"You're wrong, Lucas. I know the rumor mill has been fed by your lies," Brynja insisted. "What I don't understand is why you want to marry me so badly."

"I've wanted you since the first day I laid eyes on you. You should have married me from the start, not Thomas Calais."

"I can never love you, Lucas. Why would you want to marry a woman who isn't capable of love?"

"It'll come. You'll see."

"No it won't."

"It doesn't matter. You'll belong to me, and that will be enough." Lucas shrugged.

"I belong to no one," Brynja answered defiantly.

"Legally you will be mine. And so will this house." Lucas gestured around the room, his hungry eyes taking in the opulence of Angelica House. "I should have the grandest home around. And now I will."

"Or else?"

"Or else I'll produce proof of your dabbling in the dark arts."

"You have no idea who I am or what I do."

"Maybe not, but a woman who is a confirmed witch, or at least a woman who thinks she is, isn't mentally stable. Therefore, she can't properly care for a child, now can she?"

Brynja's body began to tremble. Lucas was threatening her daughter.

"You leave my child alone."

"I have no desire to hurt you or your daughter. In fact, I intend to take care of you both."

At the mention of Ingrid, Brynja's resolve crumbled. She would do anything to protect her daughter, including marrying Lucas Everwine.

"Very well. I'll marry you."

"See? I knew you'd come around. Let me love you, Brynja."

Lucas stepped forward and kissed her on the cheek, lingering far longer than she would have preferred. His touch made her blood run cold, but nothing mattered except Ingrid's safety.

Fighting back tears, Brynja shook the memories from her head as she entered the parlor. Like it or not, it was her wedding day. Soon she, Ingrid, and Angelica House would be in the hands of Lucas Everwine. She didn't even see it as making the right or wrong choice. The reality was she'd had no choice at all. If she wanted to keep her daughter, she would become Lucas's wife.

The minister stood in the parlor, Bible in hand, glaring at Brynja as she walked into the room. Lucas stood next to him, looking dashingly handsome and self-satisfied. His face burst into a large smile as his eyes met his bride's. Brynja's stomach lurched, and she pushed down the need to vomit.

Lucas was so sure she would grow to love him, but she knew the truth. She could never love a man who had no soul.

THIRTY-FIVE

Runa took a deep breath and knocked on Asta's door. She'd driven for two hours, never stopping once. The desire to flee Everwine Manor had been overwhelming. Now that she had some space and perspective, she started to think of Chase and all she'd left behind.

What would he think when he arrived home and she was gone? Would he care? Ever the optimist, she still held out hope that they could sort things out. She very much wanted her marriage to work.

On the third knock, Asta opened the door, surprise spreading across her lovely face.

"Runa, what are you doing here? Why didn't you tell me you were coming?"

"I wanted it to be a surprise."

Runa forced a smile. She didn't want Asta to know about her marital problems.

"Surprise is an understatement. Come inside, love."

Asta hugged her tightly and grabbed the suitcase from her hands, ushering her into the foyer.

"Thanks, Mom."

Runa tried to keep her voice light, hoping her all-too-astute mother wouldn't look too closely.

"Let's go have some tea. You must be tired from the drive."

Asta dropped Runa's suitcase at the bottom of the stairs and followed her daughter into the kitchen, where she put the kettle on the stove to boil. While they waited, Asta took the seat across from Runa.

"So tell me why you're really here, Runa. I know you too well. You're not just here to surprise me."

"What do you mean?" Runa feigned ignorance.

"I know something is going on with you. I've known it for some time," Asta stated matter-of-factly.

"How do you know?"

"A mother knows these things. I've also been having dreams, premonitions, visions."

"Mom—"

"Look, I know you don't believe in any of it, but that doesn't make it any less true."

Runa swallowed hard. "Tell me what you've seen, Mom."

Asta frowned, scrutinizing Runa's face for a couple of moments before speaking.

"What's changed? Something is different with you. You're not calling my visions a bunch of hocus-pocus anymore?"

"No I'm not."

"Runa, tell me what's happening," Asta begged.

"I will." She took a giant breath and blew it out quickly. "You're right. Something has changed, although I have no explanation for it. Will you tell me what you've seen first?"

"Very well. At first the dreams were sporadic, only happening at night when I fell asleep. Then they began happening all the time, even during the day," Asta explained.

"What do you see in them?"

"I see you. You're trapped in some sort of cage. I keep trying to find you, to help you, but I can't get there."

Runa's eyes filled with tears, and as hard as she tried to hold them back, it was no use. One by one they began to fall.

"You're right, Mom. I do feel trapped."

Reaching across the table, Asta clasped Runa's hands in her own, squeezing them tightly. "I've known all along, but I don't know how to help you."

"You can help me by telling me the truth. My marriage, your past, it all fits together somehow. I need to know everything about the Everwines, your history with them, and my father. That's how you can help me, Mom," Runa implored.

"Anything but that." Asta sighed heavily.

"But that's what I need."

Asta rose from the table, turned off the whistling tea kettle, and prepared two mugs of herbal tea. Placing one in front of Runa, she sat back down with her own. She drummed her fingertips on the tabletop for a few minutes, and Runa felt her hope slipping away. Just when she believed her mother would remain silent forever, she spoke.

"The first thing you should know is that your father and I loved each other very much. I've never loved another man in my life, and I never will."

Runa watched Asta's face take on a faraway look, as if she were seeing herself as the young, optimistic girl she'd once been. Even though Tawney had already told Runa the truth, she needed to hear the story from her mother's lips. It was well past time.

"Garrett Brewster was a force of nature. He had a smile that could light up a room, and he swept me off of my feet in an instant. We fell fast and hard, and it wasn't long before we had our whole lives mapped out. We were too young and naïve to understand that things never work out the way you plan," Asta began.

Runa held her breath, not moving a muscle for fear of breaking the spell that had come over her mother. She had waited her entire life to hear the story about her father.

"Garrett and Easton were best friends, inseparable really. Soon Garrett and I were spending all of our time together, and it didn't take long for Easton's jealous streak to show. At first I thought he was just bent out of shape because I was taking too much of Garrett's time. But then I figured out it was much deeper."

Asta swallowed hard and took a sip of her tea. Runa waited with bated breath.

"One night we were all at a party. Garrett went to get us a drink, and Easton came on to me. He told me that he'd been in love with me for years, that I was too good for Garrett, and that I should be with him."

"What did you do?"

Runa remembered how Easton had cornered her in the rose garden, calling her by her mother's name.

"I laughed it off at first, telling him he'd had too much to drink and didn't know what he was saying. I told Garrett about it, and he said the same thing. He couldn't bring himself to see the bad in his friend."

"And then what?"

"It wasn't long before I understood the depth of Easton's feelings. He became twisted, obsessed, focused only on winning my affection. He sent me expensive gifts, hinting at what my life would be like with him in it. He called me nearly every night, begging me to love him. By that point, I knew better than to tell Garrett."

"Why didn't you tell him? He might have understood. Maybe he could have helped you," Runa reasoned.

"No. Things were too far gone."

"Oh, Mom, you must have been so confused." Runa squeezed Asta's hand.

"I was terrified of Easton. He had a look in his eyes that I can't really explain, but it scared me."

"You don't have to explain. I've seen it," Runa confessed.

"Has Easton hurt you?"

"No, Mom," Runa lied. "Just tell your story."

"After graduation, I found out I was pregnant. Needless to say, I was shocked and afraid. I told Garrett. I was certain we were in it together, but I was wrong. His parents threatened to disinherit him if he married me, and he was young. I honestly don't blame him. I never did."

"But you were young, too, Mom. And you did the right thing," Runa insisted.

"It was different for me. Yes, I was scared, but the minute I knew about you, that was all I ever wanted. I had a terrible relationship with my mother. She and I didn't see eye to eye on anything, and I swore things would be different with my own daughter."

"You were right." Runa smiled.

Asta returned a small smile of her own. "I was. You're the best thing that ever happened to me."

"What about my father?"

"After Garrett broke things off, Easton came to see me. He vowed to marry me, take care of me and my child. He assured me we would never want for anything."

"Easton proposed to you?"

"Yes, and I'm ashamed to admit that for a split second, I considered it. I actually thought about marrying him. But I couldn't. When I refused, he flew into a rage, threatening to hurt Garrett. The crazy look in his eyes told me he was capable of anything. I decided the only choice was to leave Departure Cove. If I wasn't around, Easton would have no reason to hurt the man I loved."

"So you left to protect Garrett?"

"I did. But it didn't matter. He and Easton had started a business together, and a few days after I left, your father died in an accident that was later ruled a suicide."

"Do you believe Garrett killed himself?"

"No, Runa, I never believed that. And I honestly believe that Garrett would have come after me once he had time to process everything. I don't know what happened, but I've always known Easton had something to do with it."

"That's why you don't trust the Everwines?"

"Yes. They're dangerous. All of them."

"I'm having a hard time believing that about my husband. He's not his parents, Mom," Runa insisted.

"Are you telling me you've never seen anything in Chase to make you question him?" Asta raised one eyebrow at her daughter.

Runa didn't answer because she understood it wasn't necessary. Her mother already knew the truth.

"I have another question, Mom," she diverted.

"It seems to be the day for them. What is it?"

"What can you tell me about our family history?"

"Family history? That's an odd request."

"Not really. What do you know about where our family came from?"

"My mother, Celine, never spoke about her family. The only thing she ever said was that we had Norwegian heritage. Celine's mother and grandmother lived in England, but somehow Celine ended up in Departure Cove. She always said it was fate, that she was supposed to be there, which seemed like an odd statement from a woman who had nothing but disdain for the supernatural."

"What about magic in our family?" Runa swallowed hard as she forced herself to speak the words.

"Magic? My rational, logical daughter is asking about magic?" Asta chuckled. "I've waited a long time for this day."

"Tawney keeps telling me I have magic in my blood. What does she mean?"

"Celine was a staunch believer in all things rational. She was sort of like you in that respect. My mother believed anything mystical or magical was a fairy tale. I was always interested in the supernatural, and I saw my first aura when I was six. I had no idea what it meant, but before long, I was having dreams and visions frequently. I asked my mother about it, and she became angry, discouraging my curiosity."

"You must have been really confused."

"I was. It was around that age that Tawney and I met, and her family became a surrogate family to me. They were Norwegian as well, so they filled that need in me for a glimpse into my heritage."

"Tawney to the rescue, even back then." Runa laughed.

"Yes. That woman has been saving me for years," Asta agreed. "Why the sudden interest in magic? Have you experienced something?"

Runa took a deep breath and tried to decide what to say. She had no plans to tell her mother everything, but she needed to tell her something.

"I've been having dreams, too."

"What kind of dreams? Do they only happen at night?"

"No. I have them during the day, too. But I'm awake, so they're more like visions, I suppose."

"Yes, that's exactly what they are. What do you see?"

"It's always the same. I'm in a room, and I can't escape. There's a large mirror in the room, and I reach out to touch my reflection, but when I touch it, I realize it's not a reflection. It's me, but there are two of me."

Runa watched as her mother's face grew pale, every bit of color draining away. Asta cleared her throat and pushed her chair away from the table abruptly, the legs loudly scraping the hardwood floor.

"Mom, are you okay?"

"Yes. I'll be right back."

Without another word, Asta left the room.

Runa puzzled over her mother's strange reaction. Something was wrong, but she had no idea what.

Several minutes passed before Asta returned. When she did, she had a box in her hands.

"I have something for you."

Asta placed the box on the table. "Don't open it right now. I've been saving it."

"What is it?"

"It belonged to your grandmother. I found it in her attic after she died. I never understood why she kept it, but I'm glad she did. I hope it gives you the answers you need."

With trembling hands, Runa carried the box upstairs to her old room. It was inordinately heavy and felt warm to the touch. Her stomach clenched as she placed it on the bed and stepped away. She covered her ears to block out the sudden deafening roar that filled the room. Although they were miles away from the coast, she heard the undeniable sound of the ocean.

THIRTY-SIX

That night, long after Asta had fallen asleep, Runa lay in bed, a thousand conflicting thoughts playing like a movie reel in her brain. She couldn't sleep. Worry, fear, and uncertainty warred inside. Everything that had happened added up to one simple conclusion—she was losing her mind.

Her inexplicable experiences at Everwine Manor, as well as the strange things happening to her body, had no reasonable explanation. She was worried for both her safety and her sanity. Worse yet, her marriage was crumbling, possibly past the point of reconciliation. She missed Chase so badly it felt like her heart was breaking in two.

To Chase, maybe she was just a look-alike replacement of his first wife, but she loved him. She wanted things to work between them. Closing her eyes, she pictured his face on their wedding day. She tried to remember the way he'd looked at her, needing to believe he'd seen her, not the ghost of Freya.

The buzzing of her cell phone startled her. Grabbing it quickly, she was shocked to see Chase was calling. She hadn't heard from him all day, and she'd assumed he wanted nothing more to do with her.

"Hello, Chase," she said quietly.

"I'm sorry, Runa. I'm so sorry for everything."

At the sound of his voice, her pulse quickened and her eyes filled with tears.

"You're sorry?"

"Of course I am. Darling, I've been a fool. My behavior is unforgivable. I've been swamped at work, and I've been taking that stress out on you. You don't deserve that."

"I know your job is stressful, Chase. I understand. But we need to be able to talk to each other. I feel like I can't share my worries or concerns for fear of you becoming angry."

"I know. I've been a terrible husband. When I came home tonight and realized you were gone, I knew I had to do whatever I could to get you back."

"Chase—"

"Will you come home? Come back to me," he begged.

"Chase—"

"We'll go away together. We'll take that honeymoon. That's what we should have done to begin with. We need time together, to get to know each other. I'm sorry I didn't give that to you."

A thousand thoughts collided in Runa's brain. Chase did love her. He loved her for herself, not because she looked like Freya. And yet there were so many unanswered questions. She wanted him to explain away all the things she'd seen at Everwine Manor, but she was afraid to broach the topic.

But then she thought back on the occurrences and began to doubt herself. Every single instance was so farfetched, so over the top, that they couldn't have really happened. Was it possible she had imagined it all? Maybe it was all in her head. Maybe none of it was real. Chase had insisted that she should see a therapist to work through her stress. Was he right?

The only thing she knew for sure was that her husband, the man she loved with all her heart, was on the other end of the phone telling her he felt the same way. He was begging her to come back to him, back to the life they both wanted. In that moment, she couldn't throw away her marriage because of a few events that didn't make sense.

"Of course I'll come home. I'll leave first thing in the morning."

"Oh, darling, you have no idea how happy that makes me. I love you so much," he said, a catch in his voice. "I was afraid I'd lost you forever."

"I love you, too, Chase. I'll see you tomorrow."

Runa hung up the phone and dropped it on the bedside table. Chase had given her exactly what she wanted, and she wasn't going to throw that away. The rest of it didn't matter.

Too restless to sleep, she sat up in bed. Her eyes landed on the box in the corner. She'd been so caught up in Chase that she'd forgotten to open it.

She flipped on the light, grabbed the box, and sank onto the bed. Lifting the wooden lid, she gasped. Tucked inside was a small leather-bound book with an Ansuz rune symbol carved on the cover. Glancing at the ring on her finger, the one her mother had given her so long ago, she realized they were identical. Tentatively tracing her hands across the book, Runa felt a strange energy pulsing against her skin.

With trembling hands, she removed the book from the box. Flipping through it, she noticed different handwriting throughout the pages. She opened it to the front of the book, wanting to read it from the beginning. She blinked a few times, trying to decipher the words. They were written in a strange language, one she didn't understand.

As Runa concentrated on the words, she wanted very much to understand them. She thought about how badly she wanted to read the book. She touched the pages, and as she did, the blue light flickered from her fingertips, brighter and more vibrant than it had ever been. Her body vibrated with energy. As she looked at the book, the words suddenly morphed into English, and she could read them.

The book was called *Døtre av havet—Daughters of the Sea*. The first page was a sort of introduction, explaining it was a *svarteboken*, or grimoire. It also served as a family history. She flipped through the pages, reading through spells, incantations, and recipes for creating simples, or medicinal herb potions.

Then she came to the family history section, and her breath caught in her throat. The book explained that the women of this particular line had been endowed with special gifts, placed within them to help others. It warned that people wouldn't understand, therefore fearing their gifts, some doing unspeakable things to silence them.

Reading on, Runa learned about women who had visions, some who were healers, and others who could control elements. Each of them, all the way down the line, carried a connection to water. According to the book, the most special was the "generation of two," who would possess all of the gifts simultaneously yet must sacrifice something in return for such power. Runa had no idea what any of it meant, but she was intrigued.

She saw a list of women's names and began to read them aloud. As she did, the room hummed with energy.

Else, 1585
Bekka and Helga, 1600
Sofie, 1625
Nora, 1645
Ella, 1663
Maja, 1683
Thea, 1704
Leah, 1727
Amalie, 1748

Frida, 1767

Astrid, 1783

Tuva, 1803

Selma, 1825

Malin, 1843

Mille, 1861

Sigrid and Brynja, 1883

Ingrid, 1900

Mathilde, 1917

Ada, 1935

Celine, 1953

Asta, 1973

AS SHE SPOTTED her mother's name, as well as her grand-mother's, something inside her began to shift into place and understanding dawned. These weren't just random women. They were the women of her family line. They were women, like her, who had powers they couldn't explain, a special gift. They were connected to the water, had visions, and could control elements.

Runa thought back to her own strange experiences and pondered the manifestation of her gift. What did it all mean? She also wondered why her name wasn't written in the book. It seemed strange that Asta, who had such a proclivity for the supernatural, wouldn't write her daughter's name in a magical grimoire.

Maybe it was because of the circumstances surrounding Runa's birth. After all, Asta had been a single mother at eighteen. She was trying to survive. She probably hadn't had time to worry about recording her daughter's name in a book, too focused on keeping them alive.

Runa closed the book and placed it back inside the box, suddenly exhausted. Moving the box to the pillow beside her head, she drifted off to sleep.

THIRTY-SEVEN

DEPARTURE COVE, OREGON, 1904

"I t's a boy! Oh, my darling, you've given me a son. We'll call him Hawthorne, after my grandfather."

"Whatever you want, Lucas," Brynja mumbled.

"Hawthorne Everwine—that has a nice ring to it."

Lucas leaned down and kissed Brynja on the forehead.

Recoiling at his touch, she turned her head, murmuring, "I'm tired, Lucas. I need to sleep."

"Of course you do. You've just given birth. I'll take our son to the nurse."

Refusing to meet his eyes, Brynja kept her head turned until Lucas left the room, their son in his arms. Once she was alone, she gave way to the sobs she'd been holding in, finally allowing the floodgates to open.

Guilt and despair gnawed her insides, each emotion vying for top position. Brynja was miserable. Her powers had all but *left her. Although she secretly performed her rituals, it had been almost a year since she'd felt even the smallest flicker of magic.*

She was married to a tyrant who cared about no one but himself. He took what he wanted from her, precisely the reason she'd just given birth. She'd certainly never given him her body willingly.

All Lucas cared about was an heir to carry on his name, to propagate his legacy. He'd needed an Everwine son to expand his wealth. Ingrid was female and not an Everwine by blood. Now that Lucas had a son, Ingrid would never inherit the home that was rightfully hers. Lucas had stolen it, even going so far as changing the name that Thomas had so lovingly chosen. It would forevermore be known as Everwine Manor, yet another thing to claim as his own.

Now that Brynja had given him what he craved, her only hope was that he would leave her alone. He had his son and her job was done. With that thought, the guilt deepened. She'd just given birth to a child, her own flesh and blood, yet she couldn't bring herself to feel even an ounce of emotion for the infant. She hadn't even held him. What kind of person did that make her? Lucas had destroyed everything good inside her.

The only reason she kept putting one foot in front of the other every day was Ingrid. She lived for the girl, and that kept her going. Ingrid was the one bright spot in her bleak, desolate world. If it weren't for her daughter, Brynja would have no reason to live.

Lucas insisted that Ingrid would have everything she needed and wanted, and for that, Brynja was grateful. Strangely, he was kind and generous to the girl. In fact, he'd legally adopted her, making him her father in the eyes of the law.

Though in Brynja's heart Ingrid would always belong to Thomas, for better or for worse they were all Everwines now.

THIRTY-EIGHT

Locking the front door of the boutique, Runa waved goodbye to Emily and jumped into her car. She headed out of town and merged onto the winding road leading toward Everwine Manor. She'd been back home for a week, and things between her and Chase were better than they'd ever been. They hadn't argued once and were even making plans to finally take their belated honeymoon.

In spite of the fact that everything was better, she still worried, always feeling as if she were walking on eggshells around Chase. She reminded herself that it was to be expected. The couple had been through a lot in a short amount of time, and they were both still learning how to live with each other.

In order to keep the peace, Runa hadn't brought up her experiences or concerns about Everwine Manor. She also hadn't told Chase about the book her mother gave her. She had a feeling he wouldn't understand, and their truce was still too new for her to rock the boat.

She understood that marriage was compromise. When doubts and questions began to creep in, she pushed them away, telling herself that nothing good came without work. Chase wasn't perfect, but no one was. In spite of it all, she loved him and was happy she'd made the choice to return to Departure Cove.

Pulling into the driveway, she turned off her car and headed inside. Hoping not to see anyone, she went directly upstairs to her bedroom suite as usual. Although she wanted to be married to Chase, she had nothing but disdain for his parents and did her best to avoid them.

Tossing her bag on the bed, Runa slipped out of her high heels and tucked them away in her closet. She was just unzipping her dress when her phone rang. She smiled when she saw it was Chase.

"Hello, darling," he said as she picked up.

"Hey there," she replied. "It sounds like you're driving."

"I am. I'll be home in ten minutes. Are you ready to go?"

"Go? Where?"

"The fundraiser," he answered.

"Fundraiser? Did I miss something?"

Runa grabbed her calendar from her purse and flipped through it quickly. Glancing at the date, she saw nothing written.

"We talked about it a few weeks ago. It's the fundraiser for the hospital," Chase explained.

Racking her brain for any recollection of the conversation, Runa came up empty.

"I'm sorry, Chase, but I don't remember that at all."

"No worries, darling. Just put on your fanciest dress. I'll be there soon. We'll ride with Mother and Father. Everyone expects us to arrive together."

Pushing down the bile that rose in her throat at the mention of Easton and Camille, Runa thought quickly. She could come up with a million things she'd rather do than attend a stuffy fundraiser with Chase's parents. She could barely bring herself to look at them, let alone ride in a car with them and pretend to like them at a social event.

"Chase, I don't think I can go tonight. I came home sick from work. I think I'm coming down with a stomach bug or something," she lied.

"Really, darling? Are you sure you can't pull it together for just a little while? This will be our first public event together since our wedding."

"I'm sorry, Chase, but I feel terrible. I certainly wouldn't be at my best. I need to stay home and sleep."

"Then I'll have my parents give our regrets. I'll stay home and take care of you," Chase replied.

Runa imagined how angry Easton and Camille would be if she didn't go. They would be downright furious if Chase stayed home as well.

"No, Chase, you need to go with your parents. Everyone is expecting you. Besides, I'll be horrible company. I plan to take a shower and sleep the night away," she fibbed.

"Are you sure? I don't want to go without you."

"I'm very sure. In fact, I'm getting into the shower now and then going to bed for the night. Really, you should just go with your parents."

"If you insist," Chase agreed.

"I do," Runa declared.

He sighed. "Then I'll be home soon. I'll change and go with them. But I'll miss you."

"I'll miss you too. I really am sorry."

"Not a problem, darling. I'll cover for you," he said amicably. "I love you."

"Love you, too, Chase."

Runa hung up the phone and glanced outside. Tree branches scraped the windows, and the wind howled like a hungry wolf. It was a blustery, stormy night, and she was glad she didn't have to get dressed up and attend a fundraiser. It was too bad she'd had to lie to her husband in order to get out of it.

Heading into the bathroom, she turned on the shower as hot as it would go and stepped inside. She didn't feel great about being dishonest with Chase, but ever since she'd learned the truth about Easton, she couldn't bring herself to be in the same room with him.

Asta and Tawney were both convinced he had something

to do with her father's death, and Runa also leaned in that direction. Easton and Camille had hurt her mother, and they'd hurt her. She didn't blame Chase for his parents' actions, but she also didn't want to be around them any more than was absolutely necessary. She felt mostly validated for her fabrication of the truth.

She was still in the shower when Chase popped his head into the bathroom.

"Are you okay, Runa?"

"Yes," she replied. "The hot shower helps."

"I'll try not to be too late. Get some sleep and feel better."

"Thank you. See you in a while."

Runa waited several minutes before getting out of the shower, wanting to make sure Chase was gone. It wasn't that she wanted to hide, but convincing him she was sick was easier over the phone than in person.

She wrapped a towel around her hair and dried herself with another one, then slipped into her robe and padded from the bathroom to her bedroom. Plopping onto her bed, she unwound the towel and began to finger-comb her hair. Glancing outside, she noticed the wind was picking up. A nasty storm was blowing in.

Runa knew Chase and his parents would be gone for hours, and she was happy to have the house to herself, even if she'd had to lie. Although the plan hadn't been premeditated, she knew exactly how she was going to spend her evening. She'd been thinking of the portrait in the west wing ever since it had come to life. She wanted to go back, and now she had the perfect opportunity.

Pulling on her most comfortable beat-up jeans and over-sized sweatshirt, Runa slid her feet into her tennis shoes and slipped out of her bedroom. She was familiar with the route to the west wing, and her feet seemed to carry her there involuntarily.

Sneaking into the sitting room, she turned on the lights. Walking directly to the easel, she lifted the cover and looked at the painting.

It never ceased to amaze her how much the woman in the portrait looked like her. The resemblance was eerie and unsettling. Runa wanted to know everything she could about the mysterious woman.

"Who are you?" she whispered to the portrait woman.

Thunder cracked and a bolt of lightning flashed into the room. Jumping, Runa caught her breath, her eyes widening as the portrait woman's eyes began to blink. A second later, the woman's mouth began to move as the same strange words fell from her red lips.

"*Du er i fare*," the portrait woman said.

"I know you're saying I'm in danger," Runa told the painting.

"*Finn henne*," she replied.

"I want to understand what you're saying."

"*Finn henne*," the woman said again. "*Finn henne*."

Closing her eyes, Runa allowed the words to fall into the

room. The portrait woman continued repeating them over and over, and finally Runa joined in, reciting the strange words she didn't understand. The more she repeated them, however, the more they began to make sense to her ears. Soon, she understood exactly what the phrase meant.

"*Finn henne.* Find her."

THIRTY-NINE

Runa continued repeating the phrase. Her voice mixed with the portrait woman's voice, blending, tone over tone, until they became one.

"*Finn henne…* find her… *finn henne…* find her."

Another bolt of lightning shot into the room and Runa jumped, opening her eyes. When she glanced at the portrait, the woman had grown still and was nothing but a painting once again. Her heart beating loudly, Runa puzzled over what had taken place.

"Find her," the woman had implored.

Runa didn't know who she was supposed to find. She had no clue what any of it meant.

Overwhelmed by the intense need to do something, though she wasn't sure what, she left the sitting room. Glancing toward the end of the hallway, she spotted the entryway to the third floor. Remembering the sound of voices and the child crying, she knew she had to go back, if only to prove to herself that none of it had been real.

Slowly opening the door leading to the third floor, Runa took a deep breath. The darkness pressed in on her like a living, breathing thing. Before she could talk herself out of it, she ascended the creaking stairs. Her breath came in short spurts, her lungs tight, yet she forced herself to press on. Reaching the top, she turned on her phone's flashlight and shined it into the void of blackness, nervously glancing down each ominous hallway.

She allowed her eyes to linger for a moment, peering down the middle hallway. Once again, she spotted a faint glow of light coming from beneath one of the doors. Knowing she had to look but wanting more than anything to run away, she remembered the portrait woman's words: *"Find her."*

Creeping down the hallway, Runa pressed her ear to the splintered wooden door as she'd done before. Standing still and quiet, she listened. The unmistakable sound of conversation from behind the door floated into her ear.

It wasn't her imagination. Someone was up there.

Turning the knob, she discovered it was locked. Rattling it, she slammed her body against the door, pressing into it in the hopes of breaking through.

Nothing happened.

"Find her! Find her!"

The words pounded inside her brain like a hammer driving

a nail, over and over until it was all she could hear. Desperately, she began knocking on the door.

Runa didn't hold out hope that anyone would answer, but she continued to pound on the door, unable to stop herself. She stood there, crying and beating on the splintered door, the words "Find her" falling unbidden from her lips.

She knocked like a madwoman, sobbing as she begged someone to open the door. She had no idea how long she'd been there. It may have been thirty seconds, or it may have been an hour.

When the knob finally turned and the door opened, she was unprepared for the sight that met her eyes.

Standing on the other side of the door was a woman, nearly identical to Runa in every way.

Time seemed to stand still. Tunnel vision kicked in until the woman's identical eyes were all Runa could see.

The two women looked at each other, and Runa tried to make herself understand what was happening. Unable to explain it away, her fragile mind began to shut down. Suddenly everything went dark and she hit the floor.

FORTY

DEPARTURE COVE, OREGON, 1908

"*I*ngrid, sweetheart, where are you?" Brynja called into her daughter's bedroom. "I'm home."

She wrinkled her forehead as she looked around her daughter's empty room. Ingrid wasn't there, but something else was missing.

Stepping inside, she immediately sensed that Ingrid's presence, her essence, was gone. The room felt abandoned, and her stomach clenched with trepidation.

Running down the hall, she began screaming for Mrs. Stevens. She found the servant in the kitchen, bent over the counter, her head in her hands, sobbing.

"Mrs. Stevens, what is it? Where is Ingrid?" Panic rose in Brynja's chest.

"Gone, ma'am," the woman choked out between sobs.

"What do you mean, gone? I've only been in town for

three hours. She was here when I left."

"Mr. Everwine took her. He said... he said—"

"He said what?" Brynja grabbed the woman's shoulders and shook her.

Wiping her face with her sleeve, Mrs. Stevens tried to catch her breath. "Mr. Everwine said it was time for her to learn how to be a lady."

"A lady?" Brynja roared. "Do you mean that boarding school he's been talking about?"

"Yes, ma'am. He packed her things, and they left as soon as you were gone. He said he knew what was best and you couldn't see what Miss Ingrid needed. He said the school in England would teach her all she needed to know. He took her to the docks to meet the ship," Mrs. Stevens sobbed.

"He can't do that. He can't do it without my permission," Brynja said desperately as she sank into the kitchen chair.

"He said he's her father and he can do what he wishes, ma'am. I tried to stop him, but it was no use. I think he's been planning it for months and was waiting for the right opportunity to get you away from the house."

Jumping from the table, Brynja screamed, "I have to go to her! I have to find my daughter!"

"Ingrid is just fine, so calm down, darling," Lucas's voice boomed into the kitchen. "She's with her new governess."

Spinning abruptly, Brynja ran at him, throwing her small body against his towering muscular frame and pounding his chest with her fists. She had grown so thin and frail that it was *the equivalent of a fly beating itself against an elephant. It had little effect on Lucas, besides being a nuisance.*

"You're making a spectacle of yourself. But if it makes you feel better, please continue." He chuckled.

Dropping to the floor, her body racked with sobs, Brynja tried to catch her breath. Mrs. Stevens finally pulled herself together and ran to her mistress.

"Come now, ma'am. Let me take you to your room."

"Leave us, Mrs. Stevens," Lucas commanded.

"But, sir, Mrs. Everwine is distraught. She doesn't know what she's doing. Let me take her to her room," Mrs. Stevens pleaded.

"I said leave us," Lucas repeated, leaving no room for arguments.

Nodding curtly, Mrs. Stevens scurried from the room, throwing one last withering glance over her shoulder toward Brynja.

"How could you do this to me? To Ingrid?" Brynja sobbed.

"I've done nothing to you. I've done it for *you. More importantly, I've done it for her. The child needs a proper education. She needs to learn her place in society. You are entirely too attached to her. It isn't healthy," Lucas replied without emotion.*

"My baby," she cried.

"I'm her father, and I know what's best for her," he demanded.

Something bubbled up within Brynja. It had been ages since she'd felt even an ounce of her former power, but in that moment, it surged.

Slowly, she rose to her feet and raised her face to look at Lucas. Her eyes bored into his, not flinching, not looking away for even a second.

"You are not her father. Her father is and always will be Thomas Calais. You can change her name, you can call me your wife, you can take over this house, and you can believe you possess us, but we will never belong to you."

Brynja's body began to tremble, a vibration of energy causing her to shake from head to toe. She smiled as the familiar rush of power slammed into her middle, gut-punching her like a bolt of lightning. She closed her eyes and let it flood over her, remembering for the first time in years who she was and where she came from.

She remembered her mother, instructing her on the power of her gifts. She remembered her beloved twin, Sigrid, and how they had been the "generation of two," paying the ulti-mate sacrifice of losing each other. She remembered how it felt when she stood in the wind, speaking to it and calming it on her voyage with Captain Ingebjorg to the new world. She remembered the clear visions she'd had that led her to Thomas and their life together.

As she remembered, she felt her power build. It grew, rising within like the swell of the ocean. Wiggling her fingers,

Brynja felt the familiar blue light, crackling with energy as its otherworldly glow filled the kitchen.

Lucas watched his wife, concern spreading across his face as he took one step backward. He'd been married to her for years but was finally seeing her clearly for the very first time.

"Wh-What are you doing?" he stammered.

"Are you afraid of me, Lucas?" Brynja taunted as she continued walking toward him.

"Of course I'm not afraid," he insisted, backing away.

"I can feel your fear. I can taste it," she challenged.

"You've lost your mind."

"On the contrary. I've found it."

"Brynja, darling, calm down," Lucas soothed.

Raising her hands into the air, Brynja closed her eyes and summoned every ounce of power she possessed.

She began to chant, "Som du vil... as You will... som du vil... as You will."

Blue light crackled from her fingertips, arcing like lightning bolts toward the ceiling as Lucas's eyes widened with fear. She continued toward him, advancing as he retreated.

"Lucas Everwine, I curse you. I curse your family. You've stolen what rightfully belonged to me. You've taken my daughter, and you've taken my home. I curse you."

With those words, Brynja flung her hands toward Lucas, bolts of blue light shooting across the room. A clap of thunder boomed as the light made contact. Screaming in pain, he clamped his hands over his face as the flash hit his cheek, leaving a large open gash in its wake.

For a moment, neither moved or spoke. Brynja's body still vibrated with energy. Lucas, obviously stunned by the fact that she'd sliced his face open without ever touching him, was momentarily silent. When he regained his wits, he ran toward Brynja, grabbing her by the arm.

She felt her power begin to drain, her body growing limp as her energy left. She'd used up everything she had. There was nothing more.

Collapsing to the floor in a heap, she surrendered, knowing her job was done. She'd wounded Lucas, and his face would forever bear the scar she'd given him. It would serve as a reminder to everyone who came in contact with him.

In a fit of rage, Lucas scooped up Brynja's body and carried her up the stairs, down the corridor, into the west wing, and all the way to the third floor. Heading down the center hallway, he opened a door and climbed the large staircase leading to the suite of rooms connected to the turret.

Tossing her roughly onto the bed, he wiped his bloody cheek on his sleeve. She could feel the anger rolling off him in waves, but so did fear. She knew Lucas had never before seen such a raw display of power. She also knew that if he didn't contain her, she would kill him.

"You've done this to yourself, darling. I'm afraid I can't let you out of this room. You've proven to me that you can't be trusted. This is for the best."

With one curt nod, Lucas turned and walked back down the stairs, away from the turret, and away from Brynja.

When she heard the distinct sound of a key in the lock, she understood her fate had been sealed.

Rising from the bed, she climbed the stairs leading into the turret. She squinted as the sun cut through the kaleidoscope of designs in the stained glass windows. She was empty, spent, broken. Lucas had taken everything she loved, leaving her with nothing. She'd been his prisoner in many ways since their wedding day, and now he had actually locked her away.

Without Ingrid, Brynja had no reason to go on. Resolve kicked in and she knew what she must do. As she'd told Mrs. Stevens the day she married Lucas, women like her very rarely had a choice. With trembling hands, she reached for the metal vase on the table beside her. Dumping the water and flowers onto the floor below, she raised the vase above her head and slammed it against the window.

The sound of shattering glass pierced the quiet of the room, and rainbow shards fell to the floor. Brynja attempted to steady her shaking knees before stepping on the bench below the row of windows.

Placing her feet on the windowsill, she closed her eyes. Smiling, she saw Thomas reaching his hands out toward her.

Her body grew weightless, and Brynja leaned forward, falling into Thomas's waiting arms as the sound of the sea crashed in her ears.

FORTY-ONE

Runa opened her eyes, blinking quickly. She glanced around; nothing at all was familiar. She sat up, finding herself in a beautifully decorated suite of rooms. Running her hands across the velvet duvet cover, she tried to remember how she'd gotten there. Her thoughts raced as she tried to piece the puzzle together, but then it all came crashing down on her at once.

For a split second, she believed she must be dreaming. Rubbing her eyes, she willed her brain to catch up. Sitting across the room, in a large armchair facing the bed, was the woman from the portrait. Logic begged Runa to accept that what she saw was impossible. And yet, the woman was there.

"You're awake," the woman said.

"Where am I?" Runa asked.

"You don't remember?"

"I do, but… no, I don't. I mean… I think so… but that can't be right."

"Some things are hard to believe."

Rolling her body off the edge of the bed, Runa tried to stand on legs that felt like Jell-O, her knees knocking together as she walked slowly across the room toward the woman. As she approached the chair, the woman stood. Face-to-face, they regarded each other.

The similarities were startling, so much so that Runa actually reached out and touched the woman's cheek simply to convince herself she was real. As she looked closer, she saw that the woman's face, although beautiful, had a grayish pallor, and her hair, the same flaxen shade as Runa's, was dull and lackluster. It clearly hadn't been trimmed in quite some time, and rough split ends were obvious upon closer examination.

"Who are you?" Runa asked.

"I can't say," the woman replied, looking away.

"Of course you can. Tell me who you are," Runa demanded.

"No," she insisted.

Confusion and fear turned to anger. Runa needed to know who the woman was, yet she refused to explain.

"Listen to me! You're going to tell me who you are and what you're doing up here. If you don't, I'm going to tell my husband."

"Your husband." The woman smiled mirthlessly.

"Yes, Chase Everwine, my husband."

"You're so naïve," the woman said with a toss of her dull hair.

"What's that supposed to mean?" Runa stiffened.

"It means there's a lot you don't know."

"Like what?"

"Like the fact that he was my husband first."

The woman dropped the bomb without even the slightest flicker of emotion.

"Your husband?" Runa's breath came in short, fast spurts as the pieces came together. "Freya? You're alive?"

The room began to spin, and Runa reached out and grabbed Freya's arms to steady herself. About that time, a second voice, small and quiet, echoed in the room. Runa swiveled her head to the side as a little girl with blonde ringlets tugged on Freya's shirt.

"Mama, who is that?"

Runa looked back and forth between Freya and the child. The girl looked just like her, so she knew in an instant she was Freya's daughter.

"You're alive and you have a child?"

Freya sighed heavily, nodding her assent. "Yes, this is Alina, my daughter."

"I... I don't understand," Runa stammered as she backed away from them, her knees buckling as she collapsed on the bed. "You're Freya? Chase's wife? And your child... Chase's child...?"

"You've really put me in a bad place here, Runa." Freya scowled. "You're not supposed to know about any of this."

"How do you know my name?"

"I know everything about you," Freya answered cryptically.

"This is a bad dream. I'm going to wake up any minute. None of this is real. You're not real," Runa muttered to herself as she placed her hands over her eyes, rocking back and forth on the bed.

"Alina, go up into the turret room and read your book. I need to talk to the woman," Freya said quietly.

"She looks like you, Mama. I want to talk to her, too," Alina argued.

"I know. Just let me talk to her first," Freya insisted.

With a nod, Alina ran up the stairs into the circular room.

Freya sat on the bed next to Runa. "I'm sure this is all quite confusing to you," she began, her voice softening a little.

"That may be the understatement of the year."

"Look, it would be best for everyone concerned if you just went back to your life."

"Back to my life? My life is a sham!" Runa yelled.

"There's too much to explain, too much you can never know. Forget what you've seen and leave now, before it's too late. Once you know, you can never go back."

"You want me to forget there's a woman who looks exactly like me and a little girl living on the third floor of my home?"

"Yes. That's what I want. Please?"

"Well, that's not going to happen. And I'm not leaving here until I get an explanation," Runa demanded, crossing her arms defiantly.

"Fine. I'll tell you everything, but you're not going to like it."

"Talk. Now," Runa said through gritted teeth.

Freya took a deep breath and began her tale.

"I'm Freya, Chase's wife. Everyone thinks I disappeared seven years ago, but I've been up here the whole time."

"You expect me to believe you've been on the third floor for seven years?"

"Yes."

"That's not possible," Runa insisted.

"I assure you, it is," Freya disagreed.

"You let people believe you were dead? Why would you do that?"

"It was the best solution."

"For what? What could have possibly happened that the best solution was remaining a prisoner for seven years?"

"I'm not a prisoner. And I said you wouldn't understand." Freya shrugged.

Runa glanced up into the turret toward Alina. As she watched the little girl coloring and humming to herself, a light bulb went off in her brain.

"Freya, how old is your daughter?"

"Alina is seven."

"Seven? But how?"

"She was born here in this room. She's never been out of it."

Runa's blood ran cold as she considered what that meant. The little girl had never seen the light of day. Her whole life had been lived on the third floor of Everwine Manor.

"Freya, is Chase her father?"

"No, he's not."

"I don't understand."

"I don't even know if *I* understand anymore. It all made sense to me once upon a time, but now…," Freya said sadly.

"Please tell me."

"Chase and I were married for five years. From the start, he loved me more than I loved him. A lot of people said I loved the Everwine name more than anything, and maybe they were right. I was dazzled by his wealth and prestige."

"It's hard not to be. I know I was," Runa commiserated.

"I came from a good family. We were wealthy, and I led a bit of a charmed life. But then I found out that my parents weren't who I thought they were. It destroyed me. From that moment on, I was searching for something, some hole inside I needed filled. Then I met Chase. He wanted me, and I liked being wanted. I was hungry for the power that came with being an Everwine."

"So you never loved him?"

"No, I didn't. Not really."

"Did he know?"

"At first, I was good at hiding it. I let him dote on me. I enjoyed the gifts he gave me. I loved the fact that he would do anything I wanted him to do. I liked how people watched us as we walked into the room together. I loved the attention from the press. Being married to Chase was like a drug to me."

"But something happened to change that?"

"Yes. I fell in love."

"With someone else."

"Yes. With his father." Freya shrugged.

The walls began to close in as Runa processed Freya's words. "You fell in love with Easton?"

"Not long after Chase and I were married, Easton began to pursue me. Instead of being put off by it, I realized I liked it. Before long, we were meeting secretly, going off for weekends together. It was exciting and dangerous and forbidden. I fell hard for him."

"But how did that lead to you being here?"

"I wanted to divorce Chase and marry Easton. He wanted that, too. But money makes things complicated. Then I found out I was pregnant, which only compounded the problem. Easton and I knew our time was running out to come up with a plan. Chase and I hadn't slept together in months, so there was no way I could pretend the child was his."

"What happened?"

"Easton and I met to discuss our plan, but we didn't know that Chase had already found out about us. He followed us. When he confronted us about the affair, he threatened to tell everyone. Easton was worried about the Everwines' reputation, and he didn't want to see such a sordid scandal leaked to the press."

"I still don't understand why you're a prisoner on the third floor," Runa inserted.

"Easton and I wanted to be together more than anything, so we set about to make that happen. We knew it was only a matter of time before my pregnancy came to light, so we had to act quickly. Easton said he needed time to get his affairs in order to ask Camille for a divorce. He said it would only be for a little while."

Freya's voice shook, and tears filled her eyes.

"What are you talking about, Freya?" Runa still didn't completely understand.

"I agreed to the plan. I agreed to come up here. I agreed to disappear so that eventually everyone would believe I was dead. It was the only way we could be together."

"Freya, you've been a prisoner up here for seven years!"

"I'm not a prisoner. I agreed to it. I came here willingly," Freya defended.

"But haven't you figured out that Easton lied to you?"

"No he didn't!"

"He's going to leave you here forever. He's tucked his dirty little secret away in the attic. He never intended to divorce Camille."

"That's not true. Easton loves me, and I love him. We're going to be together," Freya insisted.

"He has you brainwashed. He never intended to set you free. You're his hostage."

"He's the father of my child. He takes care of us. I agreed to this plan."

"Freya, listen to me. Let me help you. Think of Alina. This is no life for a child."

"I agreed to the plan," Freya repeated numbly.

"That doesn't matter now. Just because you agreed to the plan seven years ago doesn't mean you have to agree now. I'll help you. I'll get Chase to help you," Runa pleaded.

"Chase?" Freya laughed ruefully. "You think he's going to help me? He was in on this from the beginning."

"I don't believe you. Chase had nothing to do with this. He thinks you're dead. He mourned you for years," Runa insisted.

"He knows everything. He's known for seven years that I'm here, raising his father's child on the third floor. Why do you think no one comes up here?"

Runa shook her head, trying to keep Freya's words from taking root in her brain.

It couldn't be true. Chase couldn't be in on a plan to keep his wife a prisoner. It had to be a lie, because if it was true, Runa's worst fears were confirmed.

Chase had simply married her to replace Freya, which meant he never really loved her at all.

FORTY-TWO

"I'm sorry, Runa. I know it's easier to believe I'm making it all up, but it's true. Chase is nothing but a narcissist. He couldn't accept the fact that I didn't love him. It was easier for him to pretend I was dead," Freya explained.

"Mama, can I talk to the lady who looks like you now?" Alina asked as she descended the stairs from the turret.

The little girl, with her gray pallor and dull hair, put everything into dizzying perspective for Runa. Alina was an innocent child who was nothing but a pawn in a sick adult game. She needed to be protected at all costs.

Runa remembered the portrait woman demanding, "Find her." She suddenly knew why she was there—to save Alina.

"Freya, listen to me. You have to get out of here. You have to get your daughter out of here."

"Mama, I want to go outside. I want to feel the ocean," Alina whined.

Freya looked back and forth between her daughter and Runa, her inner struggle written all over her face. Runa understood the decision was anything but simple. It meant choosing between the man she loved and her child.

"Freya, I know you think you love Easton, but I promise you, he's been lying to you all along. I understand this is hard. I'm asking you to betray the man you love. But don't do it for yourself. Do it for your daughter. Alina needs you to do the right thing for her," Runa pleaded.

"Take me to the ocean, Mama," Alina repeated.

As Freya considered, something shifted in her face. A look of resolve filled her eyes, and she nodded.

"Yes, Alina, yes. Let's go see the ocean."

"You're making the right decision," Runa encouraged.

"I just need to pack our things. I need a few days," Freya decided.

"No. You don't have time for that. The Everwines are gone right now. We need to get out of here before they come home. We have to go now."

Not giving them a second to reconsider, Runa grabbed Freya and Alina by the hands, ushering them away from their third-floor prison. When they reached the hallway of the west wing, Runa broke into a run.

"Follow me," she instructed as Freya and Alina ran behind her.

At the top of the staircase, they stopped.

"Wait right here. I'll grab my car keys, and then we're leaving. I'm not even packing a bag. We just need to get out of here. We can sort it out later," Runa implored, not wanting Freya to change her mind.

Runa raced to her room, grabbed her purse and keys, and led them down the main stairs and into the entryway. Their hurried footsteps pounded across the marble floor, reverberating off the high ceilings as they raced toward the door.

The foyer was dark, and Runa was too focused on escaping to pay attention to the fact that they weren't alone. She screamed as she slammed directly into Easton, who had just come in the front door. He flipped on the light, and shock and confusion distorted his features as he looked back and forth between Runa, Freya, and Alina.

In an instant, Easton's face registered the fact that his secret was out. Camille and Chase, standing behind him, gasped as understanding dawned for them as well.

Runa's heart pounded in her chest. Feeling like a cornered rabbit, she was overcome with fear, but she pushed it down. Freya's sharp intake of breath and Alina's small whimpers gave her the courage to push on.

"Get out of our way," Runa demanded. "We're leaving."

"You're not going anywhere." Easton laughed derisively.

"We're leaving," Runa repeated, refusing to back down.

"Freya, take our child and go back upstairs," Easton roared.

Freya recoiled, fear covering her face. "I'm sorry, Easton," she sobbed.

Alina began to cry. "I want to go outside. I want to feel the ocean."

Runa's hands shook, and a crackle of electricity flickered in her fingertips. A flash of boldness hit her in the stomach, and she knew she would fight to the bitter end for that little girl.

"Freya and Alina are never going up there again. You're through manipulating their feelings for you," Runa sneered.

Firmly grabbing the hands of the frightened woman and child, Runa dragged them along with her as she advanced toward the door.

Chase sidestepped his father, planting his large body in Runa's path, his cold smile sending shivers down her spine. "Darling, I'm afraid you're not going anywhere. You should have left well enough alone."

"No one is leaving this house. I will not deal with the scandal this is going to cause when it gets out," Camille shouted as she shoved Chase aside.

"Mother, stay out of this," he yelled.

"I told you bringing that girl here was a mistake. Why wouldn't you listen to me?" Camille shrilled.

Turning on his mother, Chase shoved her out of his way. Camille stumbled, losing her balance. Her stiletto heel caught on the corner of the Persian rug in the foyer, tangling in the tassels. She tried to catch herself, but the force of Chase's shove was too strong. Camille toppled to the floor, her head making a sickening thud on the unforgiving marble.

Stunned, Runa looked on in horror, waiting for Camille to move, but she didn't. She glanced back and forth from Chase to Easton, waiting for someone to help the fallen woman. Neither man moved a muscle. Instead, they stood motionless over her body without saying a word. It seemed both men were in shock.

It doesn't matter. Nothing matters but getting Alina away from this nightmare. Run!

The words echoed in Runa's brain, spurring her into action. Knowing she must move quickly, she grabbed Freya and Alina, pulling them out to the porch and closing the heavy front door behind them.

All at once, headlights flickered through the darkness as a car came to a screeching halt in the driveway. Asta sprang from the driver side and ran toward the house, tears streaming down her face as she screamed for her daughter.

"Runa! Runa, are you okay?"

"Mom, you're here," Runa answered.

"I knew you were in danger."

Asta's eyes widened when she saw Freya standing next to Runa. Then her face crumpled and her body shook.

"It's you," Asta whispered. "How is this possible?"

"What are you talking about, Mom?" Runa asked.

"Yes, tell her what you're talking about, *Mom*," Freya echoed bitterly.

FORTY-THREE

"What's going on?" Confused, Runa looked helplessly from Asta to Freya. "Why did you call her 'Mom'?"

"How can you be so naïve, Runa? Don't you understand? Our mother has been lying to you your whole life," Freya spat.

"Mom? What is she talking about?"

"I'm so sorry," Asta sobbed.

"Why did you say 'our mother'?" Runa asked, trying to block the truth as it pounded in her head.

"I can't believe you haven't figured it out. It's so obvious. We're twins, Runa," Freya announced.

"Mom?" Runa gazed helplessly at Asta, begging her to put an end to the lies.

"Freya is your sister," Asta admitted. "But I had no idea she was here."

"How is that possible?"

"Because our mother is a liar who only cares about herself," Freya interjected bitterly.

"I don't expect you to understand or accept my apology," Asta cried.

"I'll never forgive you," Freya hurled back at her.

"I am so sorry, Freya. I've had to live with my choice."

"Sorry? Little good that does," Freya quipped.

"Will you let me explain?" Asta begged.

"There's no explanation good enough," Freya threw back.

"Mom?" Runa repeated, horrified.

"I didn't know I was having twins," Asta said to Freya. "When you were born, I was afraid I couldn't take care of you both. I was a child myself. I panicked. I kept Runa and gave you up for adoption."

"You lied to me? All this time?" Runa shook her head, backing away from her mother, who continued to stare at her long-lost daughter.

"I'm sorry. A loving family wanted to adopt you, Freya. They had money. They promised to raise you well. I had no idea we would all end up here," Asta explained tearfully.

"Mom? How could you?" Runa shook her head in disbelief.

"It broke my heart to give you away, but I thought I was doing what was best," Asta pleaded with Freya.

"You can see how well that turned out, can't you?" Freya hurled at her mother.

Suddenly the front door opened, and Easton stomped onto the porch. His eyes were crazy and wild, and he was brandishing a shiny silver handgun.

"As lovely as this little family reunion is, ladies, I think we all know what has to happen now."

He aimed the gun toward Runa.

Impulsively, Asta moved forward, using her body as a barrier between the gun and her child.

"Put the gun away, Easton. You don't want to hurt anyone."

"Of course I don't. But you've left me no choice." His hands shook.

"There's always a choice," Asta soothed, holding his gaze steadily.

Breaking eye contact with Asta, Easton glanced toward Freya.

"Freya, nothing has changed. You and I can still be together."

"We can?" Freya sobbed pathetically.

"Of course we can. It'll be just like we planned. That's what you want, isn't it? Don't you love me?"

"You know I do. I've always loved you," Freya cried.

"Then you know what you have to do. Help me get rid of her." Easton jerked his head toward Runa.

"Don't listen to him, Freya. He's lying to you," Asta pleaded.

"Mother is dead," Chase screamed as he ran outside. "Now what are we going to do?"

Without even looking at his son, Easton replied, "We're going to handle it. Just like always."

"With another one of your plans? You can see how well that worked out, Father!" Chase yelled.

He paced back and forth across the front porch, running his hands through his hair in frustration.

Seeing her husband so agitated, Runa's stomach clenched. She couldn't believe he'd fooled her so completely.

Flinging her anger at him, she screamed, "What is wrong with you, Chase? You kept Freya a prisoner, and now you've killed your own mother."

"I've only done what I had to," he insisted numbly.

"Did you ever love me for even a second? Or was I just a replacement for what your father stole from you?" Runa sobbed.

Chase glanced from Runa to Freya, confusion and anger clouding his eyes. He shook his head slowly from side to side.

"I wanted to love you, Runa. I tried. But when I looked at you, I only saw Freya."

"Enough!" Easton interrupted, pointing at Freya. "You need to take Alina and go back to the third floor! Now!"

"I won't go back there!" Alina, who had silently observed the entire exchange, began to wail.

She shoved away from the group and ran, her shoes slipping in the wet grass. The wind howled and the rain poured, and Runa feared a strong gust would carry the small girl away. Undeterred, Alina sprinted toward the cliff.

"Alina!" Runa yelled for the child, but the little girl didn't even pause.

"Freya, we have to go after her," Runa insisted, grabbing her sister by the shoulders and shaking her.

"No, Freya. You go back upstairs now. I'll take care of everything," Easton commanded.

"Don't listen to him, Freya. We have to get Alina," Runa warned.

"You must think of your child. She's all that matters," Asta admonished.

Spinning toward Asta, Freya glowered at her. "Think of my child? Like you did? Why should I listen to the mother who gave me away?"

Asta recoiled as if she'd been slapped. "I've regretted that choice every day of my life." Tears streamed down her cheeks as she tried to reason with Freya.

"I don't care about your regrets," Freya snapped.

Knowing they were in danger, Asta thought quickly. Stepping toward Easton, she pleaded with her eyes. Slowly, he lowered the gun. She inched closer and placed her hands on his chest.

"Easton, my daughter is just a replacement for me. You don't love Freya. I'm the one you've wanted all along. This is all about me. Let her go. I'll stay with you."

Easton's face lit up, and he brushed his fingertips across

Asta's cheek lovingly. "You promise? You'll stay here with me?"

"Yes," she agreed. "Just let them all go."

"You're all I've ever wanted," he murmured, his eyes glued on Asta.

"I know I am, Easton," Asta whispered.

At that, Chase stopped pacing, clenching his fists at his side. "You stole my wife from me and you never even loved her? This was all about some sick obsession with her mother?"

Chase ran toward his father, slamming into him like a raging bull. His eyes were wild with madness, his face twisted with rage. Father and son fell to the porch, grappling and clawing. Punches flew, and primal, guttural sounds filled the air.

When the deafening sound of a gunshot rang out, Runa screamed. Untangling himself from Chase's body, Easton stood, panting.

Runa tried to stifle her screams as she watched blood gurgle from the hole in Chase's chest. Her husband was dying, but all she could think of was Alina, running scared toward the ocean. She knew she had to find the child.

Without another thought, Runa sprinted off the porch toward the cliff, leaving her mother and sister behind.

"Nothing else matters now," Easton mumbled. Turning to Asta, he gave her a chilling smile. "We're going to be so happy. Everything will be perfect."

Freya's face grew pale, her knees nearly giving out as she

finally understood the truth. "You never really loved me at all, did you, Easton?"

"No, I didn't." Easton shrugged, looking dazed and disoriented.

Asta saw resolve and determination flash across Freya's face. She knew her daughter finally understood the truth about Easton's lies. They needed to escape, and they must do so quickly.

Looking at Freya, Asta flicked her eyes toward the cliff, hoping she understood the meaning. Nodding almost imperceptibly, Freya reached out and gripped Asta's hand.

In one swift movement, both women began to run, feet pounding as they jumped from the porch and angled toward the cliff. They ran for their lives, managing to gain a bit of a head start before Easton realized what had happened. When the confusion wore off, he pursued, screaming at them to come back.

"Find your daughter and your sister, Freya. I'll stop Easton," Asta panted as she ran, pulling Freya along like a lost child.

"Easton will kill you when he realizes you aren't going to stay with him," Freya sobbed.

"That doesn't matter as long as you're free. I didn't fight for you when you were born, but I'm doing it now. Go!"

She pushed Freya toward the cliff and took off running in the opposite direction, toward the forest.

As Asta changed course, Easton followed.

With one last glance toward her mother, Freya headed for the sound of the ocean, desperate to find Alina, fear squeezing her chest. When she arrived at the edge of the cliff, she found Runa crouched on the ground, cradling Alina's small body.

"She's okay. She's fine," Runa cried as Freya approached.

Freya ran toward her daughter and fell to the ground, pulling Alina close and whispering soothing words in her ear.

Runa stood slowly, trying to catch her breath and gain her bearings. When she'd found Alina, precariously perched on the edge of the cliff, she thought her niece would plummet into the unknown. If the girl had taken one more step, it would have been too late. She'd arrived just in time, convincing the child to run toward her rather than away.

Glancing over the edge of the cliff at the swelling ocean below, Runa let the tears fall freely, mixing with the salty sea mist. Closing her eyes, she listened as the water sang a song she'd never heard yet somehow understood. Somewhere deep inside, the sound of the sea resonated in the secret places of her soul.

Opening her eyes, Runa noticed a woman walking along the shore, glowing with an otherworldly light, visible through the thick blanket of fog. As she watched, the woman drew a circle in the sand, enclosing herself inside of it. She placed various shells and driftwood in the center, forming an altar.

As she raised her arms toward the sky, shafts of blue light flickered from the woman's fingertips. Runa glanced at her own hands, mirroring the woman's exactly.

The woman turned toward the cliff, and their eyes met. In an instant, Runa understood she was the woman in the portrait.

"I found her," Runa called.

The woman nodded. Then she spoke, clear and loud, her voice cutting through the wind and rain and landing directly inside Runa's heart.

"You're the generation of two."

"The generation of two."

The words echoed in the air, drifting through the breeze and swirling in the storm. Runa remembered what the book said about the generation of two, and her breath caught in her throat. The generation of two would possess all the power but must sacrifice something in return.

Runa looked down at her hands, glowing brighter than ever, the blue light shooting like laser beams through the darkness. She glanced back at the woman, whose hands were still raised in the air. Then she saw Freya standing next to her.

A look of shock and uncertainty bathed Freya's face as she held up her hands. Identical shafts of blue light shot out of her fingertips just as they did Runa's. Facing each other, they reached their palms toward each other until they touched.

When their hands connected, a bolt of electricity shot

through them, bathing them from the tops of their heads to the soles of their feet, the force so strong it nearly knocked them over. Clasping their fingers together tightly, the women held on.

"You're the generation of two," the woman on the beach called to them.

Suddenly they heard Asta screaming as she ran toward the cliff, Easton in pursuit. His monstrous eyes flashed wickedly as he raised the gun toward the sky, firing off a shot.

As the sound echoed in the night, Freya and Runa locked eyes. In that moment, they fully understood the magnitude of their power. They were stronger together.

Asta arrived a split second before Easton, standing in front of her daughters. She was intent on saving them, willing to give up her life in order to do so.

"You will not harm my children," Asta yelled.

"Why can't you just love me?" Easton sobbed as he pointed the gun at her. "That's all I've ever wanted."

"You're not capable of love," Asta screamed.

"I did it all for you, Asta. I got rid of every barrier between us, yet you still won't love me."

"You mean Garrett? I always knew you had something to do with his death. What did you do to him?" Asta cried.

"He was my best friend. I loved him. But I loved you more. I did what I had to. Garrett was standing between us. I had to get rid of him." Easton shrugged, the gun wobbling in his trembling hands.

"I knew you killed him. You're a monster!"

Ignoring the fact that Easton had a gun, Asta ran toward him, directly in the line of fire.

Understanding what was about to happen, Freya also sprinted toward Easton, throwing herself in front of Asta at the exact moment he fired the gun.

The bullet hit Freya directly in the chest, and she staggered before collapsing to the ground.

Screaming, Asta grabbed Freya, cradling her body as she sobbed.

"No, no, no," she wailed over and over. "Not my daughter!"

"Freya!" Runa cried as she ran toward her mother and sister.

Dropping to the ground, she placed her hands on either side of Freya's face, willing every bit of power she possessed into her sister's body. She concentrated as hard as she could, visualizing her sister's healing. Sobbing, she pleaded with God, begging Him to help her.

But it was no use. When Runa opened her eyes, she knew it was too late. Freya's body was still. She was gone.

Runa felt a piece of herself die with Freya, the part she never knew existed until that night. Still, it left behind an empty hole, a vast expanse of nothingness she knew would never be filled.

Asta's body began to shake as she rose to her feet. Her

eyes skewered Easton, her hatred and disdain dripping from every pore as she screamed, "You killed my daughter!"

"You were never going to stay with me, were you, Asta?" Easton steadied the gun and aimed it toward her as he advanced quickly.

"Mom! No!" Runa yelled as she rose to her feet.

"You said you would stay with me. You promised," he spat, his eyes crazed.

He continued stalking toward Asta as she backed away, inching dangerously close to the cliff.

Knowing that in another second it would be too late, Runa summoned all the energy she possessed and unleashed it toward the gun in Easton's hand. A shock of light lit up the sky as a bolt of blue arced directly at him, knocking his gun to the ground.

Stunned yet mad with rage, Easton barreled toward Asta, who stepped out of his path. The momentum was too much for him to control, and he was unable to stop. Losing his footing, he began to slip over the edge of the cliff, grabbing Asta in the process. She tried to resist, to find her balance, but Easton was too strong. Together they fell toward the rocks below.

"Mom!" Runa yelled as she ran to the edge of the cliff. "No!"

She fell to the ground in a heap, covering her face to block out the horror. She beat the wet ground with her fists, sobbing, screaming, trying to wrap her brain around the unbelievable tragedy she'd witnessed. It wasn't supposed to end like this.

They were all dead. Everyone was gone. The price had been too high.

Runa's body heaved. Grief slammed into her like a tidal wave, and she remained there, drowning in it. She didn't know how much time passed. It could have been a minute, though it may have been an hour. Time had no meaning as it sucked her into the void.

She jumped when she felt a tug on her sweatshirt.

"My mama is gone," Alina said, her lip quivering.

Runa's heart broke into a million pieces all over again. She grabbed the little girl and pulled her close.

"My mama is gone, too. But we have each other."

Standing, Runa clasped Alina's hand in hers, determined to never let go. She looked at the shore, where the portrait woman met her gaze, nodding her approval. Smiling sadly, the woman disappeared into the fog.

FORTY-FIVE

Runa sat on the front porch of Everwine Manor, poring over the book. A month had passed since the night her world imploded. She still felt as if she'd barely come up for air, but every day was a little easier than the last.

Alina sang a song as she played on the swing set Runa built for her. After spending her entire life on the third floor, the little girl hated being inside. Runa did her best to encourage Alina's love of nature. After all her niece had been through, it was the least she could do. She didn't know much about being a mother, but she was doing her best.

It was hard for Runa to believe that Everwine Manor belonged to her, but as Chase's wife, everything was hers. Since the Everwines were all dead, she had inherited everything.

Emily had been a lifesaver, helping out with the boutique while Runa tried to pick up the broken pieces of her world. Tawney had been her rock, offering advice and moral support.

As she felt herself emerging from the fog, Runa couldn't shake the feeling that there was still something she was supposed to do. The problem was she had no idea what it could be. She'd been reading through the book the last few days, certain the answers were written there.

She hadn't been able to stop thinking about the portrait woman on the beach that night. She knew the woman had led her to the third floor to find her sister and niece. Although nothing that came after had happened the way she'd hoped, Runa knew she'd been sent there to save Alina. The little girl had become her purpose.

Runa thought about the portrait woman and remembered the painting had been dated 1900. Looking through the book, she began to piece the woman's story together. She learned her name was Brynja, and she was the first of their line to leave Norway.

Brynja had a twin sister, Sigrid, who died. They were the generation of two and had paid the ultimate sacrifice—Sigrid's life. Runa knew the generation of two possessed unparalleled power, but she believed the price was too steep. What good was such power if you lost the ones you loved the most?

Flipping through the book, she continued reading Brynja's story. A light bulb flickered on as she paid attention to the words Brynja used to describe the house Thomas built. She spoke of a turret with stained glass windows, a wraparound porch, and a rose garden in the back. Thomas had called his home Angelica House.

She read on.

Behind the garden, Thomas has planted a large field of angelica. The herb grew well in Norway, and he knows how I miss my homeland. He wanted to bring a piece of home to my new world. Always remember that angelica brings blessings and purification to a home. It wards off evil and encourages harmony. The answers are there if you look closely.

Runa noted that Brynja had written that particular passage almost as if she were trying to communicate a message. Looking closely at the page, she puzzled over the words, trying to decipher the code.

"Angelica, angelica, angelica," Alina sang as she glided back and forth on the swing.

Runa stopped reading and watched Alina swinging and singing. There was no way the child could know what Runa was reading about. So why was she singing about angelica?

"Angelica, angelica, angelica," Alina continued in her singsong voice.

Runa closed the book, picked it up, and walked across the yard toward Alina.

"Alina, why are you singing about angelica?" she asked.

"Because the woman told me you need to look there," Alina answered nonchalantly.

"The woman?"

"The pretty woman who looks like us." Alina shrugged.

Runa thought about the page in the book she'd just read.

"Angelica brings blessings and purification to a home. The answers are there if you look closely," Runa murmured.

She took off running through the front yard, around the side of the house, and past the rose garden maze. Behind it, she found a large field filled with angelica, growing lush and wild. At the edge of the field, she stopped and looked around, uncertain.

Glancing down, Runa saw a slab of stone buried in the earth. It was old, but the writing carved on it was clear. Crouching low, Runa placed the book on the ground. Then she gently brushed her hands across the stone, wiping away grass and dirt in order to read the words engraved there.

Angelica House, established 1900

Tears filled Runa's eyes as she finally understood. "Everwine Manor is Angelica House, the house Thomas and Brynja lived in. A woman of my line was the first to live in this house," she murmured.

Plopping her body on the grass, Runa grabbed the book, opened it to Brynja's story, and continued reading. Tears streamed down her cheeks as she learned the sad end of Brynja's tale, where she'd been forced to marry a man she didn't love after Thomas's death—a man named Lucas Everwine, who was cruel and stole everything from her.

She was shocked to discover that the cycle between the women in her family and the Everwines had continued well over a hundred years. Although she would give anything to change the way things had ended, she was happy the generational curse had finally been broken. She was back in the house that should have been theirs all along.

If Runa could go back and change the past, she would. But it gave her a sense of peace and continuity to know she'd somehow fulfilled a purpose. She had reclaimed the power the Everwines stole and finally set things right.

Runa glanced up and saw Alina, who had followed her to the angelica field. Ruffling the child's blonde hair, so much like her own, she smiled.

"There are so many things I'm going to teach you, Alina. The women in our family have power. I'm going to teach you how to use it for good. These gifts live in us for a reason. We must never waste them."

"I know, Aunt Runa. I feel them inside of me." Alina smiled.

"There's something we have to do." Runa grabbed Alina's hand, guiding her along.

She led the little girl into the house, up the stairs, down the hall, through the corridors, and into the west wing. Opening the door leading to the third floor, Runa placed her hands on Alina's shoulders.

"I know you don't want to go back into that room, but we need to. It's time to put the past to rest."

"I'm not afraid anymore," Alina stated bravely.

Her eyes glistening with tears, Runa nodded in understanding.

They ascended the stairs to the third floor, walked down the center hallway, and opened the splintered door leading to the turret room. When they reached the top, Runa clasped Alina's hand tightly in hers, leading her up the small stairs into the circular turret, the room that had been her prison for all her life.

The afternoon sun glinted off the rainbow of stained glass windows. The room was beautiful, but a dark, oppressive force was palpable in the air. Centuries of fear and pain had been locked inside the room. The time had come to set them free. Opening the book, Runa grabbed a pen. She flipped to the end, the section with the family history.

"What are we doing here, Aunt Runa?" Alina asked.

"This can no longer be a place of secrecy and darkness. Starting today, we're opening the windows to the light," Runa began.

Motioning toward the book, she continued, "The women in this book made us who we are. We're strong. We're survivors. Throughout history, people sought to silence our voices. They feared us because they didn't understand. We acknowledge the women who came before us, our legacy," Runa began.

Taking a breath, she began to recite the names aloud:

"Else, 1585

Bekka and Helga, 1600

Sofie, 1625

Nora, 1645

Ella, 1663

Maja, 1683

Thea, 1704

Leah, 1727

Amalie, 1748

Frida, 1767

Astrid, 1783

Tuva, 1803

Selma, 1825

Malin, 1843

Mille, 1861

Sigrid and Brynja, 1883

Ingrid, 1900

Mathilde, 1917

Ada, 1935

Celine, 1953

Asta, 1973."

PAUSING, Runa grabbed the pen and started writing.

Runa and Freya, 1991

Alina, 2011

All at once, the oppressive feeling lifted, and a glowing light filled the room.

Runa grabbed Alina's hands, smiling as she saw the faintest glow of blue light streaming from the little girl's fingertips.

R una held Alina's hand tightly as the ferry pulled into the port of Vardø. It was summer in Norway, but the temperatures were still far from warm, hovering at an even fifty degrees. She had planned the trip for months, knowing travel wouldn't be easy with a child, yet understanding it was something she needed to do.

If she had any hope of giving Alina a sense of where she'd come from, she needed to understand it herself. That meant going back to the place where it all began.

Runa had read the book from cover to cover multiple times. She knew the women's lives nearly as well as her own. She felt tethered to them in a way she didn't fully comprehend. The connection was primal, spiritual, and all-encompassing.

Stepping from the ferry, Runa and Alina followed the

crowd. The overwhelming smell of fish floated into Runa's nostrils, its pungency surprising her. The raw beauty of the stark landscape caught her off guard. She'd never felt such a complete sense of belonging as she did in that place.

Runa had arranged for a driver to meet them at the ferry, and she smiled as she saw a man holding a sign with her name on it.

"Runa Brandon?" he asked.

She was still getting used to the sound of her maiden name. She'd had it restored as quickly as possible, wanting no trace of a connection to the Everwines. She'd also adopted Alina, so the little girl bore her name as well.

"Yes, sir, I'm Runa. And this is Alina."

"I'm guessing you'll want to go to your hotel?"

"No." She shook her head decisively. "I need to see the memorial first."

"The Steilneset?" He raised one eyebrow. "You ladies are interested in witches?"

"You could say that, I suppose," Runa answered noncommittally.

They got into the car. The man nodded and started driving.

Alina rested her head on Runa's shoulder, closing her eyes peacefully. The child had been such a good traveler on their journey, wanting to see their homeland every bit as much as Runa.

Before long, the car came to a halt.

"That's it." The driver jerked his thumb toward the building Runa had seen many times in photographs.

"You'll wait here for us?" she inquired as she and Alina climbed from the car.

"Will do."

As she looked toward the memorial, Runa's stomach clenched tightly, a sense of overwhelming sadness settling in her middle. She grabbed Alina's hand, and the pair walked slowly toward the structure. The Steilneset Memorial was made up of two separate buildings, one square and one long wooden structure.

"Are you ready?" Runa asked Alina.

The little girl nodded. "This is the place?"

"This is the memorial they built to honor the people they executed for witchcraft in this town in the 1600s," Runa explained, her voice shaking.

Runa swallowed hard. It was impossible to articulate all the feelings warring inside her. The second she'd stepped foot on Vardø land, her heart felt like it was home. She was overcome with a hundred different memories of the place, none of which belonged to her. It was as if Vardø cried out to her, the blood flowing through her veins answering its call. Being near the memorial was physically crushing, its heaviness bearing down on her with an intensity she hadn't expected.

Alina and Runa reverently walked through the memorial, neither speaking, both barely breathing. A sense of sacredness filled the buildings, rendering speech almost blasphemous. As they walked along the timber walkway down the narrow corridor of the first building, Runa's eyes filled with tears as she looked at the ninety-one small windows representing those executed for witchcraft.

It all hit too close to home, and she felt the walls close in, understanding that if she'd lived during that time period, her name would likely be found among the list of the dead.

"These people were all killed for being witches?" Alina whispered.

"Yes, although most of them weren't witches, Alina," Runa replied in the quietest voice she could muster.

"Why did they kill them, then?"

Runa sighed heavily, her heart aching. "Because they were different."

They headed into the next building, the square structure built from weathered steel and panes of tinted glass called The Damned, The Possessed, and The Beloved. Runa gasped when she saw a metal chair in the center of the room, an eternal flame burning through the seat. Mirrors reflected the blaze so it danced like judges circling the condemned.

It wasn't difficult for Runa to imagine being forced into that chair, helpless to defend herself or explain her powers. She imagined the women in her family on trial for something they couldn't control, and the thought was nearly too much for her to bear. The walls were too close, the mirrors casting eerie reflections throughout the room.

She grabbed Alina's hand and went outside, gasping,

sucking in the fresh air. She had to get away. It was all too much.

Heading back to the car, Runa asked the driver to take them to their hotel.

HOURS LATER, after a warm dinner and a hot shower, Alina had fallen fast asleep. Runa pored over the book once again.

She'd come to Vardø, she'd seen the memorial, and she'd felt the pain and suffering of the wrongfully accused people. Still, she believed there was something she was missing, a bigger reason she'd felt compelled to travel halfway around the world to the place where it all began.

Sighing heavily, Runa closed the book and turned off the light. Snuggling close to Alina's warm body, she gave in to sleep.

Somewhere in the night, the dream began, more vivid and real than any she'd ever had. She walked along the Vardø shore, the wind howling, the sky as black as midnight.

As she walked, the sky began to glow, the Northern Lights illuminating the darkness, every color of the rainbow swirling through the air. Glancing beside her, Runa noticed a woman had joined her, matching her stride and clasping her hand. Their eyes locked, and they smiled at each other, familiar though they'd never met.

"What's your name?" Runa asked the woman.

"Helga," she answered with a smile.

"Do I know you?" Runa tilted her head and looked at the woman, who resembled her so closely.

"I'm your grandmother, many times over," she replied.

"You're the reason I'm here," Runa stated as clarity swam to the surface.

"Yes."

"You called me to Vardø."

"I did."

"Why?" Runa asked.

"To let you know I understand."

"You understand?"

"Yes. I know your grief. I, too, lost a mother."

"You did?"

"Yes. Her name is written on the walls of the memorial you visited today."

"Your mother… was executed?"

"She was." Helga's eyes brimmed with tears. "But she made certain I was safe, just as your mother did for you."

"Yes." Runa nodded slowly. "She died protecting me."

"Because that's what mothers do. Take this. It's yours now." Helga unclasped the Ansuz rune necklace she wore, fastening it around Runa's neck. "The legacy is yours, *min datter av havet*. My daughter of the sea. It's not about power. It never has been. It's all about love."

"I promise to pass that love on to Alina," Runa finished.

Helga nodded. "Teach her. Make sure she understands the privilege and burden she bears."

"I will."

Smiling, Helga began to fade away.

Runa reached for her, desperate for more time. She wanted to learn from the wise woman, to bask in her power, yet she was thankful for the moments she'd had.

———

WHEN RUNA FELT Alina stirring beside her in bed the next morning, she opened her eyes slowly, remembering the dream from the night before. A wave of sadness rushed over her when she understood it was all just a dream. She wanted it to be real.

Turning on her side, she watched Alina, who was drifting in and out of sleep. Runa had never set out to be the girl's mother, yet that was what she'd become. She loved Alina with a force that sometimes took her breath away. She would do anything to keep her safe and happy.

In that moment, she understood how her mother, and generations of mothers before her, had found the courage to sacrifice their happiness, comfort, and often their lives for the sake of their children. Runa knew if push came to shove, that was exactly what she would do for Alina.

Shifting her body a bit, Runa felt something on her neck, a cool metal object. Sitting up slowly, she felt the pendant fall, resting snugly just below her collarbone. Her hands trembled as she reached up to touch it.

Flecks of blue light flickered through the room as her fingertips made contact with the Ansuz rune symbol Helga had placed around her neck.

Smiling through tears that fell like raindrops, Runa finally understood her purpose.

"Så det," she whispered. "So be it."

"And above all, watch with glittering eyes the whole world around you because the greatest secrets are always hidden in the most unlikely places. Those who don't believe in magic will never find it."
—Roald Dahl

LOOKING for more unique suspenses from HR Mason? Check out **Nothing Hidden Ever Stays.**

ABOUT THE AUTHOR

Thanks for reading *DAUGHTERS OF THE SEA*. I do hope you enjoyed my story. I appreciate your help in spreading the word, including telling a friend. Before you go, it would mean so much to me if you would take a few minutes to write a review and share how you feel about my story so others may find my work. Reviews really do help readers find books. Please leave a review on your favorite book site.

Don't miss out on New Releases, Exclusive Giveaways, and much more!

Join my reader group: www.facebook.com/groups/346156819065335/

I'd love to hear from you directly, too. Please feel free to email me at heidisbooks999@gmail.com or check out my website at www.heidireneemason.com for updates.

H.R. Mason is an Ohio girl transplanted into the Pacific Northwest. She is a people-watching introvert who can be found hiding out in the nearest corner. When not writing, she loves rainy days at the beach, old houses and antiques, researching family history, reading, and getting lost inside her own thoughts. She is a lover of caffeine and a hopeless romantic at heart. A multi-published author in the Romance genre, she moved into new writing territory in 2019 when she crossed genres. *Nothing Hidden Ever Stays*, her debut Gothic Suspense novel, became an Amazon bestseller. It was the winner of the American Fiction Award for Mystery/Suspense, as well as a Finalist in the Best Book Awards.

facebook.com/hrmasonauthor

twitter.com/heidireneemason

instagram.com/authorhrmason

bookbub.com/authors/hr-mason

ACKNOWLEDGMENTS

Thanks to Becky Johnson and everyone involved with Tangled Tree Publishing. The way you all rally to support your authors is amazing. Thanks to Claire Smith of BookSmith Designs for always perfectly nailing my terrific covers. Thanks to Kristin Scearce, Editor Extraordinaire, as well as the team at Hot Tree Promotions. You are all fantastic human beings, and I couldn't have done this without you. Thank you for helping make *Daughters of the Sea* a reality.

ABOUT THE PUBLISHER

As Hot Tree Publishing's first imprint branch, Tangled Tree Publishing aims to bring darker, twisted, more tangled reads to its readers. Established in 2015, they have seen rousing success as a rising publishing house in the industry motivated by their enthusiasm and keen eye for talent. Driving them is their passion for the written word of all genres, but with Tangled Tree Publishing, they're embarking on a whole new adventure with words of mystery, suspense, crime, and thrillers.

Join the growing Hot Tree Group family of authors, promoters, editors, and readers. Become a part of not just a company but an actual family by submitting your manuscript to Tangled Tree Publishing. Know that they will put your interests and book first, and that your voice and brand will always be at the forefront of everything they do.

For more details, head to www.tangledtreepublishing.com.

facebook.com/tangledtreepublishing

twitter.com/ttpubs

instagram.com/hottreepublishing

Lightning Source UK Ltd.
Milton Keynes UK
UKHW011844010621
384770UK00006B/455/J

9 781922 359742